✿ **Also by S. K. Ali** ✿

Saints and Misfits

Love from A to Z

MISFIT IN LOVE

A Saints and Misfits novel

S. K. ALI

SALAAM
READS

NEW YORK   LONDON   TORONTO   SYDNEY   NEW DELHI

An imprint of Simon & Schuster Children's Publishing Division
1230 Avenue of the Americas, New York, New York 10020

For information about special discounts for bulk purchases, please contact Simon &
Schuster Special Sales at 1-866-506-1949 or business@simonandschuster.com.
The Simon & Schuster Speakers Bureau can bring authors to your live event. For more
information or to book an event, contact the Simon & Schuster Speakers Bureau at
1-866-248-3049 or visit our website at www.simonspeakers.com.
Interior design by Tom Daly
The text for this book was set in Adobe Garamond Pro.
Manufactured in the United States of America
First Edition
2 4 6 8 10 9 7 5 3 1
Library of Congress Cataloging-in-Publication Data
Names: Ali, S. K., author.
Title: Misfit in love / S.K. Ali.
Description: First edition. | New York : Salaam Reads, [2021] | Series: A Saints and misfits
novel ; vol 2 | Audience: Ages 14 up. | Audience: Grades 10–12. | Summary: "Janna Yusuf
and her friends are planning for her brother's nikah. But what started as a simple marriage
ceremony is turning into the biggest event of the summer—and a chance for Janna to
finally reveal her crush . . . or so she thinks"— Provided by publisher.
Identifiers: LCCN 2020038920 (print) | LCCN 2020038921 (ebook) |
ISBN 9781534442757 (hardcover) | ISBN 9781534442771 (ebook)
Subjects: CYAC: Weddings—Fiction. | Family life—Fiction. |
Muslims—United States—Fiction. | Love—Fiction.
Classification: LCC PZ7.1.A436 Mis 2021 (print) | LCC PZ7.1.A436 (ebook)
| DDC [Fic]—dc23
LC record available at https://lccn.loc.gov/2020038920
LC ebook record available at https://lccn.loc.gov/2020038921

To my daughter, Bili, because I love you,
and because you love weddings

Bismillahi 'rahmani araheem
The honor of your presence is requested at
the marriage of

Sarah Iman Mahmoud

and

Muhammad Ibrahim Yusuf

Saturday, the seventeenth of July,
at five thirty in the evening
At the residence of Haroon Sultan Yusuf
700 Lakeview Road
Mystic Lake, Indiana
The couple requests donations
to Islamic Relief USA
in lieu of gifts

Part One

THURSDAY, JULY 15
WEDDING PREP DAY

To do:

☐ Chill while waiting for Nuah to arrive tomorrow

☐ Go meet Mom at her hotel

Chapter One

❈ ❈ ❈

I'm in the water. Floating on my back, staring at the bluest sky there must have ever been in the history of blue skies.

My burkini, almost all four yards of it, swells up around me and serves as a flotation device. I'm buoyed, but—secret smile—it's not only because of the burkini.

Nuah's coming tomorrow—for the entire weekend.

And I have a plan.

Now that I'm finished with school and will be starting college in the fall, I'm ready to actually tell Nuah that . . . that . . . well, I guess, that we can be a *thing*? I don't know what else to call it when you say *yes, I like you back* to someone like Nuah, who's interested in me, but also interested in following Islam.

Which means there are rules—*but the rules will still lead to us being together.*

I spread my arms out in the lake and let my secret smile take over my face, remembering the words of the scholar and spiritual poet Rumi.

"Rumi said, 'Only from the heart can you touch the sky,'" I tell the sky, my eyes probing the blue expanse, my left hand pulling up my burkini pants, which are beginning to ride low again, their waistline weathered from overuse. "And I believe him."

"Janna, are you talking to yourself again?"

I don't need to lift my head to know that it's my brother Muhammad. And that he's on the dock, throwing our two little half brothers into the lake, one by one, each time they scramble back onto the dock in turn saying, "Again!"

He's giddy, my big brother.

In exactly two days he's getting married to the love of his life, Sarah. And it's all happening on the grounds of this lakeside estate house right here that Dad bought and renovated last summer in grand fashion.

I mean, there's even a perfect white gazebo by the water. Dad had wanted it to be his wife Linda's "sanctuary" space—with white couches and some kind of tulle hanging off the entire structure, doing double duty as a practical mosquito net *and* an ethereal fantasy thing.

But Linda is more of a chasing-after-the-kids-in-her-leggings person, so the gazebo is a neglected thing of beauty, lying in wait for its moment to shine.

That moment began a week ago when white-overalled workers descended on the gazebo to perk it up. Remove the couches, dismantle the net, give it a fresh coat of paint, fix the trellis roof.

This weekend everyone Muhammad knows, and I mean *everyone*, is driving up either three hours from Eastspring, our hometown, or an hour down from Chicago to see Muhammad and Sarah's relationship get solemnized in that gleaming white gazebo.

It's THE wedding of the Muslim community round these parts.

Wedding preparations have been going on for weeks now, led by Dad and Muhammad, as Sarah is scrambling to finish a master's degree and her family is throwing an official reception of their own next year.

But this event here by the lake is going to be a monstrous affair, and it's kind of unnerving. I can't even move around Dad's place without bumping into strangers measuring distances or erecting beams or looking me up and down as I flop around in my (signature) ripped, faded, slouchy clothes.

Big Fat Muslim Wedding is on everyone's lips. Like three-hundred-guests big—which is huge for being a private wedding in Dad's backyard.

Muhammad and Sarah are even letting me invite some of my friends, plus their plus-ones.

One of them is Nuah.

Who, being friends with Muhammad, is coming up to help him out prewedding.

Floating in the lake, I hitch up my burkini pants again, do a flutter kick to keep from sinking while doing so, and smile bigger at the sky above as I think about Nuah all dressed up for the wedding.

I haven't seen Nuah in forever because, after his freshman year ended, he stayed in California, where he'd started college for engineering last fall. But when he comes up tomorrow, it will be for the summer.

Our summer.

I close my eyes because, sappy but true—as Rumi himself knew—the blue skies have moved into my heart now.

Water splashes on my face. A truckload.

Grunting and sputtering with frustration, I flail for a moment before reaching to clear my eyes, to get ready to deal with my super-immature, forever-goofy brother.

The guy is getting married in two days, and he can't even let me float in peace?

Heaving and righting myself to stand in the shallow water, I open my eyes.

But not to Muhammad.

To a total stranger.

An unbelievably gorgeous total stranger.

I blink twice, but he's still there. Standing in water to his knees, his legs encased in long shorts, his torso encased in . . . nothing.

Smiling a sheepish smile, hands on his hips, squinting into the sun behind me, squinting at me.

"Haytham, this is my sister, Janna." Muhammad steps up to us and slaps this otherworldly creature on its bare back, and it nods at me, brown hair flopping ever so slightly forward. "Janna, meet Haytham, Sarah's cousin. Here to help with wedding prep."

"Sorry for splashing you like that," the creature says, scratching a bare, flat stomach that I will myself not to glance at. "I couldn't help it. You had this amazing smile on your face, and I wanted to see what would happen."

"Oh yeah, Sarah told me you had impulse-control issues." Muhammad starts laughing, while swatting at Luke, our youngest half brother, who's pulling on his shorts. "But Janna here is all about the impulse control. And you made her mad before you even met her!"

"Sorry again." The creature folds his arms across a chest that has seen many dedicated workouts. "Janna."

I don't say anything. Wrinkles of concern crease the wide and tall and majestic forehead belonging to the interloper. "Do you forgive me? Janna?"

(I have a thing for big foreheads. Everyone has things. Mine happens to be a frontal-lobe matter. Don't judge, and instead reflect on your own fixations.)

I nod at the forehead and pull at my burkini, clinging to my body now that most of the excess water has dripped out. I tug the fabric to stop it from sticking so ferociously to me.

Which is not a thing you should do in front of a tall, handsome stranger begging your forgiveness.

The burkini, my formerly trusted flotation friend, immediately makes a squelchy farting noise.

The noise that always makes both my half brothers, those pudglings I (used to) affectionately call laddoos after those Indian dessert balls, immediately scream, *Janna is farting!*

"Janna is farting!" they both shout on cue now.

"I'm not farting!" I yell, tugging at my swimwear again in my nervousness. Another fart sounds in the summer air, weaker and not quite as dedicated to ruining my life.

As squeals of laughter greet the lesser fart, I'm in disbelief that "I'm not farting!" are the first words that came out of my mouth in front of Haytham.

I whip my head around at the squealing scoundrels, my half brothers, products of my father's hasty remarriage, splashing nearby. "That wasn't a fart, Luke and Logan!"

"Janna farted again!" Logan shouts.

"Atain!" Luke echoes. He advances his rotund self toward me, paddling furiously in the floatation device he's permanently wedged into whenever he's in the water, and pulls at my burkini pants. Lately he's into disrobing unsuspecting humans of clothing covering their nether regions.

Uh-oh.

My old, unreliable burkini pants.

Before I have a moment to clutch at them, they fall off completely.

Haytham turns around quickly but not before letting out a laugh that he tries to cover with the back of his hand.

I am so thankful my burkini top is so long, so very, very long, that nothing showed. Thank you, Allah, for saving my butt, *literally*.

I slide down into the water. As low as I can in the shallowest part of the super-long shallow-entry lake.

And then, while trying to walk away in a dignified but quick fashion on the shifting sands of the lake bed, I trip on the pants swiftly gathering themselves under my feet and tip face-forward into the water.

Underwater, I pray that Haytham didn't turn around again when he heard the new laughs Logan and Luke let out, Luke even clapping his hands with glee.

I close my eyes and stay in place, even though it's so shallow. I have to sit cross-legged, and still my head rises in humiliation above the water, like a wounded giraffe.

One of the ways Muhammad is all right is that he gets my utter mortification pretty thoroughly. Even though he has no qualms about doing things to bother me when we're on our own, he understands, sometimes, the preservation of my dignity in public.

"Okay, we're going in! Logan, Luke, now! It's almost dinnertime!" thunders my only dependable brother.

I hear screams of "NO!" accompanied by splashes and threats and grabbings of half brothers, and then silence.

When I open my eyes, they're gone.

All of them, even *him.*

I stand and fit my feet through the legs of my pants, frowning as I struggle to find the holes at the hem.

Who is he?

Haytham?

I mean besides being Sarah's cousin?

Besides being the guy I just got completely humiliated in front of?

Lifting my long burkini top and bunching it under my chin to hold it in place, I tug at the bottom's waist and knot the excess fabric as best as I can. Mental note: *Get a new burkini.*

I'm just going to forget this "Janna farted" incident and go get showered and changed and then head to the hotel in town to see Mom, who's arriving today to help with wedding stuff.

I haven't seen her in almost a month now, so I can't wait to catch up.

It was Muhammad who guilted me into staying so long at Dad's. I hadn't been sure I wanted to spend three weeks here before the wedding. I had originally wanted to stay home in Eastspring to work and just come up the week of the wedding to help him out, but then Muhammad had pouted, his lips drooping, and he'd slouched his whole self. *So you don't want to hang out with me at Dad's before you go to college and before I become an old married man? Our last time as free siblings?*

So yeah, I'd given in. And said good-bye to Mom. And a job.

I hung around here at Dad's scrumptious home just resting and relaxing and eating good food and swimming every day and reading all the books and watching all the movies and shows I'd missed while finishing high school. And of course hanging around with Muhammad and Luke and Logan.

And it was fun. I'm glad I did it, actually.

But there's something I like even more than the comforts at Dad's: After the wedding, after Muhammad leaves with Sarah, everything goes back to normal. Exactly how I like it.

It'll only be me and Mom in Eastspring once again, the way it used to be—well, the way it used to be since my parents got divorced when I was ten, and we moved apart when I was eleven.

Before the divorce, I used to think of myself and Dad as a team, as we're kind of similar in our eye-on-the-prize way of seeing things. He applies it to the business world because he owns a food company, and I apply it to the getting-the-best-grades-possible-in-school world. Dad's goal-oriented philosophy helped him become the number one prepackaged Indian dessert manufacturer in North America. And mine landed me a hefty scholarship to UChicago to study English.

Team Dad and Janna lasted only so long, though.

When a member of our mosque community assaulted me two years ago, Mom was the one who was there for me. She got me counseling with Dr. Lloyd, pressed charges, and wrapped me in relentless love, and so we became a new team, a championship team. Dad was just a ball of anger, blaming the mosque, wanting something bigger to be held accountable. I found it hard to connect with him then.

Like Mom, Nuah helped me through that time too. He was never far away and stood by me when some people in our community refused to believe what had happened. In addition to duas, he kept sending me memes to brighten my day. And specially selected cat videos—which I have no idea where he found, because they weren't the viral ones.

So it's going to be a Nuah-and-me *and* a mom-and-me summer when we get back to Eastspring, insha'Allah.

And my world going back to being small and cozy like that is exactly what I need when this huge wedding is done.

Chapter Two

* * *

On the way back to the house a bit later, with a towel sheltering my shoulders, I notice there's a gathering at the gazebo.

It's Haytham and the laddoos, Logan and Luke. And is that Sarah's little brother, Dawud? Lying down on the floorboards with a book open in front of his face?

Haytham, clothed now in a navy T-shirt and khaki shorts, waves me over.

I tuck in the tendrils of hair that made their way out of my burkini cap, hesitating a moment, staring at my feet in the grass leading up from the sandy edge of the shore, across the huge expanse of backyard, to the patio at the back of the house. Then I turn left and make my way to the gazebo, my eyes still on my black-polished toes in yellow flip-flops moving through the neatly mowed grass, which feels cool against the skin of my feet.

When I glance back up, I see that my little brothers are holding a silver tray between them, excitement on their faces. Logan beams while Luke giggles.

There's a pink-frosted cupcake on the tray with a card beside it. In big crayon writing, the front of it says *SORRY JANNA*. Logan waits for me to reach the bottom step of the gazebo before speaking. "Janna, we're very sorry. Really sorry for laughing at you. You didn't fart."

"Reawy sowwy," Luke says, echoing Logan. "You didn't fawt."

"We were joking. But now we're sorry." Logan looks behind him at Haytham. "Is that good?"

Haytham shakes his head and points at me. "You'll have to ask Janna."

"Janna, is that good?" Logan says, walking over to me carefully with the tray. "Is the apology good?"

I climb the two steps to take the cupcake, nod, and look at Haytham.

He smiles at me, the edges of his eyes scrunching with mirth in the dappled light of the sun filtering through the leaves of the trees behind him, and suddenly the sky that was in my heart before when I thought of Nuah flies out and surrounds me.

It's like happiness is everywhere now, not just secretly in my heart.

What is happening?

I drop my gaze to the cupcake in my hands.

"Wow. Wow, wow, wow!" Dawud suddenly shouts, his face still covered with what I now see is a super-heavy book, almost like a textbook.

It says *WEDDINGS* in big letters across the top. The bottom says *TO DIE FOR.*

"Can we get this flower-ceiling thing for the wedding? It's like an upside-down garden! The one made from lilies is the best!" He lowers the book and looks at Haytham through round glasses askew. He's eight years old, so he ignores me.

"Aren't you going to say salaam to Janna?" Haytham takes the book from him and closes it.

"Assalamu alaikum, Janna," Dawud mutters to the trellis above him. "We could have the flowers hanging from up there! It's going to be so cool!"

I respond to his salaam and turn to leave. But then turn back.

"Okay, yeah, that was a good apology," I say, putting an arm out for hugs from Logan and Luke, the two temporarily reformed hooligans. "Thank you."

They descend the stairs toward me, Haytham standing proudly behind them, holding the wedding textbook.

"Ugh, you're all wet, Janna!" Logan jumps back. Luke just squishes himself into my thighs, laughing as his shirt and face get wet.

"Well, that's what happens when you go into the lake. But now let me go inside to shower and change maybe?" I dislodge Luke, who's still rubbing his face in my burkini, and start walking toward the house. "Thanks for the cupcake."

I say this to Logan and Luke, but I sneak a small glance at Haytham to acknowledge his part in reforming them.

He nods at me and smiles again, before saying, "Hey, just an FYI, don't use the bathroom on the third floor. The one attached to the alcove guest room. It's got a fan issue, and it's still steamed up from my shower just now."

I nod and head to the back patio.

Behind me, I hear Logan say, "Now finish the song, Uncle Haytham!"

Uncle Haytham? How did that happen so fast?

"'I wanna live in a land called Paradise. Wanna see the birds fly . . .'"

His voice.

Haytham's voice is unbelievable.

Deep, melodic, passionate.

I can't stop my head from swiveling. He's sitting on the gazebo steps, the kids gathered around him, and when he notices me, he lifts a pretend hat and continues singing.

Maybe I should choose a lighter, fresher color hijab to wear after my shower, instead of the raggedy black one I was going to wear today around the house and to go into town to see Mom.

I mean, I don't even have a lighter, fresher color scarf in the stuff I brought here, but I can check my stepmother Linda's closet. She doesn't wear hijab, but she has a massive wardrobe with tons of accessories. And she's always cool with me borrowing stuff—even without asking.

As I walk across the second-floor landing to knock on the master bedroom door, Muhammad emerges from his room. "Sarah's downstairs in the basement. She said she wants to see you about something."

"Okay, but then I might be late to go see Mom."

"Mom's not getting in until five—she made a stop on her way. Check your messages." Muhammad looks at me carefully. "You okay? With the laddoos laughing at you like that?"

"They apologized. And gave me a cupcake."

"Oh yeah, Haytham made those for their drive over. Sarah said he packed the car with his baked goods."

"That was a good cupcake."

Why is Muhammad peering at me more carefully now?

"Hey, listen—be careful around Haytham, okay? Especially since he's staying here in the guesthouse. Him, Sarah, and Dawud."

I turn from Dad and Linda's bedroom door to face him. "Why? What do you mean, *be careful*?"

"I mean just know that he's . . . really unaware of his magnetic qualities. On people." Muhammad laughs.

"You mean, he's a player?" I don't let my heart sink. Because this is officially good news.

Haytham is a player. Which is UGH. So I'm on firm ground— not one iota near falling for a gorgeous, baking, chivalrous, singing player. *Who's great with kids.*

"No way, no, of course not!" Muhammad looks alarmed. "Never. He's the president of his MSA. Or he was last year. And he's studying Islamic studies."

"That doesn't necessarily mean anything." I frown. As if any of it proves anything. The monster who attacked me two years ago was considered a "pious good boy" at the mosque.

"I know, but in this case it does. He's legit. The man doesn't fool around at all. And is serious about stuff like that."

"Oh." I wonder if my face looks as contorted as my heart feels. It felt tons better when Haytham could be written off. Because I write off people like that immediately—people who pretend to be saintly.

"I mean Sarah's told me he's gotten into things where people have thought he was interested in them when he wasn't. And it's all because he's cool and kind, you know?"

"Oh my God, Muhammad!" I open the master bedroom door, anger mixing with embarrassment. "Do you really think I think he likes me? I just met him! Plus, I don't even find him interesting in that way?"

"I thought you might have, you know, fallen for the you know what." He points at his brow. "'Cause I noticed the way you looked at that forehead. In the lake. It was in awe, Janna."

I go inside and close the door in his face.

Siblings know all the unmentionables about you.

Somehow I find myself in the third-floor bathroom.

I have no idea why I gathered my clothes from my second-floor bedroom and bypassed its beautifully appointed en suite bathroom and lifted my feet up the steps to the alcove guest bedroom.

It *is* steamy, but the fogged-up mirror is slowly clearing. At the edges, not the middle.

Are those words?

Someone's written something onto the mirror, into the fog.

The weight of your soul
Joined with its many kindreds
Will light upon

The rest of the verse disappears into the now reappearing mirror.

I look at my reflection in the clearing parts.

My face is lit by the light of intrigue, the beginnings of fascination.

On top of being a kid tamer and a baker and a singer, he's a poet, too?

I can't wait until Nuah gets here tomorrow.

After my shower I find Sarah in the basement, in the storage room, counting boxes of something. She immediately wraps me in a hug. "Janna! Assalamu alaikum, my Janna!"

Sarah Mahmoud, my sister-in-law-to-be, is beautiful, kind, and completely determined in a steely, iron-grip CEO kind of way, while radiating positivity. Even her clothes beam joy—right now she has on a bright mustard-colored shirt over jeans, topped with an even brighter chiffon-mustard scarf, perfectly peaked at the top of her head à la the latest hijab style, round sunglasses resting atop it all.

Her entire vibe all the time is Joy to the World (That I Plan on Dominating)!

"Wait, you didn't go into the room next door, right?" I say, worried she saw the way Linda and I decorated it for the henna party tomorrow night. It's a surprise we organized under the supervision of Linda's friend, Ms. Mehta, who's super into the latest desi decor and fashions. She showed us how to throw the "most authentic mehndi party ever," which included draping lots of brightly colored, long, sheer saris all over the walls, with twinkling lights in between them. My arms are still tired from all the work yesterday.

But, I have to say, *Yay for Ms. Mehta!* Linda and I aren't well versed in desi things, since she's from a Greek family and I didn't learn any culture, with parents from two distinct backgrounds. Dad's family is originally Indian, and Mom's is Egyptian, but they were both born in America. So we really needed the "education" Ms. Mehta gave us; though, honestly, after a while, my mind got tired from hearing all the "rules" for a proper henna party according to her.

I went along with it all because of my love for Sarah. I wanted to surprise her with something spectacular, something theatrical, even though she's Syrian American, Arab, and not desi herself. Even if she doesn't understand all the mehndi party traditions, I'm banking on the drama factor to wow her.

Honestly, she's been like a sister to me from the moment I confided my pain about the assault to her, so she needs to be blessed with an abundance of mirrored cushions artfully arranged, and a slew of Persian rugs littered with fake flickering candles.

"Why would I go in there? There's a big sign on that door that says 'No Sarahs Allowed,'" she says, her laugh turning to a frown as she opens a box to reveal bright blue party horns.

"What are *those* for?" I rifle my hands through the tassely, crinkly foil in the box, frowning too.

Sarah hefts another box up that's labeled *For Decorating* and reveals its contents. "Look at this. Balloons. For making animals."

"Like a clown does?"

Sarah nods and stares at me in pain. "*This* is why I came up early. With my brother and my cousin Haytham. You met Haytham, right? From Arkansas?"

"Yep. I sure did."

"We drove up the minute I handed in my final assignments, Janna. Because I found out only this week that things have gotten out of hand." Sarah frowns full blown now and directs it at *me*. "And you didn't even stop it."

"Me?" I make a scowly face back at her, confused. "Didn't stop what?"

"How crazy this wedding has become. It was just supposed to be a simple nikah. A family-and-friends thing by the lake. That's what your dad said." She suddenly sounds like a completely different Sarah, frustrated and despondent. "That's what he promised back in April. Remember? After the fight?"

Oh yeah. The fight.

Chapter Three

❋ ❋ ❋

THE FIGHT THAT ALMOST MADE THE NEWS

Muhammad: I got into law school at Stanford! And since Sarah's also doing her PhD there, it's perfect!

Sarah's father: Oh no, not so fast, young man.

Dad: Why? He's finally settling down to a real degree, after his aimless ways. I even moved out here to the less expensive countryside so that I can help fund his education again. And Janna's, too.

Me: Thanks, Dad. Although *I* got a scholarship to college—but if you'd pay my dorm fees, that would be great!

Muhammad: We're talking about me here.

Sarah: And me.

Sarah's mother: There's no way we will have you two going off to Stanford together without getting your nikah done.

Dad: Let's get their nikah done, then.

Mom: We can have it at the Eastspring mosque with my brother the imam officiating.

Me: Aw, I love Amu! Yes, I like this idea.

Sarah's mother: Yes, let us do the katb el-kitab with just family and friends. At the mosque where the kids met each other.

Mom: Yes, just warm and casual.

Me: Yay, so then I can wear jeans!

Dawud, Sarah's little brother: Can I wear my Pokémon shirt?

Sarah: But what about everyone we want to see at the wedding? Like our friends from Chicago?

Sarah's father: We will do the real wedding next year. The official reception. I'll host it, and it will be how you like it.

Sarah: You mean with a tasteful matte-gold-and-gray color scheme?

Sarah's mother: Yes, and we'll fly in all our relatives.

Mom: Yes, then Teta can fly in, too. For the nikah this year, we'll share dates and simple food.

Sarah's mother: Yes, it will be simple and sweet.

Mom: I can make basbousa.

Sarah's mother: I can order baklava.

Mom: Then, as a family, we can go out to dinner at a restaurant of the kids' choosing.

Dad: I have an idea.

Everyone: Yes?

Dad: Why don't we treat our children properly? Instead of like their union is a sneaky secret? Why don't we honor them with a real nikah party? I'll host it on my property with a large backyard overlooking the lake and an adjacent field that can park a lot of cars. Then they'll know that they're loved from BOTH sides of the family. What about that?

Sarah's father: You think we're doing the nikah like it's a shameful secret?

Sarah's mother: You think we don't know how to treat our daughter properly?

Sarah's father: Have you even seen the wedding we're going

to throw them next year? How great it's going to be? How many people we will feed and how beautiful the decorations will be?

Sarah's mother: How dare you act like we don't know how to honor our daughter!

Linda, my stepmom, Dad's wife: Oh no, he doesn't mean that. Right, Haroon?

Dad: A small nikah in a small mosque is not honoring *my* son properly!

Sarah's father: How could you say we are not honoring properly? We are the most honoring parents ever, right, Sarah?

Sarah, to Muhammad: I have no idea what's happening here.

Dad: Muhammad, would you like to do a nikah at the house by the lake, inviting any and all of the friends you and Sarah would like to see on your special day? Still a simple ceremony but at least honoring your union and guests with a full dinner? With Amu still officiating, of course?

Muhammad: Actually, that would be nice.

Sarah's father: Why did you only ask your son? What about what our daughter has to say?

Sarah: I think that would be nice too.

Sarah's mother, to Sarah: But you didn't ask us!

Dad: It's their nikah. Let them decide!

Sarah's father: But *you're* deciding this.

Dad: Like *you're* deciding the reception next year!

Linda: We can have two parties. It will be fun.

Mom: But how will we plan such a thing so quickly? And afford it?

Dad: That will all be in my hands. It's arranged, then. You are hereby invited to a nikah ceremony by the lake that will become a cherished memory for all who attend.

Sarah's parents: And then you will see our wedding next year, how great that will be.

"So, in between, your dad gave Muhammad free rein to make it a full-blown wedding. Without me even knowing." Sarah slides a phone out of the pocket of her jeans. Frown still on her face, she turns it on and clicks and scrolls to find something. "Look. I had to record it for myself when it got wild."

She lets out a long sigh before pressing play.

Muhammad's voice. "I can't believe you've never heard of them, Sarah. The 'Arrys! Larry, Barry, and Gary! Really, I haven't told you about them before? Look them up on YouTube. They're hilarious, but also really musical. They have their own band, and the best part is that they're friends of mine. When guests come in, they'll sing improvised comments about them, and it's insanely accurate—and funny! I don't think they've done weddings, but I was thinking it would give off a real relaxed vibe. Sort of go with the whole happy blue-and-yellow color scheme, you know?"

"Blue and yellow? Like the Pacers, his favorite team?" I look at Sarah. "Is he talking about his bachelor party?"

She presses pause on the recording and leans against the massive shelving units lining the walls of the storage room. "He's talking about the wedding. This is from our phone call on Monday."

I lift my eyebrows. I really had no idea that Muhammad had actually been running the show.

I swear I thought Dad had hired a wedding planner.

"Oh my God. No wonder he asked me and my mom to wear blue. It's to go with his color scheme." I shake my head.

This is bad.

"He asked Haytham to wear blue too, and God knows how

many others. But the true worst is that he *hired* the 'Arrys to perform this weekend. At *my* wedding," she says, scrolling through her phone. She turns it to reveal a YouTube video of three guys in matching plaid shirts and plaid pants with Civil War–era bushy beards. One of them has side whiskers jutting out so long, you can see them sticking out from the back.

"Oh my God. No." I grab the phone and watch in mortified fascination as the three guys call out random people sitting at tables, addressing them with cringey jokes. "They make fun of guests?"

"Muhammad thinks they're hilarious."

"So weird." I give her back the phone. "I'm sorry you're marrying him, Sarah."

She lets out another sigh that sounds like it's being strangled by a growl. "Janna, you have to help me take this wedding back from your groomzilla brother!"

I look at her. And see her pain.

But the wedding is in two days. "Isn't it going to be a lot of work?" I whine, thinking of my plans to dedicate all my time to hanging out with Nuah when he arrives.

"I've organized it all. How we're going to take back this thing," she assures me.

"Don't tell me you brought a clipboard." I turn to stare at her. Clipboards are Sarah's thing. Because they help her Get Stuff Done.

"Hell yeah. Five clipboards, five colors to divide up each task area." A smile spreads on her face. Obviously at the thought of clipboards.

I like seeing that smile return.

I want Sarah to be really happy.

"Are you excited? I mean, besides this stuff, are you excited about getting married?" I ask, wanting to keep that smile of hers going.

"Of course! Other than his bad taste, Muhammad is seriously the best, and I can't wait to make it forever. Insha'Allah." Her wide grin and slightly blushed cheeks assure me of the truth of her statement as she peers at her phone and starts texting someone. "The minute we met, I knew he was the kindest person I'd ever encountered."

Okay, that's true. Muhammad is extra kind and caring, maybe even over-the-top caring, and he and Sarah make a good match—because they're both extroverted do-gooders.

But the part of "making it forever" is giving me pause. Mom and Dad weren't forever. Dad moved on to Linda, which, to be fair, seems to be headed to forever. Maybe.

Mom is still single. I don't know what I'd do if Mom decided she was seriously into someone. This one time, a couple of years ago, I found a flyer for a Muslim singles meet-up in her dresser drawer, but nothing came out if it.

Sigh of relief.

I don't want to be alone. And the thought about everyone pairing up around me gives me anxiety.

The thought of Nuah cures that anxiety right away too—because I know he likes me.

But then what happens next? Once I tell Nuah I'm interested in him, too? My plan only goes as far as telling him tomorrow before the henna party, before all the other guests arrive.

But I don't think I want the next step to be to actually *marry* him.

More like I want us to be connected before I go to college. So that I feel—safe? I guess?

I know that in Islam, you don't try things out with people—like there's supposed to be no sex before marriage, so making out and things that potentially lead to sex are a no-no without a nikah—and that you're supposed to find someone who suits your nature, has your values, and the same goals, and then, voilà, just make it work. That's how Nuah wants things.

And I do too. I think.

So Nuah and I make sense.

I think.

Gah, things always make better sense in my head.

Muhammad and Sarah are lucky. They just happened to meet each other, fall for each other, and make sense to each other immediately. And now they're making it real.

I look at Sarah as she continues texting with a frown again, and a sudden burst of love for her takes hold of my heart. "Okay, I'm in. I'll help you."

She looks up, face beaming. "Love you, girl. Welcome to Team Take Back the Wedding. We're having a meeting in that gazebo in ten minutes, when Muhammad goes to get groceries. Me, you, and Dawud. And Haytham, of course."

Chapter Four

✳ ✳ ✳

For the gazebo meeting, just to prove I don't have a thing for *anyone* (except Nuah, of course), I wear my ol' raggedy black scarf, flung on my head, the ends lopsided, over an oversize but thin sweatshirt instead of the nice top I'd originally thought of wearing with my super-faded, almost-white jeans.

I brought a notebook with me for "notes." But I snuck a copy of the latest Ms. Marvel inside.

I open the comic now to the first page as Sarah lectures to catch me up on what she, Haytham, and Dawud already discussed on their drive up.

Once in a while she paces the gazebo and then pauses to look out into the distance at Dad's house, the huge white behemoth with columns in the front *and* back that everyone in our family unironically calls the White House.

I can see Sarah so well as the professor she's studying to become.

Phrases like "color intervention at the party-rental place" and "paying off the 'Arrys" and "changing the balloon artist's task to entertaining the children and *not* doing the decorating" float around me as I move my capped pen across the comic panels describing Kamala Khan's latest escapades.

It's a good distraction, because once in a while Haytham tries to include me in the proceedings, and I'm studiously avoiding looking at him.

Because he's dangerous.

He came to the gazebo meeting holding Sarah's five clipboards fanned out to serve as a tray for a plate of more cupcakes.

"Hey, Janna," he said. "I saw that you liked the cupcake, so I brought the rest. These have messed-up icing. But now that I've won you over to my baking, you'll overlook that, right?" His eyebrows had curled up almost against each other in eagerness.

I nodded, my heart sinking at his uncalled-for cuteness, and, thus compelled, I reached out for another cupcake, glad I had brought comics to read as a shield against him.

At the end of the meeting we get a clipboard each with instructions—Sarah gets two—and I scramble out of the gazebo in my eagerness to go read quietly in my room. I have a bit of time before I go see Mom in town.

In my room, I fling my green clipboard on the bedside table and flop into bed. Immediately two books fall off the other side.

I'm okay admitting I sleep with books. They collect in an almost-body-shaped mass beside me, one that I can hug, and I love it.

Books are tidy and contained and bring closure. Sometimes not full closure, but there's an arriving at a destination that's perfect.

Why can't life be like that? And, really, why can't *love* be like that?

School is, and that's why it makes sense to me. It's ordered and has a beginning and an end, and the in-between is split up by studying for this or handing these three assignments in to make up this much of your grade.

I can't wait for college to start, to bring that order back into my life.

I reach for my phone and scroll through my personal guest list for the wedding.

Arriving on Saturday are some of my people and their plus-ones:

1. Sandra and her date: her grandmother, Ms. Kolbinsky. Sandra is good without having the whole boyfriend/girlfriend thing going on in her life. And Ms. Kolbinsky is the best. (She already promised to bring me a container of her spicy Polish samosas.)

2. My partner-in-nerd, Soon-Lee, and her boyfriend, Thomas, the only forever couple from middle school that has lasted. They already have their own wedding date "circled" ten years from now.

3. Coming on Friday for the henna party: Sausun, this girl (way older than me, already done college) I edit YouTube videos for, for her extremely popular Niqabi Ninjas channel, and her plus-one, her older sister. Basically, Sausun saved her sister from a nightmare marriage, and now Sausun is not into marriages or coupling for herself at all, only into making sure her sister heals.

(Though Sausun did say in a recent Niqabi Ninjas episode that she wants to find someone in this vast universe—and she emphasized *universe* because she wasn't ruling out aliens or jinns—who one day could be worthy of her. Someone who loved her personality, didn't care that she covered her face as a niqabi and so didn't put an emphasis on how she looked, who would be a good parent to the four kids she wants to have one day. "Thus far, I've never met worthy parent material. Truly. But there are unexplored parts of the ever-expanding universe, so I continue holding out hope—but only a sliver of it," she ended the segment with.)

4. Also coming on Friday, of course, is Tats, short for Tatyana, my best friend, and her mysterious plus-one. Who I'm super confused about. I haven't seen Tats for the three weeks I've been at Dad's, but there's no way she hooked up with someone new who I don't know. Whenever I text her WHO WHO WHO, she changes the subject or replies with something wedding related (like we're picking out a suit now) but random at the same time. And I just want to pull her long, glorious hair in retaliation for each cryptic message. But she's in Eastspring, and I'm enjoying the good life under blue skies, so she's too far away to beat up effectively.

I prop two pillows behind me and get comfortable to scroll and tap slowly through all of Tats's social media stories and posts in another attempt to suss out information on this date of hers. A knock interrupts me while I'm rewatching her latest TikTok ode to Billie Eilish, this one for "Ocean Eyes."

"Janna?" Sarah's voice.

It's Sarah and Dawud. He blinks at my unhijabbed head as I swing the bedroom door wide for them to enter.

"Can you give Dawud a ride when you go into town? He's already made an appointment with the florist Muhammad hired. To ask about the flower ceiling." She pats his head, and he beams while still staring at my uncovered hair. "I'm proud of him."

"Sure." I grab my scarf from the foot of the bed, where I'd thrown it. "We'd better leave now then. But is he okay with me staying in town for a while? I wanna hang with Mom for a bit."

Sarah shoots a questioning glance at Dawud. "You okay with that?"

"As long as we get back here for the movie night Uncle promised us." He continues staring at me, almost unblinkingly. "You guys have such an awesome theater in the basement!"

"Oh yeah, my dad. I have to actually check with him if it's okay we use one of his cars. He's sometimes not cool with it."

"Just use Haytham's." Sarah holds out the keys. "He's okay with it."

I take them and slide them into my tiny backpack purse. "That's nice of him."

"I'll talk to Muhammad to get the rest of the wedding details. He and Haytham are hanging out on the front porch right now. Perfect place to tease out information!" She lights up. "I already found out the 'Arrys are free tomorrow, so maybe we can get him to switch them to perform at the bachelor party instead of the wedding!"

Dawud scrutinizes me as I wind the scarf on my head. Geez, hasn't he seen Sarah put on her hijab before?

I shoot him a scowl. I hope he's not one of these creepy eight-year-olds who has a thing for older women. Ugh.

"You have purple icing on your forehead," he announces. "And I don't even know why. Because none of the cupcakes we had at the meeting had purple icing."

I look in the mirror. There *is* purple icing on my forehead. So weird.

"There was pink icing and blue icing, so they must have mixed together. On your forehead." He breaks out into a big grin and turns to leave, clipboard in hand.

I grab my own clipboard and head to the en suite bathroom to take care of my forehead before Haytham sees it.

Tats texts me while I'm in the bathroom.

I'm changing my dress for the wedding! When we were looking for a tie for my date I found a dress JUST LIKE THE ONE LINDSAY LOHAN WORE TO THE MTV EUROPE AWARDS!!! But it's yellow not metallic gold.

Tats is going through a huge Lindsay Lohan moment. We've been watching Lindsay movies every weekend since May. She even dyed her hair ginger. Which means there's a lot of ginger around her, because Tats has huge hair.

Can I see a pic of you in the dress? And your date in his tie? I smile at the way I slid that in so deftly. Maybe I'll finally find out exactly who Tats is bringing to the wedding.

Is it okay that the dress is above my knees and off my shoulders? Avoidance in action.

Yeah, why wouldn't it be?

Because when I go to the mosque with you I don't dress like that?

It's okay. We're not at a mosque. Something dawns on me. OMG, you and I are going to match the wedding decor now. Blue and yellow.

Blue and yellow? That's kinda ew, tbh?

Don't worry, Sarah's here and we're working hard on the ew factor. Really hard.

Haytham's car is a Honda Civic, which I've never driven in my short six months of driving, so I'm kind of nervous.

As I prepare to ease it out of the long driveway, he saunters over from the porch and approaches the rear passenger's-side window, which Dawud has rolled down all the way. "Would you guys be able to pick up some Gatorade? Need it for after bench-pressing. Cool gym your dad has by the way, Janna." He holds out a fifty. "The blue kind or, if they don't have it, white. And only Gatorade, please. I'm a purist."

Dawud snatches the bill. "Perfect. This leaves enough for ice cream after."

"You guys are getting ice cream, too?" Haytham raises those compelling eyebrows at me, and I fiddle with the keys in the ignition. "I love ice cream."

"We are?" I say, shrugging, turning to Dawud.

"Yeah, that's why Muhammad thinks we're going to town, so we have to," Dawud says, folding up the fifty smaller and smaller.

"But the ice-cream truck comes by here almost every day. Because of the laddoos." I close my mouth. Oops, I didn't want Haytham knowing my endearing name for my little brothers. It feels kind of private.

"Oh man, I love ice-cream trucks more than ice cream itself!" Haytham laughs. "Did you ever notice the people who drive them fall into two categories: jolly happy souls or mean uncles? But mean uncles holding out ice-cream cones, which is the best."

I can't help laughing. Because it's true, our ice-cream guy is a mean uncle.

But . . .

"Actually, our ice-cream guy *is* a mean uncle, *but* he gets excited and ho-ho-hos when he hands you your ice cream. Like serious Santa-level excited."

"I need to see this. When does he come around?" Haytham leans his elbows on the door next to Dawud and peers across at me. "I can get your brothers their ice cream and also get further data for my ice-cream-truck hypothesis."

"Usually around seven. But he came by yesterday, so it may not happen today." I kind of want to stay home now. To wait for the ice-cream truck. With Haytham.

Of course it's only to see what he thinks of our ice-cream-truck uncle who completely defies his theory.

Maybe we can finish everything in town and make it back before seven.

While slowly rolling the car out onto the road in front of the house, I can't help glancing in the rearview.

Haytham is sprawled on the porch hammock, the one I like to read in during the day. But he's not reading, or even paying attention to Muhammad and Sarah talking at the table nearby. He's waving at us.

Chapter Five

❋ ❋ ❋

I turn on the car stereo, and after a few piano notes, Haytham's voice enters the car. "'When I was young on the Fourth of July, I'd go outside and watch the show in the sky . . .'"

It's a haunting antiwar song set to a simple piano accompaniment. I listen in silence and then turn to Dawud. "That was amazing."

"It's Haytham's entry for the Muslim Voice competition."

"Oh, he's going for that? That's impossible to win." I play the song again. "It's a global competition. Thousands and thousands of entries."

"But he's got a lot of votes! He's in the top five!" Dawud crosses his arms to say this. "And he's going to get more. Like you, right? Can you vote for him?"

"Okay. Because he—it's really good." I play it again. The words are amazing. *We can bend iron with our prayers at night.* "Did he write the song?"

"No, it's from one of Haytham's favorite singers."

I nod and play the song a third time, wondering what else there is to learn about Haytham.

It ends up being a fail for Dawud at the florist's, Ravson's Ravishing Ready-Blooms.

The owner, Hope, is all game to discuss details about Muhammad's floral order until Dawud inquires about pricing for a ceiling of lilies. "Calla lilies," he specifies.

"A small ceiling arrangement of yellow callas?" Hope looks curious. She's a dead ringer for the Disney princess Merida, an older version, so her curious look is slightly scowly. "Or white ones with blue centers? Because you realize I can't get blue ones, right? Not enough lead time."

She talks to him like he's a CEO in a business suit and not a kid in a blue T-shirt that says S'OREO FOR EATING THE LAST ONE.

"No, we actually want a big ceiling of . . ." Dawud pauses and looks at his clipboard. "White flowers only. With green foliage."

"But the order said no white flowers. Only a yellow-and-blue sprig for each table and a blue-and-yellow arch for the entrance to the path to the gazebo. I thought the theme was blue and yellow." She turns from the cash register to look through a wicker basket holding file folders. Her curly and mountainous red hair masks her peripheral vision, so I'm able to make frantic *stop* motions with my hand to Dawud, unbeknownst to Hope.

I risk mouthing, *She may call Muhammad!*

Dawud looks at me blankly and pushes up his glasses.

"Muhammad Yusuf is the name on the file. Are you Muhammad Yusuf?" She pushes up her own glasses and stares at Dawud. "Are you the groom?"

She says this with a steady glance, without irony.

He shakes his head and points at me. "Nope, that's *her* brother."

"And where's Muhammad Yusuf? And the bride, Sarah Mahmoud?" Hope turns to me and finger-stabs the names on the file. "Because this is their wedding order. That I'm delivering in two days."

"Oh, we were just thinking of doing a surprise for them. And just wanted pricing on it. Because they both love the idea of a floral ceiling but didn't think it was in their budget." I talk quickly and confidently.

"Ah, so you wanted to do a surprise floral gift?"

Dawud nods his head enthusiastically.

"Sorry, we don't allow that. Too risky to interfere with the wedding plans of the bride and groom." She turns to put the file back in the wicker basket.

"But how much would it be? In case they do want to order it?" Dawud is holding a pen poised over his clipboard, and I can't help but think that he's learned the determined, decisive ways of his sister.

"Oh, depends on the flower variety, the number, and kind, as well as size, but anywhere from a thousand for a simple cluster to ten thousand for the full deal." Hope takes her glasses off to rub her eyes. "And that's with at least three weeks' notice. No one can pull off an entire ceiling in three days, sorry to tell you."

I swing my backpack to the front and take the car keys out of it. "Thanks so much."

But Dawud doesn't budge. "What if I help? To make it?"

Hope breaks out into a grin, then gives a full-bodied laugh. "You must really love the bride and groom!"

"No, I just really, really want a flower ceiling," he says solemnly, clutching the clipboard to himself.

"Sorry, dear, I can't teach you how to be a florist's assistant in a couple of days." She continues laughing while tidying up wisps of ribbons and snips of stems on the counter.

"Dawud, I gotta go meet my mom. Let's go!" I hiss as nicely as I can. "Thanks, Ms. Ravson!"

I head to the door and then, seeing Dawud still standing motionless, push it wide open and go right out. Maybe if he thinks I'm driving away, he'll start moving.

I'm in the car with the engine running when Dawud runs to the back door and opens it. "She said I can have all the leftover flower and leaf cuttings from all her other orders. So we can make our OWN ceiling."

"Oh no," I say. "No, Dawud. I'm so not doing it."

He just writes something on his clipboard, and I see the beginnings of Sarah in him again.

But he is *so* not going to boss me around.

Since we arrive at the hotel early, Dawud and I wait in the lobby for Mom.

It's a lush lobby meant to mimic nature in a very unorganized way, so there are tons of large plants, fake and real, as well as seating made to look like it was hewn from white birch tree trunks. In the dead center, right before you get to the elevators, there's a tree that almost reaches the high ceiling, obviously fake, its branches sprouting big fluffy balls of red cotton amid the dark green leaves. I don't know what that's about, unless it links with the name of the hotel, the Orchard.

I'm scrolling through Instagram—Tats posted a picture of her prewedding look—when I see Mom enter through the automated double doors, wheeling a large suitcase behind her.

I jump and practically run over to hug her.

She looks so good, her smile, her eyes, her entire face. Like she's rested—and like I've missed seeing her for almost three weeks. We texted and talked on the phone every day, but nothing beats being back in her presence.

"How are you, sweetums?" She strokes my face and kisses a cheek before ruffling in the pocket of her thin windbreaker to find and hold out a pack of halal gummy bears. The quality, imported-from-a-Muslim-country kind.

I seize it and am about to rip it open when I remember that I'll be seeing Nuah tomorrow. Insha'Allah.

He appreciates real gummy bears.

I pocket the pack and give Mom another hug before following her to the front desk.

She has on a white sporty pull-on hijab, the kind she wears when she's doing a long drive, and, under her light pink jacket, black track pants and an old gray T-shirt with faded words, I DID 10K FOR ALZHEIMER'S.

I'm kind of surprised she's so slouchy-looking, as she's really into being presentable. Not fashionable, but neat and ironed.

The opposite of me, in fact. Except for tomorrow, at the henna party, and at the wedding itself, when I'll be in two of my favorite outfits ever. Mom and I spent a lot of time finding fancy clothes I actually liked.

"You brought my clothes, right?" I ask as she waits for the hotel personnel to activate her room key.

Mom turns to me and nods and then squints at something beyond me. "Isn't that Sarah's brother?"

Dawud is coming out of the hotel shop cradling six Gatorades in his arms. He spots us and bounds over while trying to balance the drinks. "These were almost thirty dollars!"

"What! WHY DID YOU BUY THEM HERE?" I'm incredulous. "That's so irresponsible! I was going to stop at the grocery store! Where the whole thing would have been ten dollars at the most!"

Mom looks at me with her eyebrows raised, the edges of her mouth moving up slightly, before nodding, proud-like.

Wait, did she just give me a mom-to-mom-approval look?

I turn back to Dawud, who's trying to push his glasses up while holding on to the Gatorade. I poke his glasses onto the bridge of his nose so I won't have to pick up the bottles he'll spill should he fix his own glasses. "I can't believe you! Wait until I tell Sarah!"

"I just wanted to make sure we get back quickly! So we don't miss movie night," he whines, while tolerating Mom's hand reaching over to tousle his hair, to say salaam. He responds to her with a peppy "walaikum musalam!" before lugging the Gatorade bottles to the chair he'd been sitting in before Mom entered the hotel.

That kid.

Just wasted Haytham's money.

I'm done babysitting the twerp with a mind of his own.

The automated hotel doors open again at that moment, and a tall man in a dark suit, with hair graying at the temples and a beard similarly salt-and-peppered, steps inside and gives the hotel lobby a once-over. Behind him are two girls, twins, who almost reach his height. They appear to be around my age, and I can't help staring, because they're in hijab, one with breezy red fabric flung on her head casually and the other in a dark purple trim turban worn tight.

Which is a rare sight—two more hijabis—in a town that's almost as small as a village.

My eyes trail the girls following the man, who's now headed

to the counter beside Mom. They don't notice my stare, though, because they're whispering to each other intently.

They look like they just stepped out of a fashion magazine. One is wearing loose and flowy light brown pants that go all the way up high on her waist to disappear under a short, white, squarish top with military-looking details on the shoulders and front pockets. The other girl, the one in a turban, has on a loud jungle-leaves-print jumpsuit that flares, with a matching cape attached at the shoulders that hangs behind her almost to the floor.

They walk confidently, like they're on a runway, their clothes fluttering in sync with their strut, their luggage streaming behind them.

Who are these girls?

"Husna! Assalamu alaikum!" It's the man. Talking to Mom. "Thought you were getting here earlier?"

Mom turns to him, and her entire face lights up.

Chapter Six

❉   ❉   ❉

"Bilal! Walaikum musalam!" she says with gusto. "I stopped to check my car fluids on the way, so I just got in."

"Well, I'm so glad. You'll get to meet the girls earlier than dinner, then." The man takes out his wallet and hands his credit card and ID to the front desk attendant before turning back to Mom, a smile taking over his previously pensive face. He notices me. "Oh, masha'Allah, is this Janna?"

Mom motions for me to come stand beside her. I move in, and she puts an arm around my waist. "Janna, this is Uncle Bilal. He and Dad and I went to college together a long time ago. He's here for the wedding, and these are his daughters, who're coming to the henna party tomorrow. Assalamu alaikum, girls!"

I straighten and nod at Bilal. Uncle Bilal, I mean. "Assalamu alaikum."

Uncle Bilal smiles at me and says salaam back and introduces his daughters. "Dania and Lamya. They've heard so much about you, Husna. And you, Janna. And they're good friends of Sarah's from college, just like your mom and I were, Janna. Subhanallah."

Dania (purple turban) and Lamya (red scarf) smile big and

lean in for hugs with their salaams with me and Mom in turn, and I involuntarily stiffen.

I'm not a cuddly person in general. It's only recently that I've learned to relax with Mom even, to let her hug me and show an affectionate touch. I don't know why, but it definitely isn't natural for me to just melt into hugs with people, especially people I just met. So I pull away from Lamya's and Dania's embraces quickly. They don't seem to notice and go back to smiling benevolently at me, but not talking.

"This is perfect. Now we can *all* sit for dinner together." Uncle Bilal beams at Mom. "I got my nephew to join us too, if that's okay. He was driving through."

Mom beams back at Uncle Bilal but suddenly looks nervous. "Janna, is that okay with you? Or do you have to go back to Dad's? Because Dawud is with you? And you might be expected back?"

Wait.

Does she want me to?

Go back to Dad's?

While she has dinner—that's obviously been preplanned— with Uncle Bilal and his runway-model daughters? Who've heard so much about Mom and me, while I've never heard of them?

I need to check on something my gut is raising low-key alarm bells about.

Like where's Uncle Bilal's wife?

"I can stay for a bit. I don't need to get back right way," I say, before smiling friendly-like but tentatively at Dania and Lamya. "And what about your mom? Is she going to join us?"

There's a second of silence before the three of them, Uncle Bilal and his daughters, speak all at once. "Mom's in England. With her new family." "Mom's remarried." "Mariam and I divorced when the twins were six. Then Dania and Lamya moved back here from England to go to high school, and have been with me since. It's just us three, our family. For now."

This last part trails from the joined voices.

Why do they look kind of confused by my question?

And, *for now*?

Mom grasps the handle of her luggage and glances at her room key. "We'll meet at dinner then, insha'Allah? I'd better go get settled in. I had a long drive up." She adds an awkward laugh to this. "And you had an even longer journey."

Why are her cheeks flushing? I put my arm through hers and speak confidently, not giving in to the weird vibes I'm getting here. "Where did you guys come from?"

"I flew into Chicago from New York, picked up the girls, and drove here in a rental car. We wanted to be sure to make it in time for dinner," Uncle Bilal says, his eyes lingering a bit too long on my mom's face, like he's trying to figure out what Mom's feeling—but in a tender way.

"Okay, Mom, we better go unpack. Insha'Allah, we'll be seeing you." I smile and wave at Dania and Lamya, and then take the handle of Mom's luggage and begin to roll the bag toward the Tree of Red Fluffs. Nearing the elevators, I glance behind. "What floor, Mom?"

"Fifth." She waves feebly at Uncle Bilal and his daughters as she leaves to follow me.

But they're right behind us. "We're on the fifth floor, too!" Uncle Bilal beams again and . . . is that a flush on his cheeks too?

I grab Mom's arm tighter. I don't realize how tight until she wiggles out of it as the elevator doors open.

"Janna! We have to go!" Dawud appears in front of the elevator we're assembling in, still cradling his Gatorade bottles. "It's almost six, and your dad said the movie is going to be after dinner! Which is at six! You said you'd get me back!"

We all stare at him before Mom nudges me. "Go, Janna. Maybe you can come by later? And I'm coming to the house tomorrow really early, anyhow. To help with wedding prep."

Uncle Bilal puts a hand on the elevator door to hold it open, and I hesitate before stepping out. When I turn back, it's to watch the door close on Mom and them.

To watch the door close on Mom, flushed and smiling funny, and them, flushed too. Well, one of them, that is.

The tall guy who called Mom one of his best friends from college.

Who's also divorced.

I drive back slowly, my mind turning things over, making whole scenarios up—like Mom and Uncle Bilal and Dania and Lamya having dinner together at the hotel. And then taking a summer evening stroll through the "quaint" town. And then eating ice cream at that ice-cream place by the side of the road beside the largest lake here, the one the town's named after: Mystic Lake.

Ice cream.

I glance at Dawud, who's waving his arms out the window like he's one of those floppy air-filled figures businesses use to advertise their wares.

He's the one who prevented me from spending more time with Mom. "Too bad you didn't get your ice cream."

I just want him to squirm a little. Feel a gut pinch.

But he doesn't and just smiles goofily, pointing ahead. I turn my eyes back to the road, and there, way up ahead, is the ice-cream truck, driving the same direction we are. On its way to the end of the road, which runs through a peninsula of houses filled with kids, after which he'll circle back to our place.

I speed up. I want to get home in time to prepare for jolly mean-uncle ice-cream man. So I can show Haytham the truth of the matter.

But when I pass the truck and make it to Dad's driveway, there's a car parked in the spot where Haytham's car was before.

And I forget all about the ice-cream-truck theory.

It's a car I know really well.

Nuah's.

He got here early. Today. *For me.*

Chapter Seven

✿   ✿   ✿

Dad's house is quiet when we enter. Like no one is home.

But when you step into the hallway from the foyer, there's a direct view to the huge glass doors to the patio that take up almost the entire back wall, and I see Dad and Linda out there in front of the barbecue. The doors are open, and I can smell the burgers they're grilling.

I leave Dawud behind and make my way to the backyard. Everyone must be outside, getting food.

It's just Dad and Linda out there, though. And the laddoos, who are both working on wrecking a bubble-blowing machine by pushing each other to try to stand and balance themselves on it.

"Just in time for the first burger!" Dad, in his regular summer uniform of a buttoned-up dress shirt with shorts, flips a patty and snaps the long tongs at me. "Cheese melted on it or no?"

"Where's everyone else?"

"Went for prayer." Dad peels a slice of cheese from the stack by the condiments on the long outdoor table and holds it over the grill. "Cheese?"

"No thanks, Dad. I'll eat after. With everyone." I'd better join them for Asr salat, too. "Are they praying in the family room?"

"No, they're in the basement. More friends of Muhammad and Sarah drove up." Linda holds a container out for Dad to put the burgers in. "You sure you don't want to have one with us now? They're beautifully done."

"I have to pray too. But maybe he'll have one with you guys?" I point at Dawud, who's just stepped out, a big smile growing on his face—maybe because he saw the burgers.

No, it's due to the bubbles desperately escaping from the machine under attack.

Linda nods, and I head inside to make wudu in the main-floor bathroom.

We're taught at the mosque that prayer with others, in congregation, is rewarded twenty-seven times more than prayer alone. This is a compelling reason to hasten to the basement.

Let's call my first glimpse of Nuah in six months, since he last came up to Eastspring for Christmas break, a bonus.

I joined the prayer late, so I'm still in prayer mode, catching up on the rakats I missed, my eyes closed because that's the only way I can come even one iota close to concentrating on salat, when I hear everyone else begin to shuffle up the stairs.

I finish and sit alone on the white sheet that has been spread on the carpeted floor.

I need to make dua. I need to make sure I talk to God before doing this.

Ya Allah, make this go right, this thing with Nuah. When I tell him.

I know one thing: I'm pretty sure God loves Nuah. He's kind and humble and always smiling, always friendly. That's the type of person my mom's brother, Amu, the imam at the Eastspring mosque, always says is gold to God. Whenever he says this, though, he always peers at me and not Muhammad, who already goes around with a goofy grin plastered on his face. Whereas I've been told my resting face is a perpetual pout, which is the opposite of my middle name, Ibtissam, meaning "smile" in Arabic—Mom's choice for my first name until Dad overrode her for the more anglicized Janna.

Maybe that's why Mom didn't get the smiley daughter she'd always wanted. Because I'm Janna.

Whenever my uncle sees Nuah, his face lights up and he slaps him on the back, and while talking to him, he does that nonstop smiling nod that I'm pretty sure Amu isn't even aware that he does. Whenever *I* see Amu like that, I get all glowy, because I know Nuah's already mine. So it's like someone is admiring something that belongs to *me*.

The way I'm laying it out, it's like he's perfect. Nuah. But he does have his faults.

Like sometimes he can laugh at something you said so much and so long that you wonder if he's laughing at you, too. Like his smile is ever present, so it's hard to know where the default ends and the appreciation begins. Like I've taken a while, a couple-of-years while, to get back to him about his feelings for me because, truthfully, sometimes my gut will whisper, *How for real is his thing for you, Janna?*

And sometimes it will also say things like, *He's on and off in talking to you, Janna.*

And, girl, doesn't he always keep it light and fluffy when he does talk to you?

How for real is his thing for you again, Janna Ibtissam Yusuf?

I push delete on the comments from my mean gut and fill the space with evidence. Such as his I-stand-by-you texts exactly when I needed them.

And the truth that he's never treated any other girl at the mosque the way he's treated me.

Special.

Everyone's outside on the patio, and I freeze the image like it's a photo.

Muhammad and Sarah are sitting across from each other at the long table with bench seating, a plate of burgers in front of them. Dad and Linda are still at the barbecue, now grilling corn. Haytham is kneeling in the grass, bending over the bubble machine like he's fixing it, with Luke, Logan, and Dawud peering at his tinkering.

And then there's Nuah. He's by the condiments, dressing his burger.

He's still his lanky self in a white T-shirt and gray shorts that look like they're cut-off track pants. He's grown out his Afro above his medium-size forehead. (A forehead that I've accepted with dedicated resilience because it goes hand in hand with an awesome personality.)

I even glimpse the wooden tasbih necklace he always wears, its threaded ends disappearing into his T-shirt.

When he smiles a secret smile at his burger for some reason, a smile that ends in a dimple on the right side of his face, I feel that blue-sky feeling again—but this time it's intensified by a thousand.

I'm about to slide the patio doors open when I hear steps. Behind me.

I turn.

"Hey, assalamu alaikum! Janna! Long time no see!" I'm surprised to see Khadija, Nuah's older sister.

I move in for a side-hug, relieved she takes it, instead of doing the whole big-bear-hug thing most people at the mosque are into.

I haven't seen Nuah's sister in a while as she lives in Missouri now, but I like her a lot.

Before I became old enough to join it, she used to run the teen study circle at the mosque. Whenever she found me and my friends hiding in the bathroom, "taking breaks" from our Sunday school classes, she'd tsk, shake her head, and laugh to herself, but never, ever tell on us. Then she got married and moved away from Eastspring.

She's like a taller, girl version of Nuah. Well, except for the pink scarf she's wearing.

And the huge baby bump she's sporting.

Seeing my eyes land on it, Khadija rubs her belly. "Due in a week."

"Really?"

"Yup. That's why I came up from St. Louis. Mom wanted me to have the baby with her, at home in Eastspring." She continues rubbing it, and we watch the scene outside quietly for a bit. "The only way she was okay with me coming up *here* for the wedding was that I had to promise her I wouldn't have the baby in . . . what's this place called again?"

"Mystic Lake."

"Well, that's a pretty name. So maybe I wouldn't mind Maysarah being born in Mystic Lake, actually. Maysarah of Mystic Lake." She laughs, and I get that warm feeling again of being a little girl giggling in the mosque bathroom, of being accepted with no expectations.

Linda slides the door open. "Corn's ready now."

I let Khadija lead the way and put my hand in the pocket of my hoodie, my fingers finding the gummy bear package.

Nuah's sitting beside Muhammad now, his back to me and Khadija.

When Sarah waves at us, he turns around, and I do the only thing that feels right at the moment: I immediately hold out the gummy bears, my eyes darting between them and Nuah's face.

He smiles and takes it. "Hey, assalamu alaikum, JY," he says, turning the package over in his hand. "Ah, the best ones. Haribo halal."

He hands them back to me.

"They're for you," I say.

"Me? Aw, thanks." He nods and smiles again.

Muhammad laughs. "What is it with you guys and gummy bears? Didn't *you* bring some for *her* last time, Nuah? At Christmas break?"

"They were for both you guys." Nuah turns back to his burger. "My roommate's Turkish, and he brought tons of halal ones from Turkey. And I unloaded some on you guys."

"Naw, there's something between you two kids. Admit it." Muhammad looks at me.

I head to the barbecue to get corn, to get away from Muhammad making things more awkward than they already are.

More than I already made them by just wordlessly handing Nuah gummy bears.

When I bring back my plate of corn, Nuah's ripped open the bag of gummies, and it's now being shared by Sarah, Khadija, and Muhammad.

I take a seat beside Sarah, which puts me right across from

Nuah. And then of course, me being me, I move over so I'm directly opposite Khadija, who's beside him, instead.

Muhammad doesn't miss this. "Why'd you move over? Now you can't do the gummy bear thing with your pal Nuah. Actually, NA to you, JY."

He picks up a red gummy and a yellow gummy and does a fake conversation between them, asking each other, NA and JY, how many gummy bear packages they've exchanged.

I ignore him with nuclear-powered strength, concentrating on nibbling my corn.

"Okay, cut it out, Muhammad. It's not funny," Sarah says.

"Wrong move. Surprised you haven't learned this, and you're marrying him in two days," Nuah laughs, and picks up a colorless gummy bear. "You tell him to stop it and that *at least* doubles his buffoonery. And yeah, Muhammad, this would be . . . um, I don't know, the tenth pack of gummies we're trading?"

He nods at me and hands me the colorless bear. "Your favorite, pineapple."

I take it with a smile and set it down on the edge of my plate. That simple move of his just made this whole thing better—me not saying hello, salaam, how are you, how was the drive, what's happening at school, et cetera, et cetera.

Me just gummy-bearing him has been erased by him handing me my favorite flavor.

I stare at my pineapple bear and almost tear up thinking of how much Nuah gets me. And lets me be my awkward self.

And still likes me.

"When did you get back to Eastspring?" I ask, picking a corn niblet up from my plate.

"Tuesday. Then hung out with my parents and little brother

and now here we are." He's picking through the candy, separating the pineapple ones. "Your dad said there's wedding-favor assembling happening tomorrow?"

I nod and glance at Sarah. I wonder if she knows that the favors include little blue chocolate basketballs. This I knew from Muhammad yelling "YES" last week and sharing his "amazing online discovery" with me.

Khadija beams. "And tomorrow is the henna party. I can't wait. I even splurged on a dress for it, and it's not a tent like the one I'm wearing to the wedding." She winks at me and Sarah. "I want at least one cute pic from third trimester."

"Oh yeah, I can't wait to see your foxy dress," Sarah says, laughing.

Nuah pokes Muhammad. "What are we doing? When they're henna-partying?"

"We're outta here. Maybe go into town to eat?"

"No, I'm throwing something for you and your friends. A party in the barn." Dad brings a platter of corn to the table.

"I thought we were just going to eat?" Muhammad raises his eyebrows. "Eating is fine. Eating is enough, Dad."

"There'll be eating, don't worry. I run a successful food company—you don't think I'd have thought of the eating?" Dad laughs.

"Let's keep it simple," Muhammad mumbles into his burger.

"Want some gummy bears, Uncle?" Nuah indicates the package that's now half-gone. Then he reaches over to my plate and deposits all the colorless bears on it with a smile.

Dad shakes his head and does a whistle. It's his call-the-laddoos whistle.

Linda hates it. The whole time I've been here at their house,

I've seen her getting upset about it, about how it'll make the kids think they're dogs, but now she just calls out, "Luke, Logan, come and eat. Dawud, you too, and—I'm so sorry—I forgot your name."

"Haytham, no problem." He comes over and sits on the other side of Sarah. "Hey, are those halal gummy bears?"

"Appetizers." Nuah passes the pack over.

"You mean Nuah and Janna's code for *I missed you, boo.*" Muhammad guffaws, and Sarah suddenly flexes herself from the hip down, and, from my brother's abrupt laugh shutdown, my guess is that she stepped on his foot hard.

I'm going to like having Sarah in the family.

I scoot myself over closer to her. Now directly across from Nuah again. I can't stop myself from smiling at him.

Dad, who's right behind Nuah, stares at me with his eyebrows raised.

Weird.

"Hey, where are all the pineapple ones?" Haytham is peering into the gummies bag, tossing its contents. "Those are my favorites."

"Nuah gave them all to Janna. I mean JY, as he calls her," my brother volunteers.

I make a mental note to never ever be nice to Muhammad again. I'm about to pick some pineapple gummies to put them back in the bag for Haytham when I hear it.

It's the ice-cream truck. On its way back from its first stop at the end of the road, where a cluster of houses sits across from a small restaurant overlooking the water.

"ICE CREAM!" Logan yells when he hears the "Pop Goes the

Weasel" jingle, after which Luke echoes him. "ITE CWEAM!"

Linda immediately moves into place to stop Luke from running to the front of the house. Now I get why she's always wearing leggings.

Dawud sets down his plate and makes his way to Sarah, little-brother pout on. "Can I get ice cream? I'll eat dinner after. Please?"

"Let's go check this ice-cream guy out." Haytham stands up and motions to me. "You coming?"

I look at my pile of pineapple bears and then at Nuah. He's chewing the last of his burger and gazing behind Sarah at the water.

I want to stay with him. He's just so calm, and that's what I want right now. "No, I'm going to finish eating dinner."

"Okay, then I'll report my findings." Haytham puts a hand in his pocket and pulls out his wallet. He nods at Linda and bends to scoop Luke up. "I'll take the boys. Who else wants ice cream? Dawud will help me carry it."

"I'm done with my burger, so I'll come see what they've got." Nuah wipes his face with a yellow napkin, one of the thousand Dad ordered and has now put to use in the house because he realized we didn't need a thousand for the wedding.

I stand too. "I'll come as well, then."

Muhammad lets out a loud laugh.

Nuah and Haytham and the kids have already started walking, so I turn to glare at my brother. "You are so unbelievably immature! Sarah, you don't know what you're getting into. You can still opt out, you know."

Sarah flexes herself again, and it must have been for a hard stomp, because Muhammad whispers "sorry" to her and then makes a please-forgive-me face at me. "Sorry, Janna. I mean, JY," he adds with a giggle.

I turn and stalk off. At least he won't be there at the ice-cream truck.

It'll just be me and Nuah. And the little kids.

Oh yeah, and Haytham, too.

Chapter Eight

✳ ✳ ✳

The jolly jingle stops, the window slides open, and the ice-cream-truck operator appears.

"What do you want?" his mouth, under a lush gray mustache, demands, while his eyes, under lush gray eyebrows, stay still and drooping. His face muscles are so unmoving, the only way we know he just spoke is by the words we heard, which he repeats louder now. "What? Do you want?"

The *gruff* words we heard.

Haytham looks at me pointedly and pulls out money. "Tell the nice man what ice cream you want," he says to Luke and Logan.

"Ite cweam!" yells Luke, in Haytham's arms, reaching pudgy fingers toward the window.

"He always wants whatever Logan gets. So let Logan choose first." I hoist Logan up and point at all the pictures on the side of the truck, like I do every time it comes around. And, like every time, he pronounces a new choice and then changes his mind last minute to a chocolate Drumstick. I announce two of those to the guy, who's scowling now, his eyebrows closing in on each other.

I choose a vanilla cone dipped in chocolate. Haytham mouths *great choice* to me and picks the same.

Dawud can't choose, so Haytham lets him get all three of his choices, a Firecracker pop, a Choco Taco, and an ice-cream sandwich, if he promises to share the ones he doesn't end up wanting.

Nuah goes with an orange Creamsicle. "What?" he asks Haytham when Haytham shoots him a look.

"Dude, I've never seen anyone buy those except my grandma once."

"Your grandma has good taste, then." Nuah unwraps his treat and watches Haytham paying. "Next time, it's on me."

The ice-cream-truck guy hands Haytham back his change and grunts before closing the window again. At no point did his mustache move up to allow a smile or even any sort of mouth movement.

"Aha, so I'm right. We were just served by mean-uncle ice-cream-truck guy," Haytham says as we walk back across the long lawn. He cracks the side of the chocolate shell on his cone with his teeth and scoops into the vanilla underneath. The ice cream starts running immediately, and he begins twisting his tongue all over the cone in his hurry to get all the drips.

I'm shocked at his eating manners.

"That's not how you eat those. You work your way down," I say, holding up my immaculate cone, getting slowly consumed, top down. "And you're so not right. Today was an off day for the ice-cream guy. Maybe something happened to him. Maybe to his family."

"Okay, if that's the case, we need an ice-cream-truck watch set up." Haytham shifts his cone into the hand that's holding Luke at his hip and pulls out his phone. "Write your number in here, and

I'll text you if I see the truck. And you do the same. Then we meet the ice-cream guy again and settle this once and for all."

I take his phone and send myself a message, an ice-cream cone emoji. When I give the phone back, I see Nuah smiling at me, or maybe it's us.

He's gotta know this is a dumb sociological thing that Haytham's trying to prove, so I address Nuah. "Just so you know, Haytham thinks ice-cream-truck drivers are all either mean uncles or the nicest people in the world. And I'm trying to tell him ours is both. He usually smiles when he gives us our ice cream. Right, Logan?"

Logan turns around from where he's walking with Dawud.

"The ice-cream man is nice, right? The other days? When he gives you your ice cream?" I prompt.

"I don't like him," Logan announces. "He always has the same ice cream."

"That's his truck's fault. But he smiles at you, right?" I try again.

"No, he's mean. He always gives me the same ice cream." At this, the top of his Drumstick falls off and lands on the grass, leaving him with an empty cone. We gather around, and I see that only the chocolate chunk at the very bottom remains inside the waffle still in his hand. He looks up at me, his eyes growing larger, his mouth opening into an O at the same rate.

The lip tremble will come next. And then it'll be a wail that will echo like a police siren.

I know him too well from these last few weeks.

"Here." Dawud thrusts the Choco Taco toward Logan. "You can have this one."

"I want the same one!" Logan says, crossing his arms. He

throws down the empty cone in his hand with a great flourish, and it lands pointy part up, a pitiful distance from its departed friend, the mound of melting ice cream.

A trickle, which will erupt into waterworks soon, begins falling from his eyes.

I pass my cone to Nuah and bend to grab Logan's shoulders to get him to look at me. "But remember, you didn't want the same one? You said you always got the same one from the ice-cream guy. Now you're getting a special one."

"I want the same one!"

Still holding Luke, Haytham slides down onto his knees until he's almost eye-to-eye with Logan. "It *is* the same one. But you know how the bubble machine makes different bubbles, big bubbles and small bubbles and medium bubbles?" He waits until Logan nods.

"But they're all still bubbles? The same bubbles?" He waits again. "This is the same ice cream that you like but just in a different shape."

"But *you* don't have a different shape." Logan points at Haytham's cone, now running all over his right hand. "You have the same shape. Like mine."

"Exactly. And look what's happening to it. It's wrecking my hand. And look at Luke's face." We all turn to Luke, who looks like he just got back from World War I, like something brown and muddy exploded in his face and he survived but is now irrevocably changed as evidenced by the kooky smile on his upturned face, his eyes blinking with maniacal glee. "Look at his ite cweam. Is that the same one you want?"

"No! I don't want ice cream all over my face!" Now Logan starts sobbing at the stressful idea of potentially looking like Luke.

Haytham nods to Dawud and motions to him to pass the Choco Taco over to Logan. "And with this Choco Taco, you will never look like Luke here. It's made for big boys and big girls who don't get ite cweam all over their faces."

Once Logan takes the Choco Taco, I hand my cone to Nuah again and help Logan unwrap his.

He tentatively takes a bite, and, amid the tears still glittering on his cheeks, the trace of a small smile breaks out before he turns to skip off with Dawud toward the house.

"Man, that was gooood," Nuah says to Haytham as we follow behind. "What are you, some kindergarten teacher or something?"

"Nope, just an uncle of over twelve years. I've got ten nephews and nieces."

"Uncle of over twelve years? How is that even possible?" Nuah stares at Haytham before slurping the last of his Creamsicle. "You're, like, my age."

"I'm the youngest of five—*way* youngest of five. So I became an uncle at seven."

"Is that why you're holding Luke on your hip like that?" Nuah asks, laughing. "Like a seasoned parent?"

"The best thing for your back." Haytham laughs too. And then he proceeds to hoist Luke onto Nuah to show him how to do it, but Nuah flips Luke to do the football hold, at which point Luke's ice cream falls on the ground.

Nuah, Haytham, and I look at each other with bated breath.

But Luke just giggles, flails his arms, and says "atain" to Nuah.

He's passed back and forth like a heavy football between Nuah and Haytham the rest of the way to the patio, Haytham's ice cream gulped along the way, while I finish my cone slowly and think about how people can be so crazy different.

Good thing for me that, like how I choose my ice-cream flavor, I prefer to stick to only those who make *sense*.

Right before we turn the corner of the house to go out to the backyard, Nuah says to me, "So when do we practice the roast?"

Haytham lets go of Luke, and he runs ahead, following Dawud and Logan. "Oh yeah," he says, "you guys are doing a roast of Muhammad. I'm running the wedding toasts and performances, and you're on my clipboard."

I nod. "It's a take on his favorite YouTubers, the Hearty Philosophers. They do this thing that's like, when you consider this aspect of life, blah blah blah, it's weird. But when you consider this aspect, blah blah blah, it makes sense. And they keep going, bringing up the bad and good of everything."

"And Janna and I worked out this whole routine, based on Muhammad's profile," Nuah says, laughing. "Like about his feet unsocked, their potency. And his midnight ketchup, pickle, and peanut butter sandwich runs, and other things to alert Sarah about."

Haytham laughs too. "My poor cuz."

"Hey, you should join us," Nuah says. "We need someone to pop up once in a while, like the Hearty Philosophers do, and say *AND THAT'S LIFE*. But adding *WITH MUHAMMAD!* We were going to try to recruit someone."

We were? Maybe my face looks obviously surprised, because Haytham takes a glance at me and shakes his head. "I think it sounds perfect with just you two. And besides, I'm scheduled to sing a song for Sarah. I don't want to hog the stage."

"You sing?" Nuah asks, beginning to walk.

"Yeah. Hey, can I get you guys to vote for me in the Muslim Voice competition?"

"You going for that, man? That's wild."

"He's good, too," I add. "Really good."

Haytham turns to me. "Ah, thanks. You heard me?"

"Yeah, in the car." I smile at him, and he smiles back. "And you got my vote."

"Awwww," Nuah says, grinning. "You got Janna's vote, you lucky dude."

I shake my head. *Why would he even say it like that—with raised eyebrows?* "So you want to practice later on? The roast?"

"Sure! What about tomorrow after Jumah? Muhammad's got me on a packed schedule before then." We're almost at the patio table, so I nod quickly, and the three of us make our way to everyone else.

After Jumah.

Me-and-Nuah time.

Finally.

Chapter Nine

✳ ✳ ✳

I'm staring at the ceiling of the gazebo in a reverie, my half-eaten burger on a plate on the floor beside me, when I get jolted back to the present with the words "Nuah won't be able to stay after the wedding. He's going back to Pasadena on Sunday."

Sarah lured me to the gazebo again to talk wedding, with Khadija this time, and I reluctantly came—only because Nuah had gone to town with Muhammad to pick up snacks for movie night.

Now Khadija was saying Nuah wouldn't be in Eastspring when I got home from Dad's.

I right myself. "Why? I thought he was back for the summer?"

"He got a job. It's warehouse job, but it's at the company where he wants to work when he graduates, so he's excited." Khadija shifts herself in the deck chair Sarah brought for her to sit in. "He's going to make it for a quick visit again a bit after the baby's born, but other than that, he's gone until Thanksgiving."

"Aw, then that he made it a point to come for the wedding makes me so happy! He's such a sweetheart." Sarah turns to me. "What do you think, get him in on Team Take Back the Wedding or not?"

"Maybe." I want to know more about Nuah not being in

Eastspring, so I slide my butt closer to Khadija, my heart beginning to thud with worry. "So he'll be working the whole summer?"

"The entire summer." She crosses her hands on top of her baby belly and addresses Sarah. "Don't get him involved in the prep. The guy can't keep anything to himself. If you tell him it's a secret, he'll just avoid being around *anyone and everyone*, because he knows he's going to leak the information."

Really? I'm surprised. He's always struck me as someone who you could trust with your biggest secret. Well, that was because he did keep mine before, the terrible secret of my assault, while helping me feel ready to talk about it.

But, of course, Nuah's sister would know him best.

"He's such a cutie," Sarah says, writing on the purple clipboard she's assigning Khadija. "He must be a hit at college, especially at the MSA, being so sweet and with those eyes."

"Oh, I'm sure of it. Though he's into someone. Majorly." Khadija rubs her belly now in slow, circular motions and turns to me. "Don't mind me. This is something I've read is good for the baby. You know, like a massage. Especially while I'm talking, so Maysarah knows it's her mama who's showing her this love."

"Absolutely adore that name. Especially since it has SARAH in it," Sarah laughs.

"It was Lateef's choosing," Khadija says. "He's lucky I liked it right away."

I want Khadija to back up.

Nuah. Into. Someone.

Me.

Nuah told his sister about me.

But how to get her to pedal back to the topic without giving myself away?

Lucky for me, Sarah saves the day. "You said he's into someone? That's so cute! Who?" She turns to me. "We get Nuah gossip! Which is rare. The guy keeps such a low profile."

"I don't know who it is. All he said is that she's *really hard to get*. And he's worried about that."

"Khadija. I'm so shocked you wouldn't ask details. Come on, what kind of big sis are you?" Sarah tut-tuts and crosses off something on the clipboard. "When Dawud grows up and confides something like that in me, I will immediately set out to amass a wiki's worth of information on the girl."

"He told me just as we were arriving here, like literally five minutes before we opened the car door. I'll take my big-sis cred back, thanks." She stands and stretches. "And that, girls, is not the most comfortable chair. Especially for my butt right now."

I hope I'm not turning red, or even slightly pink. Though I don't know if anyone would see. It's almost Maghrib, so there's darkness descending.

He talked about me to his sister right before he got here.

Something that feels like it's flicking on and off takes over my body. I pull my knees up close to my chest and hug them to keep the feeling from exploding out of me.

It's joy.

How am I going to make sure I don't burst with joy being around him this weekend?

But he thinks I'm hard to get.

No. I'm going to make sure he knows that's not true.

I'm going to let myself be got.

"Janna? Have you heard anything we're saying? About organizing Logan, Luke, and Dawud to pass out the wedding favors?" Sarah waves her hand in front of my face.

"That's on my clipboard. I already know about that." I let go of my legs and stand up slowly to join Khadija. The floorboards are definitely not good for butts, even unpregnant ones, either.

"But could you update it that they're to pass them out the minute the nikah is done? Because I'm adding a slip of paper with a dua we want everyone to say right after, so we have to make sure people have it on them. So they can join Amu."

I write this to-do down in my phone, smiling at the thought of seeing my uncle again. Besides officiating, he's also giving the wedding sermon—which I helped him edit.

A message pings on my phone. It's an unfamiliar number.

I open it just as Sarah's phone rings. She takes a look at the ID and moves off the gazebo to answer.

My message is from Haytham.

Taking votes for movie night: Star Wars or Stardust?

Princess Bride

Oh ok

It's on the movie schedule

Sorry, didn't know there was a schedule

On the basement fridge

Right. Ok setting up princess bride

Before I click off, I hesitate on whether to save Haytham's contact on my phone.

When I look up from adding it, Khadija's staring at Sarah. Well, Sarah's back.

She's wandering farther and farther away, phone to her ear, not toward the water or the house but to the far right of the house, where the neatly mowed field ends at the beginning of the forest that leads to a second beach, one with a firepit. Then she abruptly turns around, conversation ended.

Khadija and I watch her come back, and as she gets closer, it's obvious that she's upset. "I gotta go. I can't stay here."

"What?" I gather the clipboard and our plates and position them so I can take them back to the house. Sarah reaches over to help me, but I shake my head. "What's wrong?"

"My parents don't like the idea of me staying here, where Muhammad is, before the nikah." She begins to make a face but then clears it. "It's okay—I should listen to them. Not get them upset before the wedding. I mean, more upset."

"But don't they know you're staying in the barn guesthouse?"

"It doesn't matter. They don't like us being in the vicinity of each other overnight without being nikahfied." She grabs the chair Khadija was sitting in, folds it, and tucks it under her arm.

We follow her quietly until we reach the patio. Then she puts the chair against a pile of others leaning against the house and shrugs. "It's okay. I'll check myself into that hotel your mom's at. And then I'll make sure to get here first thing in the morning."

"If it's the Orchard hotel, Nuah and I already have a room there. Maybe you can just stay with me, and Nuah can stay in the . . . is it really a barn?" Khadija asks, curiosity flickering on her face in the patio light.

"Really? That would work. But first check with Nuah if it's okay? It's much nicer than a barn. Loft bedrooms, just no bathrooms." Sarah turns to me. "And check with your dad, too, of course."

I nod, not sure how to feel about this new development. *Nuah is going to be staying here?*

It makes me feel excited but also weird, because of the potential of him seeing me in my pj's. Which are really old, preteeny clothes that aren't flattering.

"I'll ask Haytham to drive us to the hotel, after Maghrib." Sarah pulls on the patio door and steps aside to let Khadija in.

The hotel.

Mom.

Uncle Bilal.

I stop Sarah before she goes in after Khadija. "I can drive you guys, if Haytham's okay with me borrowing his car again. I'll stop by and see Mom again too. I didn't get my clothes for the wedding from her before."

"You going to be okay driving back alone?" Sarah asks, her face wearing a slight frown. "I don't like it. You alone in the dark on those roads. I'll ask Haytham."

"But I'd like to see my mom." I think. "Wait. What if I text Muhammad to wait for me before coming back from town? And then I can follow him?"

Sarah nods, and we pass the kitchen where Dad and Linda's live-in help, Florence, is cleaning up, and go downstairs to pray Maghrib.

Perfect. Now I get to see Mom *and* Nuah in town.

I'm dropping Sarah off at the hotel. So I'm coming back to see you Mom! ❤

Perfect. I can't wait sweetums! And we changed our dinner to later, at 9:30. So join us at the hotel restaurant okay?

Oh.

Is that okay? We can talk after. Just us two.

But I'm going to need to come back here before it's too late.

I can make sure dinner is quick.

I shake the feeling of Mom possessiveness that the message activates in my heart and, instead, try to fill it with happy thoughts. *Nuah is here! We're going to have fun at the wedding!*

It doesn't work.

Mom takes up a different chamber in my heart, impenetrable by Happy Nuah Thoughts.

I really don't have that much time. I frown and add, So it's okay, I won't come.

There's a pause before she replies.

Oh, then I'll cancel the dinner.

I stare at my phone, satisfaction at her answer quelling the weirdness rising in me just a moment ago. Do I reply with *Great! See you soon*?

I start typing it and then pause and scroll up to our texts now.

My insecurity shows big time.

And I hate that.

Why do Uncle Bilal and his family have to be so disruptive?

I can just imagine Mom's face falling at the fact that she can't go through with her plans.

Janna, she just wants to meet up with an old friend and laugh about the good old days. Like if you grew up, and Thomas, Soon-Lee's boyfriend, showed up with their kids, graying at his temples, and you wanted to find out what he'd been up to all these years.

Sighing, I erase *Great! See you soon!*

No, it's okay! I'll meet you at the restaurant! Love you.

Because I do love her.

Maybe too much.

Chapter Ten

✳ ✳ ✳

All through Maghrib prayer a thought keeps beginning to interrupt me before I shut it down repeatedly because I'm praying: *If Nuah thinks I'm hard to get, then—*

When Haytham, who's leading us in salat, says salaam to end the prayer, I let the rest of the thought invade: *If Nuah thinks I'm hard to get, then who will tell him I'm not?*

Well, besides me—but it's not going to be me. Because the minute I saw him, and his cool, chill self, my brave intention to reveal my feelings to him in person retreated.

Add to that the zoolike conditions around us, with little kids crying over ice cream and a big brother bent on ruining such delicate matters, and there's no way this is going to turn out well.

I need a new plan. I need someone to help me.

I turn to Sarah beside me. She's already started making dhikr.

On the other side of her, Khadija, who'd been praying in a chair, has already started sunnah prayer.

I wait until Sarah's finished her tasbih and then touch her arm. And point to the stairs.

I don't know if this is a good idea, but maybe Sarah, with her clipboards, can help me out with a new plan.

"So *you're* the one who's hard to get for Nuah?" Sarah asks, crammed into the cleaning supplies closet in the kitchen with me. It smells like bleach.

I nod. "Because I never show my hand. So I guess he doesn't know how I feel?"

Sarah cracks up at that for some reason. "Sorry, it's just funny the way you nodded just now. So solemnly. Like it's not love we're talking about."

"Oh," I say, wondering how you nod at something that important without being solemn. "I mean, it's a tricky situation. Maybe that's why I'm being serious."

"No, it's not. It's beautiful! Nuah, the amazing guy that he is, likes you, Janna! And you, amazing you, like him back. How's that not the best thing?"

"Sh, keep your voice down!" I hiss at her. I open the closet a crack and see Florence's back as she wraps up food. She's got her headphones on like usual—she's big into podcasts—and seems to be the only one in the kitchen, so I think we're okay.

"Janna." Sarah starts giggling again. "It's so hilarious. Your face."

"Will you stop, please?"

"Can you lighten up, then? It's fun that you found out someone you like is into you. It's not an exam, Janna."

"He liked me first. And he'd text me wondering if I was ready. But I wasn't then, and now I feel like I am."

"Aw, that's the sweetest." She stares at me for a minute and then bursts into laughter again.

"What?"

"Your face is that way again. Like you're facing a firing squad." She stops laughing suddenly. "I'm sorry. I forgot what it was like to be seventeen and unsure about love."

"Yeah, especially because you were dating then. And had *lots* of experience," I add with my eyebrows raised. I found out a couple of years ago that Sarah, who I used to call *Saint* Sarah due to her ultra-religiosity, had actually been a different Sarah before she moved to Eastspring and took over the mosque's youth committee. That's why I'd opened up to her about the things I was going through back then—and I guess now, too.

"I didn't have *lots* of experience, but I did know how to navigate guys and relationships more than you, I guess." She opens up her arms as much as the confines of the closet allow. "Hug? Along with a promise I'll help you with this?"

I succumb, and as she envelops me, her shoulders start shaking. She's laughing. Again.

"So sorry, Janna! It's just that I can't forget the way you leaned over and said that to me so gravely. *I'm the girl Nuah thinks is hard to get.* You're so cute, I love it."

I let go of her. Telling her had not been my best idea. "Can you stop? It's so easy for you to laugh when these things are simple for you. I've never been in a romantic relationship. With anyone, in any way."

"Janna, it's never simple. No relationship is. It's a back-and-forth dance where sometimes you give more, sometimes you take," she says, her face turning serious.

"Well, I wouldn't know." All I know is that I'm comfortable with Nuah. "Like, I get why in Islam it's the way it is. No dating and stuff. But—"

"What do you mean? Technically, a date is a time you make to meet someone to get to know them, to assess whether they're right for you. It's not about sex, you know."

"I mean the sort of date where you're with someone and there's expectations."

"Yeah, that's why rules exist in Islam. Like don't be completely alone, in case the expectations trap you in something you don't want. As far as I'm concerned, it's just like old-fashioned courting."

"Ugh, like how you and Muhammad had me around when you guys met to get to know each other more." I wrinkle my nose. "I hated chaperoning you guys."

"We knew. But you did such a good job, and now here we are getting married." She smiles. "And here you are asking for my help with your boo. See, I'm paying it back."

I roll my eyes. But I guess it must have been gravely, because Sarah starts laughing again.

"Oh. My. God. STOP," I command.

"No, now I'm laughing about something else. It's because Muhammad was so right about you two, JY and NA. You know what I'm figuring out more and more? That he's often right. Even though he acts all over-the-top sometimes, or most of the time, he's actually very on the mark about stuff. He's really intuitive."

"Okay, now *that's* really funny." I burst out with an expertly faked peal of laughter.

There's a clamor heading to the supplies closet, and then the door swings open to reveal Dawud dressed in knight gear from the laddoos' toy box. "Hey! What are you guys doing in here? It's time for *The Princess Bride*. Haytham said there are a lot of sword fights in it, so you better get your gear on!"

Before I head out with a sigh, Sarah stops me. "You know,

Nuah is, like, the best, right? He's got the sweetest heart, and he's going to be so good to you, insha'Allah."

I nod, happily this time. And she hugs me for real when we get out of the bleachy closet.

The road ahead of us is winding and dark with no streetlights, and suddenly I'm glad Sarah intervened on me driving back alone. I'd have turned back to town if I'd had to come home solo.

Khadija is beside me, her seat pulled all the way back, her legs spread wide, her seat belt pulled slack with the positioning of one of Sarah's pillows just so. She's looking out the window, trying to tap her fingers to Haytham's voice that came on when I turned the ignition.

When I was young, on the Fourth of July, I'd go outside and watch the show in the sky.

"Mournful. This is mournful," Khadija announces, after her fingers give up trying to find a quick beat.

"This is Haytham's entry for the Muslim Voice," Sarah says from the back. "They announce the winner on Sunday."

"Why such a sad song?" Khadija pulls the seat belt even more and twists herself to look at Sarah. "About a girl dying?"

"It allows for his range, according to him."

"Well, let's change it. Permission to?" Khadija directs this at me, and I nod, even though I want to listen to Haytham singing about feeling depressed while watching fireworks. But Khadija looks like she's not having it as her hands are already on the dial. "I want something more fun. This is wedding weekend, woo!"

She turns the dial but is stopped by Sarah reaching a hand out. "Forget the music for a sec?"

I look in the rearview so I can see her, gauge what she's up to.

She winks at me when she catches my eye. My fingers immediately grip the steering wheel tighter, and I have to tell myself to breathe.

Sarah, who's pulled her seat belt loose, moves to stick her head between our seats up front. "Dish on this girl Nuah likes. Janna and I have been observing him for a couple of years now, and he's never shown his hand in that area. We're intrigued."

I'm shocked at her bluntness. *Is my face on fire right now?*

Sarah taps me lightly on the sleeve. "Right, Janna? Remember when that love-and-romance Q-and-A thing happened at the mosque and your uncle talked about late bloomers, and Muhammad said Nuah was one?"

I nod, my face burning, and then say feebly, "Yeah."

Maybe she's trying to draw me in so I look like I don't care in *that* way. I shrug and say it again, stronger this time. "Yeah!"

Sarah coughs, looks me in the rearview with eyes wide, shakes her head, and mouths *too much*. Then she turns to Khadija again. "So?"

"I told you guys. We only talked about it for literally five minutes before we got here." Khadija reaches for the radio dial again. "He told me there's this girl he's interested in. He thinks she might be into him, but he's not sure."

"And? Did he say anything else about her?" Sarah encourages.

"That she's super nerdy but also super fun. Like, she organizes all sorts of outings—some he's gone on."

I stare at the road ahead. *Organizes outings?*

That sounds like a person like Sarah. Not me.

But wait, I did do that fundraising thing last summer to bring water to five in-need villages around the world. A group of us went to offer water-saving car washes at the mall. Technically, I didn't organize it—it was Sarah—but I was sort of second-in-command. After Muhammad, I mean. But Muhammad and Sarah are one, so yeah, I was in charge. I organized it. And Nuah came to it.

"She's into books. He said she's read more than him. And that he can't keep up with all the books she talks about."

I smile. Sometimes I snap pics of my books to Nuah. And, if he has no idea about one of the titles, like *Far from the Madding Crowd*, he'll send me a scratching-head GIF.

"So he decided he's going to go hang out at the library she works in part-time and get suggestions."

What?

I don't work at the library.

Wait.

I do. At the mosque library. An hour every week shelving.

And yeah, Nuah has come there sometimes to read when I've been there. Once or twice.

I look at Sarah in the rearview and smile. But she's got a slight frown.

"And she's really into nature. And planting trees. He was just getting to tell me about that when we parked in the driveway." Khadija turns on the radio and flicks stations. "Is that enough intel?"

It's Sarah's turn to speak feebly now. "Yeah. That's a lot, actually."

I don't say anything. I'm just looking at the outlines of *trees* in my headlights, scanning my brain for when I've spoken about my love of trees before to Nuah.

Because I do love trees. And I'd love to plant them one day.

So I must have mentioned it to him.

Chapter Eleven

✵ ✵ ✵

At the hotel, after Sarah and Khadija check in and go up to their room, I follow the arrows pointing to the restaurant at the back of the lobby. When I reach the sandwich-board sign announcing the Glade, I'm hit with nostalgia for the apartment building I live in with Mom in Eastspring. Like the lobby there, it's filled with a mix of towering fake plants at the entrance with the exact same cherry-wood balustrade to keep them at bay.

When I get closer, I realize the plastic plants have paper flowers sprouting from them randomly. Some of the flowers are nice and almost origami-like, but others look like they were made by kids at school.

I seriously don't get the Orchard's vibe—it's like someone's eccentric aunt decided to open a hotel and assigned all her nieces and nephews, with varying aesthetic sensibilities, to design and make the interiors however they wanted. Hence the modern, minimalist-looking birch-bark seating paired with fraying tissue-paper flowers made in kindergarten class.

Paired with really nice hotel staff. Like this girl at the restaurant right now, greeting me in a peppy voice that matches the ponytail sitting high on her head. "Hi, welcome to the Glade at the Orchard! We're so happy to nourish you today!"

I peer beyond the host and glimpse Mom sitting with Uncle Bilal and his daughters. "Thanks! I'm over there," I say to the host, pointing.

She hands me a menu with a big smile, and I position it like armor before walking over.

There are more fake plants and flowers leading all the way through, and it's only when I get to Mom that I see that a big, weird bush has been hiding another occupant at the table. He doesn't turn when I get there, even though everyone else makes friendly gestures and slight squeaky sounds on spotting me.

Uncle Bilal stands to pull out a chair beside Mom, the one that had been keeping a gap between her and him. I kiss Mom on the cheek and sit down, nodding at Dania and Lamya.

The sixth person at the table turns out to be a guy with longish hair that's unruly in front, with most of it falling on his forehead. He's got a lined-up five-o'clock shadow on his brown jawline. When he nods at me without smiling, he reminds me of someone, but I can't place who.

"This is Layth. Our cousin," Lamya says. "He was driving through, and Dad asked him to meet us for dinner."

Layth nods again.

"Our entrees are coming. Would you like to order appetizers?" Uncle Bilal beams at me.

I shake my head. "I already had dinner, thanks."

Uncle Bilal's changed out of his suit and is wearing an old faded T-shirt that says KICK CANCER: A TREK FOR HOPE.

Did he do that to match Mom's outfit when she'd first arrived? Her I DID 10K FOR ALZHEIMER'S?

Too bad for him, because now Mom is in a flowery summer dress with sensible sandals and a silky khaki hijab.

Uncle Bilal's daughters are still in their runway clothes.

Layth's in a jean jacket with a black T-shirt underneath, a design of a wilted, yellow daisy dying on it. He catches me trying to read the words under the flower. "It says 'Cheap Thrills,'" he says wryly.

When he speaks, I instantly realize who he reminds me of. If this guy's hair were trimmed, he would look like a taller Zayn Malik, the singer. Well, an around-my-age version of him. It's his looks plus the way he talks, the way his mouth moves up on his left side more.

And the clipped way he speaks, his dark eyes reserved and framed by strong eyebrows, and how he didn't look right at me when he spoke just now, like he's somewhere else.

I nod my head at him, pretending I get it. His CHEAP THRILLS T-shirt.

"Your mom's told us so much about you!" Uncle Bilal beams again. "Scholarship! To the University of Chicago. Masha'Allah! And to study English lit!"

"With a focus on British lit," I clarify.

Is it my imagination, or did that Layth guy just smirk a little at this?

Is he sizing me up as a nerd?

I close the menu and add, "They have a learn-abroad program in London that I'm interested in doing."

"How wonderful," Uncle Bilal says. "Travel is great when you're young. The twins did a year in Italy and Sweden, Lamya and Dania, respectively."

"Yes, more travel to emphasize Eurocentrism," Layth says,

most definitely smirking now, his eyes still not on me, even though he's talking about me. "How great."

Dania laughs. "Don't mind him—he's going through a Che Guevara moment."

Ouch, the belittling sarcasm. But also so definitely needed, because how does this guy Layth know why I want to go abroad, why I want to study British lit?

For the last little while, all my English essays have been on the roots of the revival of widespread xenophobia, of the current strain of it calling for bans and walls, through analyzing the British "classics" that we're fed in school.

I'm not studying British lit to support "the man." I'm studying it to take him down. "Well, as Che himself said, 'The first duty of a revolutionary is to be educated.'"

Layth gives me a surprised stare before turning away.

"We have a few friends at UChicago," Lamya says, folding her arms on the table. "We can send you their contacts. And we're at Northwestern with Sarah, well, where Sarah *used* to go, so we won't be too far."

"Yes, get contacts. You don't want to be lonely on campus," Uncle Bilal says, nodding at Mom. "It's the worst thing. Remember? Freshman year, before we all met each other?"

"Oh yeah. I don't know what I would have done if I hadn't met Magda. And she hadn't made me come to that dinner . . ."

Mom and Uncle Bilal drift off into a conversation about the old days across from me, and I open the menu again. Because it's something to read.

"Do you like to dance?" Dania asks me.

That was out of the blue. "Sometimes? With my friends?"

"We're doing a surprise dance for Sarah at the henna party

tomorrow. A bunch of us, like twelve people, have been practicing on Zoom, because the girl has friends all over the place. Do you want to join us?" Dania says earnestly. "It's just a simple mehndi song. And we've shortened it even further because there are a lot of non-desi people dancing."

"I don't think I'll have time to learn it."

"It's super easy. This girl named Zayneb, you must know her— Sarah's good friends with her? MSA president? She put it together in like twenty minutes."

"She called the Bollywood moves funny names so that every-one can understand them. Come up to the room after dinner and we can show you!" Lamya says excitedly, adjusting her scarf so that it peaks at the top perfectly, her loose silver watch sliding down her slim arm as she does so. "It will be special for Sarah if her sister-in-law-to-be is involved, you know?"

When she puts it like that, I pause. Of course I want to do something special for Sarah.

But it's just not my idea of fun: spending time with these people I barely know, dancing in their hotel room. "I kind of have to see when my brother's ready to drive back. I'm following him to my dad's."

"They had appetizers with us," Uncle Bilal says. "Muhammad and Nuah. And your brother invited Layth to the wedding too."

Layth shakes his head. "But I'm not coming. I gotta get to Miami."

"You need to get to Miami by Tuesday night," Dania says, shaking her head. "Sleep in on Saturday, and we'll make sure to remind you to leave the minute the wedding is over to sleep some more. And drive all day Sunday."

Lamya pipes up too, animated. "Come on, Layth. You have

to spend at least a couple of days with us. Not just a few measly hours."

Layth doesn't say anything. Just looks down at his plate. And then looks at Uncle Bilal, his expression now strangely sad. "You sure you want me sticking around?"

Uncle Bilal looks uncomfortable for a second. "Of course. Why wouldn't I? I think you should stay. Meet my old friend Haroon and hang out with your cousins a bit more. We got two rooms here. I'll ask to be switched to a room with two beds, and you can stay with me."

At that Layth raises his eyebrows.

I look at Mom discreetly. Clearly there's some family drama going on that we have no idea about.

These people are strangers after all.

Of course Muhammad being Muhammad would just invite any- and everyone he meets. He probably invited that perky restaurant host with the high ponytail, too.

I go to meet Muhammad and Nuah at the front of the hotel, while Mom continues on to dessert with Uncle Bilal and family.

I left the restaurant relieved, because it was evident that Uncle Bilal is just an-old-pal-from-college situation. And nothing like what my imagination was trying to lead me to believe.

Nuah jumps out of the car when Muhammad pulls up in front of the hotel. "Do you want me to drive, and you can take a ride in here with Muhammad?"

"No, it's okay." I take Haytham's car keys out. "I'll be okay as long as I'm following you guys."

"All right. We won't go too fast." Nuah gets back in after giving me a thumbs-up.

He hasn't changed his sweet self at all.

As I get in the car, and all the way on the drive, I imagine what it would have been like if it had been me and Nuah in the car alone.

I catch my own eyes in the rearview and tell myself, *Girl, that's going to be in your future. You and Nuah, together.*

Chapter Twelve

✽ ✽ ✽

We enter the dark home theater right as one of my favorite movie scenes ever begins: Vizzini choosing which potentially poisonless goblet to drink from as masked Westley watches and a blindfolded Buttercup listens.

I fold myself into the lone sofa at the back while Nuah and Muhammad each take a comfy armchair, one of the many arranged in rows in front of the 105-inch TV.

I've seen this scene in *The Princess Bride* so many times that I whisper-echo all of Westley's retorts to Vizzini, who's analyzing his choices out loud. For some reason, "Truly, you have a dizzying intellect" doesn't come out in a whisper but as an outburst—which causes almost everyone turn around to me.

That gives permission for the floodgates to open, and there's a rendition in unison of "As you wiiiiiiiiissshhhh" as Westley rolls down the hill and then, for the rest of the movie, commentary erupting from various parts of the room at different times.

As I sit in the back and listen to impassioned takes on the best fighting moves and the possibility of Andre the Giant not having actually died, I realize that because Linda opted out of movie night, I'm the only girl in a room full of guys aged three to fifty.

Luke (snoring, but still), Logan, Dawud, Nuah, Haytham, Muhammad, and Dad.

I text Mom. Don't forget to bring my clothes okay?

Yes, first thing sweetums!

I send her a row of various happy emojis. I love that she answered so quickly even though she's still probably with Uncle Bilal's family.

Dad gets up to get more popcorn for Logan, and I get a jolt thinking of Mom being here in the morning. With Dad.

Tomorrow will be the first time they've been together for longer than thirty minutes since their divorce. What's going to happen?

Will they act awkward or like they're acquaintances? Or even like they're strangers?

But they're not strangers. At some point they were in love. Such deep love that they wanted to live with each other for the rest of their lives. *Said* they wanted to. Committed to it.

And then . . . they didn't stay true to their words. They said adios to each other, to a life together, when I was ten and Muhammad was sixteen, turning seventeen.

The cynical part of me wants to believe that this proves that love isn't reliable. That it isn't something that becomes real and true once you say so.

But maybe Dad and Mom's love was forged too quickly. The story I always heard was "We met as third-year students, at a friend's house off-campus, on Eid." They got married before their last year of college, and Mom had Muhammad right away.

That seems fast. Maybe that was the problem.

Then there's that other thing Muhammad told me, that Mom

never told me herself. About Dad and Linda getting together before Dad got divorced. Way before, according to Muhammad.

But is my brother even reliable?

I think about Mom's face earlier today, flushing on seeing Uncle Bilal.

Ugh. I don't want to think about her like that.

That she would have feelings like I do for Nuah.

Now, even in the dark, I notice that Nuah's head is down. He must be looking at his phone.

He's been quiet. He's the only one who hasn't contributed to the movie discussions, who didn't parrot "My name is Inigo Montoya. You killed my father. Prepare to die" over and over, who doesn't even look up now when Muhammad, sword-less, gets up to mime Inigo's sword fight with Dawud, who's got his short and blunt plastic sword all drawn and ready.

Logan howls with laughter in response to seeing Muhammad getting stabbed repeatedly on his butt, but still Nuah's head stays down.

Hey, were the gummy bears *nice enough*? I stare at the back of his head with a ready smile after texting this, but he doesn't turn to me. Our thing is he's super nice and I'm always saying I'm not and so we don't match. So he used to periodically ask via text So JY, are you nice enough yet?

He continues staring at his phone for a few more minutes and then shifts in his seat, pocketing the phone and watching the movie to its happily-ever-after end.

"Kumbaya, my Lord, kumbaya. Kumbaya, Rab'bi, kumbaya," Haytham sings, with his guitar.

It's really late but we're sitting around a fire by the lake because the laddoos can't go to sleep without a campfire every night. Muhammad's convinced Haytham to sing.

I close my eyes and listen. He's got such a fantastic voice, and it actually makes my heart beat slower, makes me feel more mellow. Like nothing's going on in my head. None of the racing thoughts that take over when I need something to happen, when I need to achieve something, like get an A on a test, pass my driver's exam, or get into my first-choice college.

Or tell Nuah the truth finally.

When I open my eyes, he's looking at me.

Haytham. But then, when he sees I've noticed, he looks away while still singing.

Nuah is leaning back into his chair, his hands behind his head as he looks at the dark sky, speckled with stars.

Maybe *his* head is racing. Because he's in college now. And he's got a ton of things going on.

He doesn't see me looking at him, so I don't stop.

I feel a weird sense like someone's staring at me, though, and when I pull my eyes from Nuah and scan everyone around the bonfire, I see that it's Dad. He's kneeling in front of Logan's chair, holding Luke in his lap, directing the marshmallow on a stick protruding from Luke's clutched hands.

But his eyes are on me. I do a what's-up smile, but he doesn't return it and just looks at Nuah.

Uh-oh. Does Dad suspect something?

Well, there is *nothing*. Yet.

Just our feelings for each other.

Haytham switches chords on his guitar. After humming for a bit, he begins another song, this one in Arabic, "Tala'al-badru 'alayna, min thaniyyatil-wada'."

Muhammad joins in on the traditional Muslim song, and Dawud bobs his head to the tune.

Nuah turns to Haytham, and I can tell it's in appreciation for his voice. He opens his mouth to sing as well, and I notice the rock next to him has become empty, maybe abandoned by Dawud, who's now dancing to "Tala'al-Badru."

I get up and take the seat.

Dad immediately turns his head. *Is that a slight frown on his face?*

I raise my eyebrows at him.

I mean, I'm surprised at him if he *is* frowning. It's Mom who's always been more *be careful about boys* and *I don't want anything happening until you're finished with college and I declare you old enough* and *tell me everything if you like someone and I'll explain those feelings away.*

Dad always acts like he's totally cool with *everything* as long as I do my schoolwork. He's always said he wants us, me and Muhammad, to have *fun.*

He hasn't really described his idea of what *fun* entails, but I just got the vibe that it's different from Mom's idea of it.

And that boys and I were okay.

So why is Dad still staring at me across the fire while pretending he's not?

I turn to Nuah. "I didn't get to ask you how the end of freshman year went."

He looks surprised to see me beside him. Did I approach that stealthily? "Oh, yeah, it's been amazing, actually."

"Good to hear," I say. "'Cause, you know, I'm starting school soon."

"Yeah. You ready?" He tilts his head while waiting for my

answer, and this thing goes right through me. Like I want to reach over and twist my arm through his to find his hand. To link fingers.

I need to suppress that—because that's not going to happen for a long time.

"Sort of. Did you miss everyone when you moved away from home the first time?" I ask.

"I did. A lot, actually."

"Yeah, that's what I'm trying not to think about. Because right now I'm excited—about my own space, my dorm and things, but then I think about not being home and get worried."

"Text me. Whenever you feel worried. I got a million more cat videos lined up." He laughs.

I laugh too, but, really, I want to ask why he's going back to California on Sunday. But then it'll show how much I care, and I'm weirdly still unprepared to do that.

I look away and, ugh, catch Dad's eyes again.

Okay, now *that's* a full-blown frown on his face. And—oh my God! "DAD! LUKE'S MARSHMALLOW!"

It's on fire, as always happens, but this time Dad hasn't been paying attention, and the fire is moving up Luke's stick.

Dad grabs it from Luke's hand and flings it into the sand and then throws more sand on it. It goes out along with Haytham's singing.

Luke starts screaming and flailing in Dad's arms. "MY MAMALLOW!" he sobs.

Muhammad plops another marshmallow on a fresh stick and passes it to Dad. Then he whispers something to Haytham.

Haytham nods and sings, "A one, two, one, two, three. 'Baby shark, doo doo doo doo doo doo . . .'"

As though controlled by a remote, Luke stops crying, gives a huge smile, and flails his arms, this time in dance.

"I think I'm ready for college. After this summer, I think I'll be ready for anything," I say to Nuah, laughing.

"That's good. Let me know if you need anything, okay?" He gets up and stretches. "That song, man. I think it's my cue to call it a night."

What?

Is he leaving?

But I just got here. Beside him.

"Guys, I'm heading to bed. Thanks for the songs. Great camp-fire, Uncle." He nods at Dad.

I get up too. Maybe Nuah and I can talk more on our way back. "I'm tired too. We have an early start tomorrow," I say.

Haytham stops playing, looks at Dad and Muhammad, and slides the guitar strap off his head. "Okay if I turn in too?"

Dad nods and picks up Luke. "Yeah, this guy needs to sleep. Muhammad, take the kids in? I'll put out the fire."

Muhammad continues singing the baby shark song while grabbing Luke from Dad, which makes the handover seamless.

My brother will make a good father flits through my head, as I begin to ascend the sandy slope to where the grass before the grove of trees starts.

"You want to help me, Janna?" Dad calls out, his eyes widening at me when I turn. "Deal with this fire?"

No, Dad, I don't want to. No way, not after seeing that expression on your face that lit a baby's marshmallow on fire.

"Sorry, Dad, I gotta get back into the house. I forgot to put on mosquito repellent, and they're killing me." I don't look at him when I say this and just proceed to follow everyone else as they make their way along the forest path to the house and the barn at its side.

I'm not going to let Dad's obvious perturbation get me down.

I'm also not going to let Nuah's weird curtness and abruptness ruin my thoughts.

"Hey, Haytham, you're on first for ice-cream-truck watch. How about you're on duty until five, and then it's my turn?" I call out as I hold Logan's hand so he doesn't trip on the sprinkler heads sticking out of the grass in the field on the other side of the cluster of trees.

"As you wish!" Haytham calls back.

Dawud buckles over in laughter on hearing this. Logan shrieks with him, though I'm pretty sure he doesn't even get what he's laughing at.

"Ha-ha! You. Are. Buttercup. And. Haytham. Is. Westley!" Dawud singsongs in a weird staccato.

I wrinkle my nose at his silly shenanigans. "Okay, whatever."

"Oh boy," Nuah says to me, a grin on his face. "And he's even a stable boy. Haytham."

Haytham stops and turns around. "This is factually true. I am indeed a stable boy, as I sleep in the barn."

Muhammad's already gone ahead and wouldn't have heard this stupid conversation anyway as he's deep into shark-doo-doo-doo-ing to keep Luke subdued.

Nuah laughs some more. "And you, Janna, *are* indeed the daughter of the squire of this land."

Why is Nuah linking me with Haytham?

It's just a dumb joke, Janna, the calm part of me whispers. So I laugh along, pretending I'm having fun too.

As Nuah, Haytham, and Dawud head over to the stable turned guesthouse, I notice that Nuah pulls out his phone, reads something on it, and smiles.

He didn't even respond to my text to him earlier, the one I sent during the movie.

Part Two

FRIDAY, JULY 16
HENNA PARTY DAY

To do:

- [ ] Tell Nuah

- [ ] Spend time with Mom—without certain people intruding on our conversation!

- [ ] Assemble wedding favors without losing patience with Muhammad

- [ ] Go to Jumah

- [ ] Practice wedding roast with Nuah (!!!)

- [ ] FINALLY FIND OUT WHO TATS'S DATE IS

- [ ] Surprise Sarah with the best henna party ever

Chapter Thirteen

❋ ❋ ❋

There's an arm around me when I wake up the next morning. I'm disoriented until I see the wrist with its familiar silver bracelet. And hear the familiar light snore.

Mom kept her word.

I glance at the bedside alarm clock. It's seven forty-five.

I shift, and she dislodges her hand tucked under my shoulder and opens her eyes. She still has her scarf on, but it's fallen back, and tendrils of brown hair, with graying roots here and there, peep out.

"Morning, sweetums. Did I bother you when I got into bed?"

"No, but Mom, I didn't know you meant *this* early when you said early." I groan and then laugh. "Seven a.m.?"

"Six thirty, actually. I left the hotel right after Fajr." She smooths my hair and then runs her fingers through it, combing it, and after letting her for a bit, I shake it off. Mom can get very babying if I don't stop her.

I once heard her tell a friend that she'd wanted five kids because she always wanted some that were young enough to baby when the others got older.

She ended up with two kids in real life and, no, I'm not willing to be perpetually babied.

"Did you pray Fajr?" she asks, turning onto her back. "You were snoring when I came in."

"No, missed it. I'll make it up now."

Her head swivels. "Have you been doing your prayers here, Janna?"

"Yeah, just not Fajr on time always. Only when Muhammad wakes me up sometimes."

She sighs and tuns back to the ceiling. "Okay, I'm not going to lecture you now. I came early to spend some happy time with you in peace before everyone wakes up."

"Wait, are you even my mom?" I flip on my side to face her. "Did you forget that I'm not a morning person? I thought you meant eleven or something."

"Even just lying here with you is spending time. You're my baby, so, you know, breathing you in is enough. Even your morning breath."

"Ugh." Still groggy, I let my eyes settle into opening by gazing beyond Mom, at the photo on the wall above the tall dresser, an aerial shot of a beach, one of the generic pictures on the theme of "vacation" that Dad has hanging here and there throughout the house, and I think about love. And the different things it means to different people.

I don't know if I would be excited about breathing in my kid in the morning is what I want to say.

But what about your one true love, the person you wake up next to every day?

Would I want to breath in Nuah? is what I really want to ask.

Um. I don't know. He makes me feel so good—when I think

of him, when I look at him, when I'm around him (well, except for yesterday), but I don't know if I'd want to breath him in like that.

I don't want to breath anyone in.

I'm okay admitting I have proximity issues.

"What's going on in that brain of yours?" Mom asks. "Your eyes became so still suddenly."

I shake myself out of my reverie and am about to give my standard answer of "nothing" when this sudden, uninvited thought enters my head: *Hello, what about telling her the truth?*

And maybe it's this disruptive thought, and maybe it's because I'll be going to college in a month, going away from Mom after having been away from her for three weeks already, that I can't stop myself from blurting out, "Nuah. I'm thinking about Nuah."

I cringe. Did I just do that? Tell Mom about Nuah?

She flips herself to face me now. But I put a hand out and gently turn her back so that she can't see me.

Then I lie on my back too. "Can we both stare at the ceiling so we can forget what I just said?"

"We can stare at the ceiling, yes, but no, I'm not going to forget what you just said." She turns only her head. "Can I look at you at least to talk?"

"No. If we're going to talk about this, we have to look at the ceiling."

"Okay, looking at the ceiling. Talking about Nuah." She pumps her fists in the air above her. "YES. Nuah! A perfect first crush! Janna, I'm proud of you!"

"He's not my first crush, Mom."

"I know, Jeremy was your first crush. I mean a perfect first *proper* crush."

"What?" I look, no, stare with hints of glare at her. "How did you know about Jeremy?"

Jeremy's this guy that I lost my mind to two summers ago. He of the perfect forehead, but unperfect academic aspirations and, ultimately, unmatched faith. We parted ways after what must have been the shortest foray into tentative potential love ever.

The Jeremy thing taught me that I have to be strategic in who I choose to set my sights on in the future. That it was kind of wasting my crush time to put all my pining into a train going nowhere.

The Jeremy thing, and a brief detour to this other guy at school who also didn't cut it, taught me that Nuah made sense all along.

But I thought I'd kept the entire reconnaissance mission to discover the potential mines and pitfalls in a girl's route to true love from Mom. "Ugh, how did you know about Jeremy?" I ask again.

"Moms know. And remember when he came by the apartment? With Tats, to see if you wanted to go hang out? I saw your face, Janna, and I knew. Anyway, Nuah! He's so special! And he treats you so well, kindly, always. I've seen it!"

"Mom, he liked me for a long time."

"I know. I know. I told you—moms know these things. Well, this mom knows things. He didn't come over all the time just to hang out with Muhammad, you know."

"You *knew*?" This was making me feel a bit weird now. That Mom was in the background, rubbing her hands together, thinking, *Perfect. Two Muslim kids—one a true gentleman, the other my precious baby—falling for each other.*

"Yes, and I'm happy."

"You *are*? Why?" I'm not sure I like this. I hadn't wanted to tell her, but I hadn't expected this, either.

"Because he's a good kid and I—I don't know—it makes me

feel safe, to know *my* kid likes a good kid." She sits up and fixes her pillow so that it props up behind her before she leans back on it. "I think it's because he values the same things you do. It's easier to build a life together when you share the same values."

I continue lying down, looking at the ceiling. I still don't like her being so enthusiastic, but now at least I understand it more. She's just excited because he's a good person.

"When I first met Dad, I thought we were similar, but—" Mom stops talking. "I'm sorry. I shouldn't have brought that up."

I sit up too. "No, tell me. Please? I want to know."

"When I met Dad, he was just getting into Islam. Uncle Bilal got him into it, actually. And Dad was all excited about it—super excited. And I got excited, because you know I come from a very religious family." Mom strokes my head again. I'm going to let her pet me all she wants if it keeps her talking. "He kept it going for a while, his interest in faith, but then a year after we got married, he started to lose his commitment to the deen. By then we'd already had Muhammad and we tried for a bit; then you came along, and we had this truce where we wanted to provide a stable family for you guys . . . but then our different beliefs caught up with us. Like he didn't want me to wear hijab, be visibly Muslim, or even take Muhammad to Jumah or make sure you guys learned deen. That wasn't the way Dad grew up, those weren't important things to his own family, and, ultimately, he didn't believe they were important for ours."

I wonder if I should ask. About what Muhammad told me previously, about Dad and Linda starting their relationship before our parents divorced. When Mom thought they were still trying to save the marriage. "And then Linda happened?"

"And then Linda happened," she says, and at this, her eyes

close briefly and her mouth presses together a bit more tightly, and I feel horrible.

"I'm sorry, Mom." I fling myself into her, throwing my arms around her waist to wrap her like I've never done before. So she knows I'm sorry. For saying *Linda happened?* and for her going through all that with Dad, and me not even knowing that she'd felt such pain. My shoulders heave, and then I'm crying.

"It's okay. Janna. Stop." She removes me from her and looks at me still sobbing. "I'm not sad about it. It's been seven years since the divorce, and if you want the truth, four years since I stopped feeling sad about it all. Don't cry. Because I'm not."

I wipe my eyes, still streaming tears, and lean my head on her shoulder. She wraps her arms around me and we stay quiet and it's really warm and comfortable and my heaving slowly subsides until I can breathe without a catch. "I'm so sorry I brought it up."

"I'm glad you did. Because now you know more," she says. "And I'm happy that Dad and Linda are happy. Truly. Look at this house, their adorable kids, Dad's ability to host the nikah with such generosity. And Linda being so hospitable."

I tilt my head to look at her face, to check for the truth.

I see no tears or sadness.

I nod like I get it, but—I don't know—if I were Mom, I wouldn't want to be okay with it all.

I'd want Dad to pay. I'd want to have all the things that Dad has too.

And not have a life like Mom has now, renting a small apartment, with fewer kids than she'd wanted.

Alone.

A sudden thought invades my attempt to collect my emotions: *Is that why she's so excited about Uncle Bilal?*

Should I ask? About the weird vibes I got yesterday?

There's a hard, rhythmic knock on the door that can only be Muhammad. "Mom? Breakfast is ready, and Sarah's here too."

"Let's go. If I remember Dad properly, he's got a good breakfast ready. His breakfast game was always on point." Mom strokes my hair once more, for good luck, or maybe for strength—for me . . . and her?—and swings her feet onto the floor.

I better go wash my face and get it arranged so it looks like I still like Dad.

Checking my phone, I see a ton of messages from Tats and Soon-Lee and Sandra and even Sausun (Make sure there's some kind of wudu facility okay? I like to refresh my wudu before every prayer! To which I reply, Dad has two entire restroom trailers set up! And you're personally invited to use *my* bathroom!) but nothing from the person I really want to see a text from: Nuah.

Chapter Fourteen

❁ ❁ ❁

On the pretense of letting Mom use the bathroom in my room, I go shower and get ready in the alcove bathroom.

There's a tiny part of me that wants to see what Haytham's been up to.

The mirror holds verses again.

Some bloom with much care
But I need only your glance
To fill a garden

Wow. I wonder who he's thinking of when he writes this stuff.

I count the syllables in the poem, remembering that the first one I'd seen was similarly short.

A haiku.

He writes haikus.

How is it that I'm getting to learn more about Haiku Haytham in this short little while than Nuah?

Why is Nuah suddenly hard to get ahold of?

I erase the poem with one sleeve swipe of the mirror and look at my reflection in the cleared glass.

I look startled, my eyes enlarged, my mouth slightly open.

Or is it sadness? Or worry?

Like my gut is starting to whisper something?

In the shower, I wash the startle/sadness/worry away.

I'm going to be spending all day around Nuah and then the evening with Mom at the henna party, wearing our special clothes. That's enough to wash all the bad feelings away.

After I get dressed, I post a pic on Instagram of my henna-free hands, a before, and promise my friends an update tonight after the henna party, for which Dad hired professional henna artists.

I see that Dania and Lamya have requested to follow me. I click accept, follow back, and check them out.

Sure enough, both their accounts are beautiful. I click like on some posts and then am about to close Instagram when I get two notifications.

Two more requests to follow. Simultaneously.

Haytham.

And . . . Layth? Dania and Lamya's smirky cousin?

I've already checked out Haytham's account, but when I give another peek now, I see that he's posted a new poem:

Some bloom with much care

But I need only your glance

To fill a garden

Ah, so the mirror is his sketchbook. For his instapoet auditions.

I click like on the poem and then go check Layth's account. But his is private, with a very Zayn-like unsmiling profile pic commanding the space above his ninety-eight followers. He follows twenty-two people.

Weird that he wants me to be his twenty-third follow.

If I approve him, then do I request to follow back? Because it feels kind of weird if he can see my stuff and I can't see his?

I decide to not approve him. He's a guy I saw once in my life and am going to see a second time tomorrow, and then he'll disappear from the face of my earth. Plus he's kind of cranky. So nah.

I approve Haytham, though, and become his six thousand and seventeenth follower.

We're ice-cream-truck comrades.

Before I leave the bathroom, I look in the mirror again.

I think I look good. I'm in my favorite color head to toe. Black jeans, thin black oversize shirt that's short in front, with sleeves that reach almost to my fingertips, and falls off one shoulder but then has this false second shirt peeking underneath, also black, and, to top it all, my only scarf that sits amazing on my head even when casually thrown on. I think this black scarf knows my head the best, so it just molds to my skull in the best way.

Then I have on dewy lip gloss, and I did my eyelashes really carefully.

I'm ready to have an amazing day.

When I get to the top of the stairs, the back-of-the-house ones that overlook the kitchen and family room, a cozy scene greets me.

Near the oval, marble kitchen table, Dania and Lamya are clustered around Sarah, their hands reaching out to touch her occasionally, excitedly talking, while Mom leans against the island and watches, beaming. She looks so proud. Happy. Nothing like how I'd imagined she'd be standing in Dad's kitchen.

Speaking of Dad, he and Linda have matching black aprons on and spatulas held ready, waiting on a huge rectangular griddle filled with perfectly round pancakes. Dad's wearing his jolly face, and Linda looks like she got dressed up. Gone is the uniform of leggings and T-shirt she's normally in, replaced with a strappy blue gingham summer dress with matching strappy sandals. Her curly hair is clipped back at the sides but hangs down to her shoulders—the opposite of its usual tight bun. She extends her spatula and flips a fresh pancake onto Dawud's plate.

Mom's right—they are super generous and hospitable. I take it for granted because I'm their family, but they're also extra giving to anyone connected to me and Muhammad in any way.

Muhammad and Haytham are at the table eating, Haytham with his towel still around his neck for some reason. Dawud carries his pancake past them to the adjacent family room, where the laddoos are watching Pokémon. Dawud's a Pokémon fanatic and has been slowly indoctrinating my little brothers into the ways of the Pokémon universe from the moment he arrived.

Leaning on the frame of the doorway to the family room is Layth, scrolling on his phone.

I'm surprised to see him here.

He's in jeans and a black T-shirt with an upside-down black apple on it.

Why is *he* here so early?

He looks up at that point, like my frowning gaze penetrated the top of his head, and I relax my expression and allow a small nod.

He looks back at his phone.

"Boo!"

I give a start and turn around to see a bit of Nuah peeking from the side of the two stacked boxes he's holding, grin on his face. "Thanks for scaring me." I feign sarcasm, even though I know he probably saw my eyes light up.

"Sorry, JY. Your brother asked me to get some boxes of wedding favors stuff from his room. We're starting the operation right after breakfast. You're in, right?"

I nod, a glow already starting its bloom inside me (and I'm sure spreading across my face). It strikes me that this is the first time we're getting a moment to ourselves. Sure, it's in full view of the kitchen and its occupants below, almost like we're onstage, but still, it's an *opportunity*.

Finally.

"Hey, I heard you're going back to California? On Sunday?"

"Yeah," he says, lowering the boxes so I can see his whole face. "Got a job. Plus, my roommate can't handle the rent on his own, so this works out. He's awesome, so it's best to keep him happy. The Law of Landing a Good Roommate."

"Right. I just thought you'd be spending the summer in Eastspring." I don't care that I'm showing that I'm upset.

He leans the stack of boxes against the banister. "When you leaving for UChicago?"

"I'm moving at the beginning of September." It sounds whiny, but I can't help adding, "I thought, you know, I'd see you in August. And also, it's weird you didn't tell me when we were e-mailing about the roast?"

"Ah, got it. Sorry." He smiles. "Well, what about when I come up to see Khadija's baby? You could drop by our place then too? My mom would like that. And Khadija too, I'm sure."

What about you? the whiny voice wants to add, but I squash it by nodding. "That sounds cool." I pause. This may be our only time before things get hectic. "Um, I also, um, wanted to tell you something."

I pull on my sleeves, my hands working them in turns so that the frayed black cuffs cover my fingertips again and again.

Oh my God.

Why am I so nervous?

I glance down to make sure no one's watching us, but, other than Dad, who lifts his eyes right then, everyone else is busy in their own conversations or phones.

It's almost like I wished people had been all staring up at us so that I'd be able to cut this conversation short and just go downstairs.

Gah, this is hard. Because I have no desire to make things happen in the real world. Or, I should say, it takes me a while to *decide* to make things happen.

I like everything to stay in my head. The world up there feels better.

But I need things secure now, out in the open, before I go to college.

"Yeah?" Nuah asks, his body still positioned against the boxes to keep them fixed on the banister railings. He raises his eyebrows expectantly, like he's really interested in what I have to say.

But there's something different about those eyes under his eyebrows.

Or am I imagining it?

"Just wondered why you didn't answer my text last night?" *Way to go, Janna. Pour more whine.*

"Oh, sorry. My phone is on an auto timer that shuts down messages in the evening. It ended last night at ten before you texted me." He talks fast, like it's nothing, so I relax. "And then this morning, I just rolled out of bed to follow Muhammad and his tasks."

"Okay. Anyway, it was just nothing. It was about the gummies.

Whether they were nice enough for you." I try to laugh, but it comes out like a swallowed sob.

"For sure." He shifts the boxes and glances down.

Does he want to go?

Okay, this is like ultimate cringe now. Me trying to get to something deep but making it about gummy bears.

Cut it short and go down and talk to him when you practice the roast later.

I reach out a hand. "Want help taking stuff down?"

He looks sort of relieved. Exactly how I feel.

"No, I'm okay— Actually, you know what? Take this little bag that's dangling?" He holds out a plastic bag that he had hanging off his wrist. I take it, and we head to the kitchen.

I'm halfway down the stairs, a smile of strained relief on my face, when I see Dad.

His spatula's raised, he's watching us come down the stairs together, and Jolly Dad is gone.

He's been replaced by Strangely Upset Dad.

Chapter Fifteen

❋ ❋ ❋

I'm chatting away with Lamya, Dania, and Sarah (well, listening more than chatting) in the kitchen when I get a nudge.

"I've put together a plate of your favorite breakfast things. And set up a nice table for us outside—just you and me. Come out to enjoy it?" Dad's still in his apron but his spatula is gone, so his arms are able to make perfect Vs as his hands rest on his hips.

That's not the posture of someone who wants to "enjoy" a "favorite" breakfast at a "nice" table with his daughter.

"I actually thought I'd eat with Mom, since, you know, I haven't seen her in a while?" I scan for Mom.

"She's eaten already and is helping Muhammad organize stuff for the favors. They're headed to the basement," Dad says, undoing his arms. But then he folds them across his chest. Real friendly-like.

"I'm actually not very hungry."

"You need to eat. And wow, I didn't know you were so averse to eating with your dad. Who you don't see most of the year." At this, his face looks genuinely hurt. And he unfolds his arms and puts his hands in the pockets of his shorts.

I really don't want to be with Dad right now.

But then he's Dad, the guy who always wants everyone to like him so much.

I know he feels like Muhammad and I have grown to love Mom more. When he and I were a team, I was his princess, and because we saw him less—and he was so lax about some things— spending time with him used to feel like a treat. But now that I've been with him for almost a month, it's not the same.

He's pretty exacting about how he wants things to be. Which can be exhausting.

But I'm leaving on Sunday to go back to Eastspring with Mom. And I won't see Dad again until maybe Thanksgiving or even Christmas.

The least I could do is have breakfast with him now. "Okay, maybe I'll eat a little."

I follow him out onto the patio, trying to push away the feeling of getting ready to rip off a Band-Aid quickly.

"Excited about college?" Dad's asked me this several times already over the past few weeks, and I answer the same way each time ("Can't wait! But also nervous!"), but today I add in, "Yes, and I'm feeling a bit less nervous because Dania and Lamya are going to introduce me to some people."

It's actually nice here on the patio because the sun isn't unbearably hot yet.

"Ah, great. They're nice kids." Dad takes a forkful of scrambled eggs. "And I'm glad you brought that up. Meeting people."

I cut a piece of pancake and dunk it into the puddle of maple syrup on the side of the plate. Everyone else looks at me funny when I eat pancakes this way, but it's the perfect way to ensure your breakfast doesn't devolve into a mess of soggy dough.

"You're going to be meeting a whole lot of new people. But make sure you keep up your friendships from before," Dad says.

"I know. Tats and I have already planned our meetups." We're going to get together every six weeks in alternating locations that will be around halfway points between her college and mine. We already scouted and mapped the first series of diners on Google Maps.

"And when you meet new people, make sure you check that you make sense for each other." He clears his throat. "I'm talking about romantic relationships. Make sure you're of similar upbringing."

"Dad. Why are we talking about this?" I'm irked, but it's in an I-knew-it way. So his scowls *were* about BOYS. "I'm not going to college to get a boyfriend."

"I'm not saying that. But it's inevitably going to happen. People meet people in college all the time. Mom and I did." He looks at me pointedly. "So I'm just telling you to be aware of how important it is that your backgrounds sync. Whoever you meet."

How is it that Mom and Dad are giving me the same advice? *Make sure you've been brought up the same way as whoever you're falling for.*

I'm not impressed to hear it coming at me again. "Okay, Dad. Got it. Can we move on?"

He clears his throat a second time. "It's important culturally, too."

"What? What's important culturally?"

"That your backgrounds are similar."

"What do you mean? That we're both American? Don't fall for an international student?" The irk's taking on a different strain. "Be nationalistic? USA! USA! Is that what you're trying to say?"

"I mean heritage-wise. That you're not from vastly different cultural backgrounds."

I put my fork down. "I can't believe you just said that."

"I'm giving you advice as a father. Isn't that my role?" Dad puts his fork down too and reaches a hand out as if to quell something in the air. "To help you not run into problems? And I'm just saying if you choose someone from the same background, Desi or Arab—well, better if they're Egyptian like Mom—it's less problems."

"I'm not listening to that advice. Ever." I don't know why, but I feel tears welling in me, and they're the hot kind, the kind that are mixed with anger. "I'm not listening to prejudice."

He stares at me without flinching. And it's with such an I-know-what-I'm-talking-about gaze, with the "White House" in the background, that it just tips me over into full-on-angry territory.

"I'm glad I'm more like Mom. She'd *never* say something like what you just said."

"Well, it's because of your mom that I'm saying it. Because of how her family treated me due to my Indian background. Because I'm not Arab. And the same thing is happening to Muhammad. The way Sarah's family is treating him. Because he's not Syrian."

I shake my head and pick up my plate. "I don't believe that. And even if it was true, I don't care. It doesn't make what you're saying right!"

"Janna, I just want to save you the headache I've been through!"

"You're not saving me! You're condemning me to your racism!" I stand and look at his always-coiffed self. "And I know it's because of Nuah you're bringing all this up. Because he's Black!"

Dad doesn't reach a hand out this time, just crosses his arms, and I rush away.

Chapter Sixteen

❈ ❈ ❈

I hold my plate of one remaining unsoggy pancake and walk by the gazebo. Straight ahead is the dock, but I'm not heading there. It's in view from the patio, and I don't want to be anywhere Dad can see me.

I take a sudden left turn and follow the path through the trees that leads to the water.

In the lush grove, I pause for a moment and look up at the treetops. Leaves are fluttering here and there, and there's a persistent hum from an insect.

I decide to sit right here, in a patch of grass next to the worn path, and eat my breakfast.

Dad's racist.

He can't stand the idea of me liking Nuah.

Tears sting my eyes, and big thoughts invade, like *I'm going to leave this place. I'm going to stay at the hotel with Mom.*

I'm never going to talk to Dad again.

I take my phone out and text Tats. When are you getting here?

She's supposed to bunk with me in my room here after the

henna party. Maybe I can squeeze her in with Mom and me at the hotel instead.

> I'll be late because my date can only drive me after work so at like 7
>
> That's ok. It starts late anyway. Your date's not staying over, right?
>
> No
>
> We're staying at the hotel with my mom
>
> Whyyyy I want to swim in the lake. I even bought a BURKINI
>
> What
>
> Because you and Sarah would be wearing one so you know
>
> Sarah is not going to be swimming on her wedding day
>
> But I want to. I got the same burkini as Lindsay Lohan.

I fork another piece of pancake and chew while staring at the path ahead of me. There's something black in the spaces between the trees farther up.

> We'll talk when you get here

I leave the plate with half a pancake on it and make my way forward on the path as it inches to access the lake, and the black thing grows bigger.

Oh.

It's Layth's back.

He's sitting facing the water, headphones around his neck. The back of his T-shirt says CHEAP THRILLS in teeny writing, which I can finally see clearly because I'm literally a bush away from him. The bush I'm hiding behind.

I make the mistake of sighing loudly at this stupid thing I'm doing after getting into a fight with my racist dad.

Layth turns around. Doesn't say anything and just turns back to the water.

"Just so you know, I wasn't watching you. I just wondered who was sitting here."

"So you snuck up?"

"Well, yeah. It's not like I could honk a horn or something. I just followed the path."

He doesn't say anything.

"Why are you going to Miami?" I don't know why I even want to know.

He looks back at me, one dark eyebrow raised, before turning away again without answering.

Burn.

But I'm in such a weird mood after Dad's grossness that I spew more. "What's Cheap Thrills? Your band or something?"

"Nope."

"Well, then why do you always wear Cheap Thrills shirts?"

"Because."

"Why are you having your Che Guevara moment?"

"Not."

"Okay, why'd you ask to follow me on Instagram if you're not answering me?"

He lifts his phone, presses, scrolls, swipes, and presses again. "There, unrequested."

"Thanks. It was bloating my requests."

He lets out a snort. "Why're you studying dead white people literature? Why're you excited about going to study abroad in a place the whole world knows too much about anyway? Why are you sneaking up on me to bother my peace and quiet?" He stands and picks a backpack up from the ground and then turns to me. "Tell Dania and Lamya I'll pick them up later. Leaving now."

"Why? Because I scared you off with my questions?" I cross my arms. He's standing with his back to the water, and something about the way he squints slightly in the sunlight filtering through the trees behind me gives the impression of a deep melancholy.

No, it's not his expression. It's the way his pose is resigned, the way his hands are positioned protectively, one hand on the strap of the backpack on his shoulder and the other hanging down cradling his jean jacket, the same jacket he wore at the restaurant.

He looks alone. That's it.

He looks like he's not completely a smirky crank.

"I'm studying British lit because I want to take it apart, starting with the white man's burden myth repeated over and over in our favorite classics, that we overlook all the time at school or wave away as being inconsequential to the greater contribution that these quote unquote 'beloved' authors make, but that ultimately cements in our consciousness the idea that we brown and Black people will never be consequential. I mean, so many people have studied this, like one of my oldest friends, ninety-three years oldest, who wrote an entire manuscript on Shakespeare's othering of nonwhite peoples. Actually, he's the one who got me thinking about all of this. And my thing is going to be to tie it all in with what's going on now. The way we're so publicly hateful in this country. That's why I'm studying British lit."

He relaxes his squinting, and his mouth relaxes too. And the corners turn up, the left side more noticeably. In a non-smirk. In a smile. A genuine one.

Why do I notice that he's got a really nice smile? And that his lips, like his eyes and jawline—and okay, eyebrows—are his best features?

I just realized I named all of his facial features. But that's because they became animated just now, not like when he was at the restaurant, when he was all closed.

I wonder how many girls like him. And are among his ninety-eight followers.

"So *you're* the one actually having a Che Guevara moment." He doesn't say it sarcastically, like Dania had done to him. He says it politely.

"It's not a moment. And it's not Che. It's that I don't want America to not correct its course." I think about the book I just finished reading last week, *The Autobiography of Malcolm X*. How people are still grappling with the same racism today that Malcolm described over sixty years ago.

Wait, I actually got that book from *Dad's* bookshelf. How does that even make sense?

"I wear Cheap Thrills shirts because I've only got three shirts and they're all Cheap Thrills. Because it was a friend's attempt at running a T-shirt company while he was studying graphic design. And he gave me his three prototypes. Three good-quality cotton prototypes." He lifts his hand holding the jacket across his chest to his backpack strap and sets it higher on his shoulder. "I only have three shirts because I got rid of everything except for what's in this bag. And I'm taking this bag with me to Miami to catch a flight."

"Where you going?"

"To Ecuador. Moving there."

"Wow. Moving? As in *moving* moving, for good?"

"Yup. Selling my car in Miami—already got a buyer lined up—and then it's Mera, Ecuador. Hopefully for the rest of my life."

I don't know much about Ecuador except what our class studied in middle school geography. "Do you have family in Ecuador?"

"None. Just me." He looks away and adds quietly, "The way I like it."

"I've never traveled alone," I tell him. "Actually, I haven't traveled much even with family."

"I thought that you'd have been to tons of places. What with your dad being some kind of mega-rich dude." His smile crosses into contemptuous territory again.

I frown at his scorn, now blatant on his face. "I'm not rich."

He raises his eyebrows. And makes a movement, like he's really leaving.

I'm going to follow him because I hate his expression right now—like he knows everything about me based on the few glimpses he's gotten. I need to straighten this guy out, and with all the stuff Dad stirred in me, I'm ready to get in any boxing ring. "You don't know me. You think you do, but you're clueless."

He stops moving, just hitches that backpack up higher.

"You think I'm rich because my dad's rich?"

"I think you're rich because you *are* rich."

"And I think you're an asshole because you *are* an asshole."

"And you'd be right. Because I actually am." He raises his eyebrows at me. "See, we're both right."

I hate this guy. Because he makes me want to just keep talking and telling him everything to prove him wrong. He's like a prosecutor who's got all his facts incorrect, and I'm the defendant, representing myself. "I live with my mom. She works in a library shelving books, hoping she'll become a librarian one day even though she didn't get to finish her degree because she had my brother young. We live in a two-bedroom apartment that my mom pays rent for. My rich-dude dad pays for certain things for me and my brother. Like college for him, which is amazing—I'm going on a full scholarship. But day to day, I'm not rich. My mom's been a single mom for a long time." I try to say all this matter-of-factly, but then I glare at him. "There, now do you feel better?"

"Why would I feel better?"

"Because you feel out of place or something with all us 'rich' people?"

He just looks at me. Then shakes his head. "Sure, Jan."

Jan is what my friends call me at school, so I can't stop the snicker that comes out of my mouth. And then I'm shaking my head and full-on laughing.

He stares at me and loosens his own expression. "What?"

"Jan is my actual nickname."

He tips his head back like he's caught and allows a smile, again an actual smile, to take over his face. And then he laughs.

I relax. When he's not all scorny and rude, he looks like a person I'd talk to in one of my classes. Though in class he'd be considered hot, and surrounded by people, so I'd probably never actually get a chance to talk to him. "So my brother's wedding tomorrow will be your last party in America?"

"Yeah, but maybe I'm not even going to it." He shrugs and begins walking toward the path. "Your brother's nice to invite me and all, but I usually avoid weddings. I'm not a big crowd person."

I nod and let go my crossed arms and begin walking too. "Why Ecuador?"

"I volunteered in an animal sanctuary near the Amazon a few summers, and now I'm returning to work at the same place, training volunteers."

"Are you in college? Taking a break?" I spot my half pancake waiting for me under the trees. "From studying veterinary sciences or something?"

He laughs, and this time it's completely sarcastic. Again. "I'm not going to college. I'm not going to an institution that's out to colonize your mind."

"That's not the reason I'm going either. I'm going to get my degree."

"Uh, okay. Everyone says that. And then they come out as programmed zombies living for the weekends." He turns to me as I pause to pick up my plate on the ground. His face is open again. "I'd rather live every day."

We walk quietly for a bit until we come to the entrance to the path, and I spot Dad up ahead on the patio, arranging the picnic tables into one long one. He's not alone, though, as Nuah, of all people, and Haytham are helping him.

I stop abruptly. Layth almost bumps into me.

I turn and he steps back. "I can't go out there yet. I just got into a fight with my dad, and I can't be around him."

He nods and brushes his hair from his eyes with the hand still clutching his jacket and then looks up at the trees.

I do too, and it's weird, but after staring at the aspens, birches, and oaks and the bits of sky above it all for a while, I get this feeling of not being *here*.

I don't mean of not being here, in this place.

But of not being in the angry feelings of before.

Like I'm completely good, strong, capable of being me and taking on Dad. Of getting in the boxing ring with *him*.

Because he is wrong, and I know it with a certainty that makes me feel like I can be anywhere, in any situation, and stand tall. Like his racism just gave birth to more of who I really am. And who I'm definitely not.

I'm not him and never will be.

I look at the trees and think, *Yes, I do like trees the way Nuah described me to Khadija.* They've been around for millions of years, seen tons of crap, and still stand strong and graceful, sure of their worth to the world.

"Fighting makes you smile, huh?" Layth says, interrupting my trees-are-my-Patronus aha moment.

"I'm smiling?"

He nods.

"Maybe it's because I'm ready to go back to help my brother get ready for his wedding," I say. "Do you have siblings?"

He shakes his head. And then says faintly, "Used to." And shakes his head again.

We make our way out of the forest.

Dad, Haytham, and Nuah look up at the same time at Layth and me walking toward them.

I smile at Nuah. Huge.

So Dad can't miss it.

Too bad for Muhammad this wedding is going to turn into a little war.

Chapter Seventeen

❋ ❋ ❋

We're half an hour into putting together wedding favor boxes—an eerily silent half an hour for nine people gathered around a long table—when the ice-cream truck chimes. Haytham and I look at each other.

It's ten o'clock. Ice cream has never arrived this early before.

"Permission to take a short break, sir?" Haytham raises a hand to salute Muhammad. He nods at me. "For Sergeant Janna, too?"

"You want permission to break the delicate assembly line we got going here?" Muhammad drops a blue-foiled chocolate basketball into the box in front of him. "You're the candy almonds. Everyone loves those."

"Ugh. Not me." Dania shakes her head and, with the blade of a pair of scissors, curls a ribbon that ties the dua paper to the favor boxes. The dua says *May God bless you both and shower blessings upon you and unite you in all that is good* in Arabic and English.

"I'll take over the almonds. They're right next to me. I can do a double shift," Nuah says, using an elbow to nudge the bowl of pastel almonds right next to him. "Haytham, you owe me."

"And Janna's dates?" Haytham's already standing up. "Who'll do her dates?"

"Seems to me that you're doing that? Dates with Janna?" Muhammad says to Haytham, smirking.

I can't believe Muhammad. And wait, is that a smile on Nuah's face as he shakes his head at Muhammad's "buffoonery," as he always calls it? Why would he be smiling at a stupid joke like that?

I stay seated as Haytham hits Muhammad on the back.

"I'll do Janna's dates," Layth announces. He's sitting diagonally from me, having been cajoled to stay and help by Dania and Lamya, who are seated across from each other at one end of the table. Lamya puts little packets of fennel candy into the boxes before passing them on to Dania to add the finishing touches.

I look at Layth, but he's not looking at me. He's unfolding the bright yellow cardboard that makes the boxes and propping them open to lay a small square of blue tissue inside. His hair is off his face, tied back by a tiny elastic, and I see his forehead.

I don't want to look at it.

I push the bowl of unripe yellow dates closer to Layth and get up. That's when he looks at me, and I notice his eyes don't hold the blank look that I first saw on him, that his eyes are kindly when they turn in my direction.

Is he thawing?

"Anyone else want ice cream?" Haytham asks. "Where are the kids?"

"They went into town with Linda to get groceries. Dawud said he needed to get something, so he went with Sarah too," Dad says from the head of the table, where he's working on his laptop, apparently updating wedding things. "And of course nobody wants ice cream at this early hour."

"You can't assume that," I say sternly. "Anyone want ice cream?"

Everyone shakes their head. Dad shoots me a look—a smug one. Again.

"Dania? Lamya? It's really good ice cream," I say, pressing. They shake their heads. Haytham's already started walking away, but I'm not going to leave until I prove Dad wrong. "Mom?"

I make a pleading face at her.

"No thanks, sweetums. And how will we eat it while we're doing this?" Mom says, dribbling chocolate kisses into the three open boxes in front of her.

"But you love Firecracker Popsicles."

Mom looks taken aback. "But not now."

Somebody has to want ice cream so that Dad's not right. Somebody. "Layth?"

"Okay, get me an ice-cream sandwich?" He puts his hand in the pocket of the jacket on the bench beside him and pulls out a ten. "And get Dania and Lamya snow cones. They're just being polite, but they love ice cream in the morning."

He glances at Dad before holding out the bill to me.

I take Layth's money, grateful.

The window slides open, and the ice-cream-truck driver is . . . a woman. A woman with a huge smile on her face, under a base-ball cap.

"Hi, friends! What treat may I bestow to brighten your day?" she asks.

I trade glances with Haytham. "Two snow cones and one ice-cream sandwich, please."

Haytham gives his order, which is another ice-cream sandwich, and then adds, "We didn't see you yesterday. New to this route?"

"Yeah, just filling in for Alex. He's taking a rest. Poor guy's sick." She adds syrup on the crushed ice in the paper cone and then holds it out to me. "I'm his sister, Katarina."

"Oh, sorry to hear. Is he okay?" I take the cone. "We thought he hadn't been feeling his best."

"It was his migraines. They've gotten worse in the last few days. Yesterday was terrible, so I told him I'd do his run today." She hands me the second slushy cone and tilts her head. "He'd been extra grumpy, huh?"

"Which wasn't like him," I say, and look at Haytham pointedly. "He's usually so jolly."

"Really? Alex, jolly?" Katarina laughs and opens the freezer to take out two ice-cream sandwiches. "That would be news to me. I always say what a perfect job this ice-cream truck is for him, in an ironic way, mind you."

Haytham lets out a laugh, shoots me an *aha!* glance, and accepts the sandwiches.

I ignore him and decide to get this settled once and for all. "Do you think he'll be well enough to come out tomorrow? My brother's having an informal weddingish gathering here, and it would so cool for the kids to get ice cream after."

"You know what, I think that can be arranged." Katarina leans against the window and smiles at us. "Did you guys know this is Alex's favorite route? He calls it the Golden Peninsula, this bit of road that goes out into the water. He says you guys on this street are always buying ice cream. I'll come with him to help out for your event."

"Perfect, then we'll see you tomorrow. Preferably around seven, if it's not too late?" I say. She nods, and I spy the soft-serve machine inside the van. "Wait, one more ice cream, please. A vanilla cone dipped in chocolate. Actually, also a Firecracker Popsicle."

I'm going to add coconut flakes on the cone in the kitchen and give it to Dad. I hope he gets the ice-cream commentary on his prejudice: that he's a coconut. Brown on the outside, white on the inside.

Sometimes when Muhammad and Dad used to fight before, Muhammad would mutter "coconut," and once Dad heard him. My brother stopped saying it that day, but I know it hurt Dad.

And I want to hurt him now.

And then I'm going to give the Popsicle to Mom and say, *Because you're the best, Mom!*

When I return from the kitchen detour to dress his ice cream, Dad receives his customized coconut cone with a confused look on his face. Mom does the same when I gift her with a Popsicle, but because I follow hers up with a hug, she pauses from her assembly-line work to unwrap her treat.

I'm so glad no one asks about the whereabouts of my ten a.m. ice-cream cone.

I don't want to admit I agree with Dad that it's a weird time to eat it.

I don't want to admit to having *anything* in common with *him*.

After we finish boxing three hundred favors, Mom announces that she needs to leave to get ready for Jumah. That opens up a whole discussion of how everyone will get to the mosque, the one Muhammad and I go to for Jumahs when we're with Dad, twenty minutes from Mystic Lake. In the end, we decide on a caravan of cars with a combination of people in each car.

Dad watched all this organization to go to Friday prayers from over the top of his reading glasses, over the top of his laptop, ice cream completely melted into his coffee cup, and I couldn't help saying aloud, "So glad to go with *you*, Mom!"

Mom hugged me, oblivious to my intent to wound Dad, but Muhammad gave me a look.

Now, as everyone scatters to get prepped to leave, and we go inside the house to change, Muhammad beckons me into the family room.

Once I'm inside, he pulls the pocket door closed. "Okay, what's going on with you and Dad?"

"What do you mean?"

"I mean, the ice cream thing? When you said, 'Here's a coconut cone, like you'? And the other digs?"

"It's not my fault Dad's racist. And you used to call him that! A coconut!"

"What?" Muhammad looks surprised. "Racist? I called him a coconut because he wanted me to not use my hands to eat and stuff. When he wanted me to be more bougie."

Oops. I shouldn't have blurted it out. This means he's going to know about Nuah.

And he can't know about Nuah.

He'd never let me live it down.

But, wait, that's only if something had to be lived down.

I mean, once all goes well, Nuah and I will actually be okay with people knowing. Right?

I look at Muhammad. He's still staring at me with his eyebrows knotted in confusion.

"Dad doesn't like that Nuah likes me. You know, in *that* way. Because he's Black," I say. And when I finish this short—not simple—statement, my eyes fill up immediately, my hands making their way to my eyes to try to stop them from spilling over.

The next thing I know, I'm blubbering.

Because it's awful. Horrendous. Despicable.

That Dad can sum up someone based on their race.

When I shift my hands away from my eyes, Muhammad has moved to sit down on the couch, his face still. "I can't believe it. But I can, at the same time."

"That Nuah likes me?"

"No, dummy, that Dad would be prejudiced like that." He leans back.

"He gave me some BS about how if you're not of the same cultural background, you get treated like crap by each other's families." I sit on the sofa across from him. "He said he wasn't treated well by Mom's family because he's Indian and they're Arab."

Muhammad shakes his head. "Not true. You know Amu and Teta and everyone's not like that."

"Yeah, exactly. He's just justifying his racism. And then he said Sarah's family doesn't treat you well because you're not Syrian like Sarah." I lean forward. "BS."

Muhammad doesn't say anything.

"BS, right?"

"That doesn't matter. What matters is that you don't listen to Dad on this. He's completely wrong. You don't choose someone based on their culture, ethnicity, race, or some superficial thing like that."

"Duh, I know that."

"Okay, then you're good. Why are you crying? And trying to pick a fight with him?"

"Because I hate that he's like that. It's so wrong!" I'm fired up again.

"So you thought Dad was perfect before?" Muhammad lets

out a sarcastic laugh. "Nobody's perfect. You work with what you've got. He's still our dad. You just write him off, and I mean *completely*, as capable of giving you any sort of advice you'd respect on these kinds of issues. I did that a while ago. Remember when you couldn't understand why for a long time I was arm's-length with Dad? This is why."

I slump down, thinking of Dad's frowns aimed my way all day yesterday.

Ugh.

Muhammad laughs again, and this time it's his familiar teasing laugh. "NA and JY, huh? See, I was right. I'm always right!"

I shake my head and stand to go open the door and get away from the inevitable teasing to come when I remember one of my wedding-clipboard tasks. "Hey, you know that group that you're getting to perform tomorrow? Your friends, the comedian-singers?"

"The 'Arrys? Yeah?" He gets up.

"What about, as a special surprise for Sarah, you get Haytham to sing instead? And ask the 'Arrys to perform tonight for whatever Dad is throwing for your friends? Sarah will be so wowed."

He thinks for a minute. "But they're looking forward to doing a show at the wedding."

I stand in front of the door and give him a piercing stare. "Muhammad. It's way more important how Sarah feels. And do you really think Sarah is going to love the 'Arrys?"

"What are you talking about? They're hilarious!" His face is incredulous. "They're getting gigs all over the place now!"

"But at *weddings*?" I press.

"This is a nikah. It's just our friends and families getting together. The official wedding is next year."

I don't take my gaze away from his face. "But admit it—it's

become weddinglike. Everyone calls it a wedding."

He doesn't say anything, so I go on. "Think of Sarah's *parents* . . . think of their faces as the 'Arrys introduce them. Think hard." I pause. "Think about the future."

His shoulders slump before he lets out a sigh. "I'll see if they can switch."

YES! One more thing crossed off my list! "Her *parents*," I emphasize again before sliding the door open and indicating for him to go first. "After the groom-to-be, of course."

He goes through but then backs up and wraps me in his signature bear hug.

Chapter Eighteen

❄ ❄ ❄

Dad tries to stop me to talk when I'm heading to Mom's car, which she's driving into town to pick up Sarah, Khadija, and Dawud on our way to the mosque.

"Hey, listen, let's not fight now." He stands on the porch, by the white balustrades, his hands in his pockets. "It's Muhammad's wedding."

"I'm not fighting." I don't look at him but go down the steps slowly so he can hear me. "I just hate that you're being racist."

"I'm not." He lowers his voice. "Okay, I said something wrong. But it came from trying to protect you."

"How is it protecting me when *you* married out of your culture, Dad? In case you didn't notice, Linda's Greek—but is that okay to you because she's white?" I turn at the bottom of the step. "And when Muhammad first told you about Sarah, a couple years ago, all you asked him was 'Is she fun?' You never said anything about *her* culture being different. Is it because she's kinda white too?"

"No, it was because Mom is Arab too. So Muhammad's partly from the same background as Sarah."

"But you're not the same background as Linda! In any way,

shape, or form!" Oh my God, I'm getting hot and teary again. I don't want Mom to see me like this. "It's racism—actually, it's anti-Blackness, since all the other cultures seem okay to you. Don't talk to me, Dad, until you figure that part out yourself!"

I leave Dad and rush back in the house to wash my face before Mom sees.

Luckily, she parked in the driveway at the side of the house and so she didn't witness the whole thing.

I don't want to spoil her happiness about this special weekend for Muhammad and Sarah.

It's only later when I'm in the car, in the back with Sarah, a talkative Dawud between us, that I remember I forgot to tell Muhammad not to say anything to Nuah. About *us*.

Muhammad and Nuah are driving together to Jumah.

I pull out my phone to text but then remember that Muhammad's texts blare on top of his locked screen. Nuah would see it if Muhammad has his phone lying around in the car while he's driving.

I can't even call him. It will go on speaker. And even if I break out in the little Arabic I know, Haytham, who's in the car with them, will understand it.

Urdu.

I know Urdu even less than Arabic, but Muhammad knows it more than me because he's tighter with our only cousins on Dad's side, Imran and Adnan, who are flying in tomorrow from California. Muhammad claims he's almost fluent (which I don't believe) due to their calling each other names in Urdu.

Dania and Lamya can help me. They speak Urdu too.

I text Dania and, when she doesn't reply, text Lamya to ask how to say *Don't tell N what I told you.*

She replies, N ko nahi batana meine aap ko jo bataya.

I copy the message and send that on to Muhammad.

The rest of the way to the mosque, I tolerate Dawud going on about the "tons of stuff" the florist is bringing for him tomorrow morning for the floral ceiling he's going to make, how he's got amazing ideas because he's getting "tons of stuff"—which was his whole reason to go into town this morning. Sarah hugs him in delight periodically.

Up front, Khadija and Mom are deep into a discussion of childbirth positions.

I look out the window and think about tonight.

Tats will be there. I'll be wearing a sari, which Mom's friend Auntie Maysa is going to come and wrap for me. It's a very dark green chiffon one with tiny black and silver crystals on the edges.

I wanted to wear a sari because I'd seen a picture of Mom in one when she took a trip to India to see my grandmother on Dad's side, who passed away when I was five.

Mom had looked regal, like royalty from a picture book—but mysterious and elegant, which is what drew me to her outfit.

After watching countless YouTube videos on the elegance of saris, I asked Mom if I could wear one to the henna party. I wanted to wear one with a short top, so a girls-only party was the perfect place to debut a sari. That's when Auntie Maysa, expert of all things Bollywood, got involved.

She's supposed to arrive two hours before the party to help me get ready.

✿ ✿ ✿

After Jumah, we all gather in the parking lot of the mosque to discuss lunch. Differing opinions from no lunch to pizza to choosing a nice restaurant lead us to split up and reorganize the cars.

Dawud wants to rush off to work on designing his floral ceiling, and to keep this a secret from Muhammad, he says he wants to eat leftover burgers at Dad's, so Muhammad offers to drive him back. Sarah goes along because she has a hair appointment to get ready for the henna party.

Because pregnant Khadija's craving deep-dish pizza, Nuah's going to drive Mom's car, with Haytham on board.

Mom, Dania, Lamya, and Uncle Bilal want to eat "proper food," so they're going to find a nice restaurant nearby.

I'm torn. Something about the way Mom flushed immediately on seeing Uncle Bilal after Jumah is reawakening my imagination regarding them.

I want to go with Nuah, but, yes, I want my mommy.

More specifically, I don't want my mommy to go with Uncle Bilal and his family without me.

"Husna, you won't believe it. There's an authentic Italian halal restaurant nearby, and it's called Magda's." Uncle Bilal looks up from his phone, his eyes seeking Mom's earnestly. *"Magda's!"*

"We *have* to eat there. That's where we met in college. It's meant to be!" Mom says. Her face is lit up a million watts, and its light turns to me—because I'm practically leaning over to peer at her. She adds brightly, "It's where *all* of us met each other, at Magda's apartment. Your dad, some other friends, everyone."

I decide to go to Magda's too.

But Khadija entwines her arm through mine. "Can I interest you in some ooey-gooey cheese-a-licious pizza?"

"Actually, I'd like to see what authentic halal Italian's like," I say. "Never had it, except for pizza, of course."

"But deeeeeep dish," she says. She looks around and pulls me to the side. "And, also, deep dish about Nuah's girl. I found out more intel."

She raises her eyebrows at me. With high significance.

My cheeks are flooding. It feels like every bit of blood from my toes and up is making its way to my face. I can't talk, so I just stare at Khadija's mauve hijab intently.

"Layth, what about you? Halal Italian or deep dish?" Uncle Bilal calls out.

I turn away from Khadija to see Layth coming out of the mosque's intricately carved wooden doors. He's putting his phone in the pocket of his black jeans.

"Deep dish," Layth says.

"Janna? You're coming with us, right?" Mom asks.

Khadija's arm is still tangled in mine. The heat on my face is settling down, so I squeak out, "No, I think I'll do pizza."

Before Mom leaves, I go up to Dania—well, I think it's her, because she's in a turban hijab—and, pointing at Mom and Uncle Bilal, I boldly say, "Can you watch those two?" I add a buoyant laugh to make it light.

Dania blinks at her dad's back and then looks at me, something dancing in her eyes.

"Will do," she says with a smile.

Oh no.

Does she think the opposite of what I'm thinking?

Is she going to *encourage* those two?

✿ ✿ ✿

After a hard time figuring out how to seat ourselves so the wrong people don't end up being squished beside each other (as per Islamic rules about physical contact), I end up driving with Khadija beside me.

I'd been secretly hoping for me, Nuah, and Khadija to be in the back, but that would have meant pregnant Khadija sitting in between me and Nuah, her legs squished on the middle bump on the floor of Mom's small Mazda, which would have been cruel.

So I drive with three guys in the back.

At stoplights, whenever I glance in the rearview, I glimpse three sets of eyes.

Three completely *different* sets of eyes.

But *I* only have eyes for one.

And he's the only one whose glance I don't catch in the mirror.

What's happening—with me and Nuah—hits me when the big pizza we ordered arrives and Haytham plates a slice and presents it to me with a flourish. He nods at me encouragingly with a smile and says, "Enjoy!"

Nuah thinks *Haytham* likes me.

And that I like him back.

Proof: his recent laugh when Muhammad joked about Haytham's "dates" with me and the comment he made matching us to Westley and Princess Buttercup in *The Princess Bride*.

Uh-oh.

That's why Nuah's not responding to my texts. That's why he's not looking for opportunities for us to talk, like I always am, and like he *used* to whenever he was around me before.

That's why whenever I look at him when everyone's talking, he's not paying any attention my way.

Why he doesn't even look at me now as we sit in this rounded booth, me at the end and him smack in the middle, beside Khadija next to me.

I cut a piece of my pizza, but when I raise it to my mouth, I realize I can't eat. It feels strange, like there's something burbling inside that'll push the pizza right out again.

My phone buzzes in my pocket. I slide it out and see it's a text from Muhammad.

Meine aap ka paigham dair se dekha. Meine Nuah ko mangni ki mubarak baath de di. Bohat bohat mubarak ho behna! 😊

This looks important. Obviously because it has the word "Nuah" in it.

I look up for help deciphering this dispatch—maybe a waiter?

None of them look desi.

Layth. He's sitting across from me eating a slice of pizza calmly while Haytham and Nuah discuss their theories of how you make deep-dish pizza, with Khadija interjecting, laughing, at their more ridiculous suggestions.

But I don't know Layth's number.

I could just pass him my phone? I clear my throat and lean forward.

Which makes everyone at the table fall silent for some reason.

I don't care, I decide. I'm good at ruses.

"Layth, can you translate this Urdu for me? But like text me the meaning? It's for this thing for the henna party tonight." I glance around at everyone after passing Layth my phone. Haytham nods his head, and Khadija smiles.

Nuah looks at his pizza and then at Layth, who's peering at my phone.

Layth reads and then—ugh—immediately looks at Nuah. And then at me.

He touches my phone and then pauses. "Can I get your number from here?" And when I nod, he scrolls and swipes and then picks up his phone and texts me before handing my phone back.

Saw your message late. I already congratulated Nuah on your engagement. Congrats sister! ☺

Chapter Nineteen

✳ ✳ ✳

Muhammad's phone rings and rings.

I'm in a stall in the pizza place bathroom.

"Janna, what's with you? Calling incessantly? I was driving, just dropped Sarah at her appointment. Can you guys pick her up at the hotel after?"

"What did he do when you said congrats?"

"What are you talking about?"

"Nuah," I whisper into the phone in case someone comes in. Someone like Khadija. "Tell me everything."

"He got quiet. And told me to shut up. And then I said, no seriously, man, I'm excited about you guys getting together."

"And then what happened?" I whisper again.

"He just kept saying shut up. Then Haytham came up to us in the prayer hall because he'd finished his sunnah. Why?"

"Nothing." I stare at the flyer on the back of the stall. It says *Glow Nights Party All Night with DJ Mousefire, Girls Dance Free, General Admission $15*. "Okay, bye."

I hang up and stare at the flyer some more before leaning my head on the stall wall.

Why is this becoming unbearable? My ability just to talk to Nuah?

I scroll through all our messages after he went away to college, and it's a long scroll that actually starts when I got this new phone for Eid-ul-Adha last year. Before that, the stream of messages in my old phone was ironclad proof of the slow-burn buildup of *Me and Nuah, the Love Story.*

Wait.

I slow my scrolling.

There are a lot of messages in the beginning. Silly things like What is a nerfherder? I figured you would know this geeky thing I encountered (from me) and Yo English nerd, if you (if I) say that that's someone's "shtick" does it mean something negative or can it be positive too? (from him) to Before I pass out from eating so much, Eid Mubarak! (me) and I posted my #BlackOutEid pic and you didn't say a word. Pout on (him).

And then it peters out.

The petering out started in March. No, maybe even a bit before.

I guess I didn't notice because we hung out so much at Christmas break. And I thought we were both busy with school—because I *was*. Getting all my things in before graduating.

We still liked each other's posts and he still watched my Snapchat and IG stories, like I did his. And we shared laughs.

And, last month, we did that whole e-mail thread about Muhammad's roast performance. We even practiced on FaceTime a couple of times to get the delivery right.

But yeah, we didn't talk about anything except the roast on those calls.

Because Nuah was always busy and had to leave right away when I'd try to bring up other topics.

Which I chalked up to being a freshman—but which my gut had whispered doubts about all along.

I sigh and lean against the stall again. *Glow Nights Party All Night with DJ Mousefire, Girls Dance Free, General Admission $15*

Was that easier? To show up at a club and be purposeful and find a guy, and you both wanted each other and wham—there he was, *your* guy?

Ugh. I would be the person hiding in the corner in a club, hoping no one looked at me.

I couldn't make eye contact—especially in that way—or small talk.

Basically, you need to be some kind of It girl to make things happen that way. Which is unfair and based on looks and some kind of elusive thing that you need to be able to project.

We mousey girls tend to fade until a Nuah finds us.

And my Nuah did . . . but what happened?

I close my eyes and let the thudding voice deep inside grow. The one that made itself known faintly this morning.

As it speaks with confident clarity, *Janna, it looks like Nuah doesn't like you anymore*, and a hot tear falls, the bathroom door opens, and the unmistakable footsteps of Khadija sound.

I wipe my eyes and stand up straight.

"Janna? You in here?"

"Yeah, just coming out."

"Wait for me. This baby makes me pee the minute I drink something."

I pretend chuckle.

"Wait, okay? Remember I had to tell you something?"

I don't want to wait. I don't want to hear the "deep dish" Khadija has.

On *the* girl.

She starts talking even though she told me to wait. "So Nuah met this girl at Caltech, in his program, actually. She's Muslim too. Her name's Sumayyah. And remember he wasn't sure she liked him back? He just found out, like yesterday, that she does. Isn't that wild?"

I close my eyes again.

DJ Mousefire.

It's so stupid, but, when I open my eyes and look at the club flyer again while trying not to cry, it makes the utmost sense to me.

It *is* perfect, in fact.

Like a sign. A haram nightclub sign, yes, but still a freaking good sign.

I'm going to be DJ Mousefire. A mousey girl on fire.

I'm not going do anything I don't want to do.

I don't want to continue to stand here listening to Khadija.

I unlock the stall, head to the sink, wash my hands and face, dry them with a paper towel, and walk out of the bathroom.

I slide back into the booth and finish my pizza slice that's greasy as hell but also the right kind of fatty for deadening my emotions. I drink my Coke, slurping down to the icy bottom.

And laugh whenever one of the three guys makes a stupid joke. Even Layth is joking now.

And he's beating everyone in sarcasm levels. To the point that if Muhammad were here, he'd be standing up cheering.

I make it a huge point to never once look Nuah's way. Even when I'm laughing at his one-liners.

When Khadija returns, I get up and ask if she's finished eating, because Auntie Maysa's coming to do my sari and I need to get back.

Once she nods, everyone rises and pitches in for the pizza, and we're out of here.

The cracks and digs and funny stories continue in the car, and I never once look in the rearview.

DJ Mousefire gets everyone to Mystic Lake in twenty minutes. Because being on fire means keeping her sights on the road right in front of her.

She needs to get this henna party done and this wedding done, and then she's going to collapse at home in Eastspring.

When we get to the Orchard to drop Khadija and Layth and pick up Sarah, she's standing in front of the hotel with her arm around someone.

After we park and Nuah and Haytham go inside to use the bathroom, Sarah rushes over to the driver's door and opens it. She's got her hijab on big and loose, sort of helmetish, and I know it's because she's trying to preserve the hair she just got done.

"Here she is in person! Janna!" she says to the girl still on her arm. "Janna, this is a friend of mine from school, Zayneb."

Zayneb bends down and peers at me, big smile on a face encased in a trim blue hijab tucked into a white buttoned shirt over jeans. "Janna! I'm such a huge fan! Assalamu alaikum!"

I smile back, because she's got that kind of contagious smile, but I have no idea what she's talking about. *Fan?* "Walaikum musalam. Great to meet you, but I'm drawing a blank as to why you're a fan?"

"Aren't you a Niqabi Ninja? Like you edit the videos and fill in sometimes for Ruki?"

Oh. She's talking about my work for Sausun, for her YouTube channel, the Niqabi Ninjas.

"Sarah caught me bingeing nostalgically one weekend and I was like, I live for these videos, and then she drops the news that she's getting married to the brother of a ninja and I was like, YOU ARE GOING TO INVITE ME TO THAT WEDDING!" Zayneb laughs. "So I'm here for *you*! And, yeah, a bit for my girl Sarah."

I get out of the car, feeling this glow ignite inside, drying teeny bits of the dampening that happened earlier.

Zayneb leans over but then pauses. "Hug? Handshake? Or none of the above?"

I'm impressed. She actually asks.

I put out my hand, and she takes it and shakes it lightly and then puts her hand on her heart. "Mentally checking off my bucket list. Met Janna, a favorite YouTuber."

This girl. She's one of those rare people who you can actually soak sunshine from. Like I can tell everything she said just now was the truth and not some attempt to sweet-talk me. "Aw, thanks. But maybe you'll be happier to know that an *actual* Niqabi Ninja is coming to the nikah tomorrow. Sausun will be here."

"Wow!" Zayneb raises her hands in victory. "I can't believe it! Okay, I'm going to tell you right now that I may tag along with you guys. Be a groupie. Because you're doing amazing work."

"Thanks," I say. "But it's really Sausun that's doing everything. I'm just helping so she can keep doing it."

"What are you talking about? The editing is so cool. Like the time you pretended her cat was taking all the footage? And proved that animals were the ultimate humans?" Zayneb starts laughing. "Oops, I'm going to be fangirling all weekend, so I'd better do it in smaller doses, spread it out, or you'll get sick of me."

"Janna is amazing but too modest." Sarah puts her other arm

around me, and I swallow the feeling of claustrophobia at being held in a tight circle with Zayneb. "Come up to the room for a bit. Zayneb brought all these treats from when she went to visit her fiancé in Ottawa, and we still haven't gotten to the ketchup chips."

"Ketchup chips?" I make a face.

"They're AMAZING!" Zayneb shouts, walking backward in the parking lot toward the hotel's front doors. "Oh, Sarah, you know he's coming tomorrow, right? Adam? We flew down from Ottawa together, and he's staying with my brother now who'll be driving him over tomorrow to be my plus-one. My *date*, finally, ooh-la-la!" She makes a mischievous face and laughs.

"You mean I *finally* get to meet the man?" Sarah's face lights up. "Now I'm really looking forward to my wedding!"

"What about the guys? Haytham and . . . them? They said they need to get back to my dad's." I want to get back too. And just close the door on the world for a while.

"We'll leave in fifteen," Sarah promises, a bounce in her step as she follows Zayneb.

I lock the car door and tag after them, thinking maybe Zayneb's a good distraction.

When we leave the hotel, it's with the addition of Zayneb, who whispered to me—when Sarah was in the hotel bathroom—that Dania and Lamya said I'd promised to join in their dance at the henna party tonight. "I'll come back with you to the house and I'll show you all the moves before we get dressed. We'll hide it all from Sarah."

To the car, Zayneb wheeled an orange carry-on suitcase that had her henna party clothes and was filled with Canadian treats (ketchup chips, Kinder Surprise eggs *with tiny toys in them*, something called a Coffee Crisp bar, and various other things I was assured were unsurpassed in perfection) that she promised we were going to eat while we practiced dancing. I just nodded, because it took less energy to nod at the things Zayneb wanted to do.

Because Dad and Linda had insisted Sarah get ready for the party in their bedroom and had even hired a friend who was a professional makeup artist, Sarah also brought a suitcase with her with all her party clothes and stuff.

Haytham drives with Nuah up front, and Sarah asks Haytham to play bits from his Muslim Voice audition samples for Zayneb so she can get her network at college, which is apparently huge, to vote for him.

I'm by the window and luckily looking out when I hear these lyrics, because the next thing I know, I'm crying silently:

> *She's like a boat that's caught in the storm*
> *Sees the sun through the clouds but she can't stay warm*
> *Now she's in pain and she can't bear the load*
> *But she don't know there's something better down the road*

I understand why I fixated on Nuah all this time.

He was the rainbow in my heart after the storm.

After the assault.

He was the one who let me be—angry, in pain, sad. He just let me find my way out of it. On my own, while always being in the background if I needed him. Sending me a million pick-me-up videos, memes, messages.

It was like I relied on him to always be in the background.

And now he's gone.

> *Now she's in pain and she can't bear the load*
> *But she don't know there's something better down the road*

I thought Nuah had been that "something better down the road" who came into my life when I needed someone to.

But he wasn't. Isn't.

Zayneb unknowingly saves me by getting me out of the roast practice Nuah had scheduled for after Jumah.

Once Sarah goes into the house, Zayneb tells everyone, "Janna and I are going to work on a surprise for Sarah."

In the driveway, Nuah nods and says, "JY, we'll squeeze in practice tomorrow, then, okay?"

I don't know if I agree or not, in my haste to get inside the house, in my haste to get away from the world I made up in my head.

Chapter Twenty

❈　❈　❈

"Yeah, use both hands! Screw those lightbulbs twice up right, then bring them to your left and screw twice!" Zayneb directs me as we watch ourselves dance in the mirror in my room. Zayneb's teaching style is comprised of translating all the Bollywood moves she's choreographed for this dance into mundane, everyday things. "Now turn those arms into streamers and stream them to your right! Now to your left! And lightbulb screwing again! Now streamer those arms and spin around! And back to spreading that jam on your hand, now the other hand!"

I changed into pajamas in the hope of curling up to mourn the state of things alone with one of my books, but then Zayneb had knocked on the door to say that Sarah was getting her nails done so we had to practice *now*.

A song with the Urdu word for henna, "mehndi," being repeatedly sung is sounding from Zayneb's phone. *Mehndi hai something something*.

At least it's a simple beat and really repetitive. And on loop, because it fades then starts again.

"You're a fast learner!" Zayneb looks at me proudly. "You already got all the first moves."

"Maybe it's because I know how to screw a lightbulb and spread jam?" I do the my-arms-have-turned-into-streamers move that Zayneb demonstrated previously, while keeping up with my bopping on one foot, and then turn slowly like she did.

"You're a natural!" Zayneb leans against the dresser and watches me dance for a while, nodding her head to the beat. "How about we position *you* in the middle? Currently it's me because everyone insisted. But I can see you in the middle. Sarah will be wowed."

"No, I can't." I stop dancing. "I'll fumble."

"But you're amazing!"

I shake my head. "You in the middle."

I'm not very coordinated. Why am I good at this?

I look in the mirror and see my eyes are still sort of red. I explained them away to Sarah, who asked, as allergies. Maybe I'm dancing well because I don't care? About anything?

"What are you wearing to the mehndi?" Zayneb asks.

"A dark green sari, because my stepmom's friend who's organizing the whole thing told us that in Indian culture you wear green or yellow or orange to henna parties and no way was I going to wear yellow. Or orange. Can you imagine?" I make a face.

"I'm wearing orange. It's my favorite color. The brightest orange suit I could find, in fact!" Zayneb announces.

"Oh, sorry. I didn't mean—"

"You're wearing an *actual* sari? Like the kind that you drape?"

I nod.

"You can't dance in that really well, unless you've had a lot of practice." Zayneb considers me for a moment. "The rest of us in the dance are all wearing pink or orange, the theme colors of our dance. I brought some extra clothes with me in case our other dancers didn't have the right stuff. If we roll up the top of the shalwar, you can wear one of my suits? Just for the dance part, which will be at the end."

I shrug. All this trouble to do a dance? "I don't know."

"Wait here. I'll go bring my suitcase."

Before I can protest, she's gone.

The song comes on again. *Mehndi hai rachnewaali* . . .

I close my eyes and streamer my arms and screw lightbulbs and spread jam.

And try to forget about Nuah.

Zayneb comes back in, wheeling her luggage behind her, with an iPad in her hands. "Oh my God. Haytham's in the lead now! And I haven't even messaged everyone yet!"

I come over and peer at the screen.

It's the Muslim Voice video summary of the three singers in the finals. A fifteen-year-old Malaysian girl with a ukulele who weaves Arabic and Malay into her covers of popular songs, an elderly man from Sudan whose renditions of traditional nasheeds are haunting, and then Haytham. They give a sample of some of his submissions for the contest, and I hear the song that made me cry in the car.

It's called "Hold On." The original is from a singer named Kareem Salama.

I look up the song on my phone. *Country* music?

I thought there was something different about it.

Zayneb unzips her suitcase and hands me folded clothes. "Try this. Just for the dance."

I balk. Whatever she's holding out is hot pink with gold

embroidery, really extra-gold embroidery, at the edges. "I don't do those colors."

"But it's not for anything IRL, you know? It's like a costume for a play. Imagine we're doing a performance just for Sarah." She unfolds the outfit. "This one's beautiful. It's a cut called Anarkali. A traditional suit that's an ode to the past. Look."

When it's unfurled, it's a dress with a high, embroidered bodice, gold again, from which the soft skirt falls full with tiny pleats almost to the floor, ending in a wide, heavily beaded ribbon of a hem. She pulls out a pair of skinny ruched pants that are shocking pink as well, dotted with gold circles, before holding up the dress full-length in front of me. "When you twirl like you did just now, with your streamer arms, the skirt will flare in a circle, and you'll look amazing."

I look in the mirror. It *is* beautiful. The dress.

And *so* not me.

But maybe it's DJ Mousefire?

I take the dress to the alcove bathroom as Zayneb is also changing to show me her "outrageously orange suit," as she calls it. She assured me it's an Anarkali cut as well. "We're going to match," she said excitedly. "I just want Sarah to be happy. Because she makes so many people around her happy, you know?"

I nodded, remembering how Sarah hadn't let go of asking me if she could help me when she'd thought something was wrong before, when I'd gone quiet after the assault. And then, when everything had come to light, she'd called me every day. Even if it was for like a minute to say salaam.

I love her, and I'm going to do this thing all the way for her.

Before I try on the clothes, I find the original version of "Hold On" and play it while I change.

She's like a boat that's caught in the storm
Sees the sun through the clouds but she can't stay warm

I wish I could write *those* words on a steamed-up mirror.

But it's okay. I'm going to will myself to be warm, to be on fire, to rock this dress, this dance.

I unhook the loops at the back of the pink-and-gold neck, slip my T-shirt off, and slide into this thing.

The dress part, the kameez, is a little too big on the shoulders because Zayneb has a slightly bigger frame than me, but otherwise, I'm surprised at how epic I look.

I look like I stepped out of a fairy tale.

I've never worn something so extravagant, and I don't think I ever will again, but something about this outfit makes me feel like I'm not the old me.

Even though I can't do streamer hands, screw lightbulbs, or spread jam to the beat of this country song, I try out the moves Zayneb taught me, and when I'm finished twirling, I stare at myself and say yes.

Yes, I'm going to dance tonight in this shocking pink dress.

Everything in life is born then it dies
After the storms the rooted plants do rise
So let pain die and plant yourself deep
Till this whole wide world falls down at your feet

Mom comes over with Auntie Maysa, who spends thirty minutes draping me in a sari and making sure I know how to walk in it. It's a good thing that the henna party is all women, because the black top I'm wearing is midriff baring and has a scooped back, and shows a lot more skin than I'd like.

Auntie Maysa declares me proficient in walking, adds a ton

of black and silver bangles on both my wrists and long glittery earrings to my ears, and Mom approves the way I did my hair (in a bun with two curled tendrils on either side of my face), and so they allow me to go check on Sarah, who's moved on to getting her makeup done. Linda said the makeup artist has been hired to make over me, her, and Mom, if she wants, as well.

The master bedroom is full of Sarah's friends, including Zayneb, Khadija, Dania, and Lamya. Everyone's outfits make a cacophony of color and shine and shimmer, but Sarah, sitting in a chair by the window, is just the most beautiful vision of all.

Her jilbab is peachy pink and hangs down to the floor, laden with heavy beading and embroidery in matte gold and gray. It's cinched at the waist with a matching, similarly embellished belt that's tied at the left side, the long golden-tasseled ends reaching her hem. The neck is scooped low to allow all her jewelry—several traditional necklaces and a heavy set of earrings—to shine. Atop all this, her hair lies in descending waves framing her happy, beaming face.

Sarah usually goes without makeup, and is stunning bare, but now, with the help of the makeup artist's touches, she looks utterly amazing.

She reaches out a hand when, in the mirror in front of her, she sees me enter. When I go over, she squeezes my hand and comments on how beautiful *I* look.

"Sarah, stop. This is YOUR day. You look unbelievable but also believable because you're you." I give her a hug—carefully, since she's crusted with gold and her face is done. "Can I take a picture? Muhammad's going to want to see this." Once she nods, I hold out my phone and snap several while Deirdre, the makeup artist, adds a layer of powder to her face. After she finishes, Sarah stands so I can take full-length pictures of her.

And then all of us girls in the room gather around Sarah, and Deirdre takes more pictures with our various phones and cameras.

"Hey, remember, everyone! No posting pics anywhere! Most of us here are hijabis!" Zayneb calls out. Her long curly hair is in ringlets all the way down to her waist. She looks amazing.

Khadija grabs me to exclaim over my "sophisticated" outfit, but I can't stop from squeeing over *her*. She's in a deep burgundy sheath dress that hugs her belly proudly and falls off her shoulders. It's a shimmery fabric with an underlaid orangish sheen to it, so when she moves, it's like another dress. Her hair is tied up high and then falls in thin braids that skim her bare shoulders, which are grazed by long—super long—twinkling, gold earrings.

Dania and Lamya, in matching suits, Anarkali as well, but in pink and orange respectively, come to fawn over Khadija with me.

EVERYONE LOOKS SO GOOD.

"I confirmed that the house is free of male presence right now. So we can go practice in the basement before Sarah comes down." Zayneb speaks low so that Sarah, near the window still getting pictures with Linda and Mom, doesn't hear. "She's only going to appear downstairs when her mom, aunts, and cousins have arrived, so we have time."

"How am I going to practice in this?" I indicate my sari to Zayneb. "You said I can't."

"Just don't do the feet movements. We'll be mostly just going over our placements anyway. And guess what? We got someone for the middle." She ta-das her hands toward Khadija. "Khadija's going to be the seated queen at the center."

Khadija nods. And does the screw-lightbulbs move for me as Zayneb goes to gather more dancers.

"And we're going to drape pink and orange dupattas on her so she matches," Dania says. "We already tried it out and it's perfect."

Khadija nods again and spreads jam on her face, then on her belly, before speaking. "This is Maysarah's first official henna party."

"The next one will be when Nuah gets hitched!" It's a girl I don't know well who says this. A friend of Sarah's. And apparently a friend of Khadija's, too, from the way she sidles up to her and puts an arm around Khadija after she speaks.

I keep my face still. But when I see Khadija switching her gaze to me, I feel my resolve crumbling.

"Let's go." Zayneb comes back, whispering. "I told Sarah we're just going to check out everything downstairs."

As we head out, Khadija starts walking closer to me, and one glance at her face tells me she's going to bring up something I don't want to hear, so I look around for an escape.

I back up and head to the chair by the window. "I'll catch up with you guys. I'm next to get my makeup done."

Chapter Twenty-One

❋ ❋ ❋

After Deirdre finishes working on my face, I go back to my room and throw open the closet doors.

I need to get away, and I need a cloak to do so.

What I'm looking for is all the way at the back of my closet, in a pile of clothes I threw on top of my suitcase. A long black abaya with a hood, ties at the waist, and deep pockets at the side for a phone. An abaya I brought up with me to Dad's in case I needed an extra coverall for praying.

But it's also the perfect coverall for a brief, necessary getaway.

I tuck the two tendrils of hair into the claw clip holding my bun in place and then put on the abaya, tie the sash to close it, and lift up the hood. It falls forward onto my forehead, and when I look at myself in the mirror, I see that the hood casts a long shadow over the top of my face, so only my nose down is revealed.

Good. Because I don't want anyone seeing my heavily done eyes with fake lashes and some kind of eyeshadow layering that makes me look like a manga character.

I open the door a crack and check if the coast is clear.

Then I slip off my shoes and go downstairs quietly. I hear some movement from the family room off the kitchen. I don't wait to see who it is but open the doors and walk fast, barefoot, until I'm between the house and the gazebo.

Then I run.

I can feel something happening to the sari, some kind of loosening, but I don't care, because I want to get to that secluded spot by the water to hide alone.

It's not to cry.

It's just to *not* see anyone who wants me to be smiling when I can't right now.

The waves lightly lap the shore, and I follow their rhythm for a while before I look up at the sky.

The sun's setting. I watch it and then decide to pray Maghrib right there in a patch of grass by the sand, with the water sounds nearby and the stillness of the approaching night.

By the time I finish, I can tell my sari's in serious disarray.

I stand and fix my robe and tie the sash tighter and reposition my hood.

I need to get back before they notice I'm missing, before it becomes a source of drama.

I'm hoping I've swallowed enough of the stillness of this spot by the water to fill me with the serenity I need tonight.

The truth is that my insides are still tangled, but maybe this moment to myself, bringing the rhythm of the waves with me, will help.

I just don't want this setback to open that other wound in me. Because anything bad happening in my life always somehow leads to that tiny dark space the assault opened in me.

I repeat the prayer I made after Maghrib: *Ya Allah, don't let this lead me where I don't want to go.*

It's dark now through the grove of trees so I use my phone's flashlight to light the path.

When I come out, at the side of the house between the barn and the driveway, it's to Nuah and Muhammad standing there talking, leaning against one of the many cars parked on the grass.

Then the worst-case scenario happens, because I look up straight into Nuah's eyes.

I try to do the nod-and-walk-away thing, but Muhammad calls out to me. "Is that you, Janna?"

I nod again but without turning.

"Why were you out there by yourself?"

I keep walking toward the driveway.

Great, he's (they're?) following. "Hey, stop. What's wrong?"

"Can I talk to her?" It's Nuah's voice. "Janna?"

I freeze. *How am I going to talk to him?*

"Janna, I'm sorry you found out from Khadija." Nuah's voice is low. "She told me."

"Found out what?" Muhammad sounds bewildered.

I'm not moving ahead but not turning around, either.

"I seriously didn't know you liked me back," Nuah says. "Honestly. I mean, I knew we were friends, but that's it."

I try not tear up at that. I can't open my mouth.

It's because I'm feeling the sting of humiliation.

"Khadija told me she told you about Sumayyah. She didn't know about me and you, and still doesn't." Nuah clears his throat. "Sorry, I guess we just never had it out in the open."

I turn around at that, but my voice is so soft, I don't know if he's going to hear it. "So, all the times you were asking if I was nice enough for you yet . . . that didn't mean what I thought it meant?"

Maybe I'm saying it so softly because this question is more for me.

But he hears it. "It did. But it was like a wish for me. Like from the first time we met. Then things changed." He says this gently.

"It was a wish for me, too." I can't hide the sadness in my voice.

A pause. And then he takes a breath and lets it out in one exhalation before speaking again. "I'm also just going to come out and say it. It was obvious from the beginning your dad wouldn't be too into it."

I close my eyes. *Nuah knew all along. He could feel it.*

My heart closes tight for him—the feelings of humiliation fleeing, replaced with waves of sorrow.

Sorrow for the kind of world where Nuah understood instantly how he was perceived—and in a space that should have been safe.

A Muslim space.

Muhammad's words come to me. *So you thought Dad was perfect before? Nobody's perfect.*

This is not about perfect.

Muhammad comes closer now, the driveway lights showing his furrowed forehead.

"Nuah? What's going on?" Muhammad is still confused. "Who's Sumayyah?"

"I met someone at college. And we've been talking."

I don't look at Nuah, but the way his shadow's moving on the ground tells me he's fidgeting.

A car is turning into the driveway right then, jolting us with its sound, and all three of us move closer to the house to hide from the approaching headlights.

We're pressed against the house, breathing quietly, and all I can think of is how many times before had I wished that Nuah and I could have had moments like this together.

I glance at the driveway and see the car doors open and Tats step out of the passenger's side.

Jeremy steps out of the driver's side.

Oh my God. This is like a weird dream. Maybe a freakish nightmare.

Jeremy?

I turn to Nuah. "Is it okay if I'm alone now? Please?"

He nods and leaves, heading to the barn.

"You too," I tell Muhammad. "Please?"

"Naw, you don't look good." He stays unmoving.

"But it's your bachelor party thingy. Please just go."

As he's leaving, I can't stop myself from adding, "And you said Dad wasn't perfect. But you're wrong. It's not about imperfection. This is more heinous than that."

Muhammad turns around and his face tells me he's processing what I just said. Then he nods at Tats now approaching us and mouths to me, *We gotta talk more. Later.*

"Janna?" Tats is wearing a simple green shalwar kameez Auntie Maysa had lent her. "What's wrong? And I thought you were going to be wearing a green sari?"

"Tats, you going to be with her?" Muhammad asks. "She needs someone."

"No I don't," I protest, my voice coming out insistent yet pouty. "Muhammad, it's your party, so please just go."

He leaves, with a nod to Tats.

Tats is beside me, and when I turn my gaze to her, I see Jeremy looking at me with the car door still open, his arm resting on the top.

Tats and Jeremy?

I turn away and lean on the house again and then slide down until I'm sitting on the driveway with my legs splayed, a big bunch of green chiffon wadding up in between the front opening of the abaya. My feet are still bare and now dirty.

I'm sure my mascara's running. One of my fake eyelashes must be loose, because I feel something heavy flicking at the side of my right eyelid.

"Okay, thanks for the ride, Jeremy! See you tomorrow!" Tats waves at him. And then she sits down on the ground beside me. "What's going on, Janna?"

I don't say a word. Because I don't know what words to say.

Like:

When did you hook up with Jeremy?

I mean, he means nothing to me.

But why wouldn't you tell me before?

And, um, how do I even begin to tell you anything like the truth about Nuah? When you thought it was weird all along that I liked him and he liked me but we wouldn't go out with each other?

And now I found out that there was an elephant in the room— namely anti-Blackness—that I had the privilege of not knowing about but that Nuah felt all along.

Something about this opens the wound.

The scab that always gets picked at when I come face-to-face with sad things I can't hide from.

The hurt I asked Allah not to open undoes itself at the seams.

Tats lets me cry silently, sitting beside me, rubbing my arms or putting her arms around me, and every time I feel like I'm going to talk and say, *Okay, I'm done. Let's go inside. It's Sarah's party*, a new wave of tears comes with a memory of something from that time.

"Should I go get your mom?" Tats asks finally. "You need to call Dr. Lloyd."

I shake my head.

"Janna, please?" Tats's voice is soft.

"It's not about that," I whisper. It's not really.

I don't think it is.

"Then what is it?" Tats says, taking my fingers in hers and lacing them. "I'm here for you."

I stay quiet. It sounds ridiculous when I think of saying it.

Nuah doesn't like me and I thought all along he did and that we were going to have a great summer but then he had to go and meet someone else. And my dad is someone I don't—I can't—like anymore.

But then I just blurt it all out. All of it.

All the way back, from our texts and communication to Nuah making it a point to ask me if I was still interested at Christmas. To the way Dad revealed his racism.

And how Nuah felt it the whole time.

That feels like the most heartbreaking thing of all.

Car lights come and go with new henna party guests arriving, and still we sit there in the shadows, unseen, me just unloading.

When I'm done, I've been petted repeatedly and offered soothing words, along with tears of empathy.

I look at my dirty feet and wadded-up sari and wonder how it ended up that I'm sitting here in disarray like this. I need to get back to the party.

My eyes go beyond my feet to the patch of grass in between us and the car parked the closest.

That's when I notice someone else's feet. In hiking boots.

They're slightly sticking out of the side of the car that we can't see.

It's a car I recognize from today.

From our caravan of cars heading to Jumah earlier.

I motion to Tats to quiet down. And then I stand slowly and walk over, gingerly, to those boots, with Tats following behind.

It's Layth.

He's sitting in the grass, leaning back against the car, holding his phone in his lap, earbud in—but only in one ear.

Chapter Twenty-Two

✳ ✳ ✳

"I promise I didn't hear anything until you erupted. I thought it was a fox in distress. Seriously." He takes the other earbud out of his ear now and wraps the wires around two fingers. "That's when I pulled my earbud out. To figure out what it was. That crying."

"Then you heard *everything*." I'm slumped down on the ground again, across from him this time, leaning against another car. Tats sits beside me.

"I swear I put my earbuds back in and just took them off periodically to make sure you were okay." To his credit, he doesn't laugh when he says that. "And I swear too that the only reason I didn't walk away was that I thought you'd be more upset. If you saw me."

Tats leans into me to whisper, "Who is he, and why is he hiding here?"

"Layth, and no idea why he's here," I say.

"Uncle Bilal forced me here for the thing your brother's having. His party. But there's some strange band setting up, practicing, and I needed to get out." He taps the phone in his hand. "Just catching up on some friends' updates. From the sanctuary."

"Sanctuary?" Tats asks, reaching up to her hair. It's in a bun—we decided to do similar hairstyles—but now she's unclasping something. If she lets her giant hair down now, it's going to dwarf her face.

"Yeah, animal rehabilitation sanctuary in Ecuador. There's no electricity, no Wi-Fi except on Friday afternoons when they go into town, so they've just uploaded a bunch of videos." He holds out his phone to Tats. "A rescued kinkajou."

It's an animal that looks like a weasel. A cute weasel with a long tail. It's scampering around with mad energy while a guy, his bushy blond hair held back with a headband, tries to get it to eat from a slop bucket he's kneeling beside. The guy occasionally shoots a goofy grin at the camera. There's a girl making encouraging noises off camera who must be the one taking the video.

The kinkajou suddenly slows down and tentatively approaches the bucket. And then shoots away again to climb a tree nearby. It stays there for a bit and then comes back down and attempts the bucket approach again.

"They get hunted for their pelts or to be exported as exotic pets," Layth says. "This one got hurt, so he's still on edge after a few weeks at the sanctuary."

It's weirdly calming to watch the animal slowly come to trust the slop bucket. And eat finally.

I find my breathing's slowed down. I look up from the video and meet Layth's gaze. He nods at me, his eyes kind, not judgy in any way.

I decide to forgive him for sporadically eavesdropping. He's going to leave the continent soon anyway.

"Aw, it's adorable," Tats says, handing the phone back.

"And calming," I add. "And satisfying. To watch that kinkajou trust again."

"It's like a drug." Layth plugs his earbuds into his phone again. "The high."

"The high?" Tats says, ever pushy. Her hair is not in a bun anymore. But it's still up—now in a high Ariana Grande ponytail, which, because Tats is an Audrey Hepburn doppelgänger, makes her look like Ariana's sister or something. "And you would know? About highs?"

He shoots her a look that says he knows.

"So when you go to this sanctuary place, you're not going to have any *electricity*? Or Wi-Fi?" I ask.

"Nope. Can't wait."

"But what about lights? And phone charging? And family and friends?"

"There are candles, and they fire up the generator twice a week so we can charge our phones, though the service is not good as we're actually in the rain forest. Wi-Fi is in town once a week." Layth pockets his phone. "And family, I only have my mom, who flew to England last month to be with my aunt—Dania and Lamya's mom. My friends, they know where to find me."

I remember him muttering "used to" when I brought up siblings before. But it would be weird to ask him about that with Tats around.

What did that mean, "used to"?

I could never imagine not having a sibling—well, Muhammad.

Like how he didn't want to leave me earlier until he made sure Tats was with me.

Will I ever be that good of a sibling to the laddoos?

To Muhammad?

I stand up slowly, holding the opening of the abaya closed tight over the wad of sari cloth that is now even bigger and dragging on the ground.

I'm thinking of Sarah in her glittery jilbab, resplendent at her henna party.

I try to push my loose fake eyelashes back into place and look at Tats. "We'd better go. I wanna dance for Sarah."

She nods and gets up too.

Before we leave, I look at where Layth's still sitting. "I'm pretty sure that band my brother got for his party, the 'Arrys, should be done now."

"Nah, I'm okay here." Layth shakes his head.

"Can I ask you something? Where can I see more of those rescue animal videos? From the sanctuary?"

"I can send you the link. It gets updated weekly."

"Thanks." I nod at him. "'Cause they're calming, you know?"

He looks up at me, nods, and adds a smile, and I'm 100 percent sure that I got him wrong before. He's not a crank at all.

Chapter Twenty-Three

Tats and I go to Linda's room, and I use makeup remover and clean my entire face and take off the fake eyelashes. Then Tats unravels my sari, and I change into Zayneb's shocking pink suit. Tats helps me put on fresh makeup that's not so loud.

I line both her wrists with all the bangles Auntie Maysa had given me, which gets her giddy, and then I hug her tight, because, truly, there's no best friend like her.

The other girls in the dance with us come up from the basement, and we practice in the family room quickly, under Zayneb's direction. We decide that Tats will join in at the end and do a ta-da flourish of different TikTok dance moves to get Sarah to laugh.

Tats hams it up, and we laugh so hard at her antics that we're all in high spirits as we head downstairs to perform. I swallow everything I felt earlier, but I don't push away all the memories that were opened from that awful time.

Instead, I draw the memory of the moment when Sarah learned that I was trying to hide my assault. How she took me out for fancy cupcakes to bond with me, to show me she cared about me, and I took a picture of her in my head.

Of her loving smile under a big thick frosting mustache.

I'm going to dance my heart out for Sarah.

The room is a long rectangle, and, except for the dance space in the middle, the floor's covered with the Persian rugs and mirrored cushions Linda and I set up on Wednesday, so guests are sitting here and there on the floor. There are a few chairs at the edges for those who can't sit on the floor, but most people are seated low and spread out.

We line up in three rows of four, with Khadija seated in the middle, for us to dance around at the chorus part. Sarah, sitting on a red velvet chair Ms. Mehta loaned us, gives a huge smile on seeing our group all arrayed. I know from Zayneb that we're the third dance performing.

The music comes on, and Zayneb nods to get us hopping to the rhythm before we add our arm and hand movements, when the words join the beat.

Mehndi hai rachnewaali.

We spread jam on our right hands in unison while hopping our feet to the beat.

We spread jam on our left hands in unison.

We screw lightbulbs on the right. Then left.

We streamer our arms to the right, then left.

We screw lightbulbs on the right. Then left.

We streamer our arms and spin.

And continue for the rest of the song, coming together to dance around Khadija whenever the song swells.

I can't believe how good it feels to do something perfectly

synchronized, where even when we mess up, we all laugh and help one another get back on track. And then, when Tats comes in at the end and jingles the bangles on her arms dramatically before launching into a mashup of TikTok dance moves, while the rest of us look at her theatrically perplexed, our hands positioned in front of our mouths, it's just the perfect ending.

While Tats finishes, I sneak a glance at Sarah and am thrilled at the delight on her face. She's so happy, she's actually tearing up, watching all of us.

I tear up.

She's not *going to be* my sister.

She always was.

After the dance Sarah grabs me for a hug, laughing with happiness. "Janna! You're an amazing dancer!"

I hug her back tight. Because she's *mine*, someone I'm completely comfortable hugging. "Thanks! But I'm actually just good at following directions."

"You have to do it again at the reception next year! Because it'll be split women and men, so we can dance our hearts out!" she says excitedly, before turning to hug Dania, Lamya, and Khadija. "I got some great selfies to share with Maysarah. Her first henna party!" Khadija tells me before I move from them. She adds a wink. "And to bless Lateef's eyes with."

I smile and make my way to someone I spotted while spinning around.

While carefully picking a path through the crowd, I see Sarah's mom and aunts on the chairs at my right, so I go over to give salaams. Only one of them hugs me, even though I veto my no-hug instincts and start out by trying to tentatively hug Sarah's mom. She gives me a small pat on my back in response.

She has the same look on her face as when I first saw her at the mosque in Eastspring a few years ago, when Sarah's family moved there. It's the same slight frown that's greeted me each subsequent time.

The frown that I previously attributed to a facial tic.

But now, without me summoning them, Dad's warning words run through my mind: *The same thing is happening to Muhammad. The way Sarah's family is treating him.*

Is it because we're not Syrian that Sarah's mom always scowls at me?

Why didn't Muhammad answer the question when I brought up what Dad had said about the way Sarah's family treats him?

After forcing myself to smile at Sarah's mom one more time, I head over to the person I really want to see.

Sausun, seated on the floor niqab-less, grins big when she sees me coming and stands up to open her arms to receive me. After we hug, she points to someone still seated. "Nada."

I bend to shake hands with Sausun's sister, who I've met a few times since Sausun helped her and her toddler son escape an awful situation in Saudi Arabia. Now Nada lives with Sausun and is still adjusting to her new life. She's mostly quiet, like right now when she just whispers salaam to me and doesn't add another word, even when I ask her how she's doing.

Straightening up, I make the mistake of looking beyond Sausun.

Sarah's aunt is scowling at me *from across the room* and whispering something to another of Sarah's aunts. Then the first aunt gets up from her chair to move toward us.

"Uh-oh," I say to Sausun. "Don't look, but I think there's trouble headed this way."

Sausun is cool as a cucumber, so she doesn't flinch. She just tosses her jet-black, dead-straight hair behind her shoulders and looks at me calmly from under her fringe of long, severely level bangs. Her eyes are hazel and big and there's no escaping their probing, and I can tell she's already assessed that I have a lot of things to tell her soon.

"Janna? Right? Muhammad's sister?" It's Sarah's aunt who owns several salons and who's always giving me and Mom advice on facials on the few occasions we've met. I think her name is Rima.

I nod and smile. Sausun begins to turn to Auntie Rima, but, before she completes the 180, she loops her arm through mine.

"Can I ask something? As Sarah's aunt?" Auntie Rima says.

"Sure," I say, stiffening, wondering if I'm the right person to represent Muhammad and our family. Should I call Mom over?

I look around for her and notice she's at the food table with Auntie Maysa and Auntie Ameera, her best friends.

"Why are you wearing this Indian outfit? Did your dad tell you to?" She's cocking her head like she really wants to know. "I'm not trying to offend you—I hope you know that. It's just something our family is wondering. Why you couldn't have honored our traditions."

I'm stunned. I look down at the carpet and then at her face again, to see if she's being serious.

She's awaiting my answer.

"Janna, you don't have to answer that." It's Sausun.

I turn to her. Her gaze is unmoving from Auntie Rima's eyes.

"You don't have to answer offensive questions," Sausun continues.

"Excuse me, I just told her I'm not trying to offend anyone. And who are you? You're not family." Auntie Rima's eyes flash angrily.

"And neither are you if you're coming to a happy occasion and then asking my friend, who's a part of YOUR family now, why she chose the happy, beautiful clothes she did," Sausun says, her voice growing louder. She turns to me. "Because they are, Janna."

I nod as it sinks in how awful this is—being accosted for the clothes I'm wearing. "I'm of dual heritage. And I think I can honor the part of my culture I want to." I say this quietly, wishing I could be as firm as Sausun.

"When are you going to honor *our* culture?" Auntie Rima shoots out. She sweeps a hand over the basement. "I don't see anyone here doing that."

"Not true," I say. "Sarah's honoring her culture beautifully. Everything she has on is of her culture. And it's beautiful."

"But many of the songs, the dancing, and most of the clothes are all from your father's background. Even your stepmom has on Indian clothes!" Auntie Rima thunders.

It's a good thing there's music on. Otherwise everyone would have heard "even your stepmom has on Indian clothes!" and turned their heads to us.

"So? Maybe everyone's choosing to wear whatever they think goes with the vibe they're feeling. Who are you to police them?" Sausun indicates her own clothes, a kaftan dress in pale, barely there mint green with silver beadwork. "I'm of dual heritage, and I'm wearing Arab clothes. Because my sister Nada and I are going to do a traditional dance from my dad's side for Sarah. And you know what? I don't think Janna's mom's going to have a problem with that. Or her dad."

Well, Dad might, I think. He and Auntie Rima may get along just fine.

I mean, just fine in their opinions on the world, but not culturally.

I look over at Mom again to see if she can rescue me, and realize that she, an Egyptian American, and Auntie Ameera, who's Somali American, are both wearing Pakistani suits like Auntie Maysa (who *is* Pakistani American). Auntie Rima is probably affronted by that, maybe thinking it's a planned emphasis on one culture—while I know that Mom and her friends just wanted to match each other and that they saw a deal at a desi store when they took a trip to Devon Street in Chicago together.

I need to exit this situation. "Oh, look. The line's cleared around one of the henna artists. She's the one I've been waiting for. I'm going to get my hands done."

"And it's time for my dance, I think." Sausun holds Auntie Rima's gaze. "You're free to join us if you want to. We're dancing to an old Arabi song you may know."

Auntie Rima shakes her head.

I point out the henna artist near Mom and her friends to Sausun. "I'll watch you guys dance while I get my henna done."

"Let's catch up later." Sausun winks at me.

I nod and leave Auntie Rima.

Before I get to the henna station, though, I feel a hand on my back. It's another of Sarah's aunts, Auntie Razan, who's older, maybe almost as old as Teta, my seventy-six-year-old maternal grandmother. She leans in to whisper to me. "Habibiti, don't worry. You've brought so much joy. Don't listen to Rima. She's feeling things wrong. We're so happy to be here together. There's so much joy here."

Then she strokes my hair and I feel like I'm with Teta and her warm love.

Mom comes to sit beside me while I'm getting hennaed.

"What happened over there with Auntie Rima?" she whispers. "I was going to come over when I saw your face, but then you left."

"You don't have to whisper, Mom," I say, indicating the henna artist with my chin. "She's got headphones on."

"So what happened?"

I fill her in, and she shakes her head when I'm done.

"I'm sorry that happened." Mom sighs. "But you know Sarah's mom's not like that, right?"

"Then why does she look so disapproving all the time?"

"That's her personality. She's like that with Sarah, too. She really loves Muhammad."

"Mom, can I ask you something?" I draw my right hand, now complete, away from the henna artist and shift myself to lay my left one in her palm. She positions the henna cone in the middle of the back of my hand and starts the same beautiful design of paisleys swirling in and around a larger, slender paisley that extends from below my wrist to the tip of my ring finger. "Did your family treat Dad like that? Like how Auntie Rima is behaving?"

I want to know how this assumption about cultural superiority plays out in our family. Like, I know it's there in the world; I've seen it with my own eyes—at school, at the mosque, the Muslim community—it's out there, everywhere.

I'm not that naive.

But I want to know about its existence in *my* family.

Mom doesn't say anything for a bit. Then she sighs again. "Most of my family didn't want me marrying Dad. Except for

Amu, who helped us get married. And Teta, who is Teta, always kind—you know how she is. But everyone else wasn't very happy, especially Grandpa before he died. That's why I'd only take you and Muhammad for visits. Why Dad wouldn't come."

"Why? Was it because Dad wasn't religious? And your family is?"

"I thought that was why for the longest time. But then one of my cousins married a completely unreligious person, but he was Egyptian, too, and they welcomed him with open arms. And Dad saw that. And it was early on in our marriage."

I shift again, uncomfortably this time. "What did you do?"

"I got angry. But I couldn't change them. To them, it's about the fear of losing something—culture, history, language—and not what the Qur'an says about why God created diversity." Mom leans me against her gently. "So that we may come to know our differences and love each other for them. When you see the world as divided, when you're prejudiced, it's not about expanding hearts— it's about shrinking your capacity to love. Which is really bad for our systems, physical and spiritual."

Is that why Dad and Auntie Rima are like that? Their capacity to love has been restricted by the way they see the world? Even though Dad acts so generous, *is* so generous, in other ways?

How does it make sense that Dad, who has felt the effects of prejudice himself, is dishing it out now too? Is it because it's the kind of prejudice, anti-Blackness, that's been ingrained in our cultures, South Asian and Arab, the kind that's so insidiously prevalent that Dad didn't hesitate to blurt it out like it was nothing?

Chapter Twenty-Four

✿ ✿ ✿

Tats and I slip out quietly with Mom when she leaves Dad's after the party, just after one a.m., after Sarah's family takes her back to Chicago, where they've all gathered. They're going to make their big entrance for the nikah tomorrow as a family procession around the bride. It's going to be quite dramatic according to what I've heard from Sarah. Having met more of her family tonight, I don't doubt it.

To stay in Mom's room at the hotel I packed an overnight bag, which, at Tats's insistence, includes my burkini. She found out from Mom that the Orchard has a pool, and she claims we're going to get up early in the morning to go swimming.

Dania and Lamya are in the car with us to go back to the Orchard.

With Tats in the back with them, acting like a talk show host (she's actually going to junior college to study broadcasting), we're getting a lot of information about their lives.

They even bring up Layth. How he's their cousin on their mom's side.

How he's had a rough life.

And how they hope his going back to Ecuador will help him out. Because the summers he spent there were the best years of his life.

We even learn how his family fell apart after a car crash, when Layth's only sibling, a younger brother, died.

Oh.

That's why he said "used to" about siblings.

When we get out, Dania stops me as everyone else goes on ahead.

The matching scarf for her pink outfit is wrapped around her head turban style, allowing massive gold hoop earrings to glint in the light from the parking lot.

"Guess what?" Dania's beaming. "Remember how you asked me to keep an eye on your mom and my dad?"

I nod, but tentatively. Her big smile is throwing me off.

"So the whole time, at the restaurant at lunch, they were reminiscing about college, right? And so Lamya and I kept asking questions, and we got a crucial piece of information that we wanted to share with you as well." She's practically laughing, the way her mouth's turned up so wide while she's talking. "We found out that Magda— Remember the famous Magda? Whose apartment everyone gathered at for Eid that fateful year long ago? She'd actually been trying to set *our* dad and *your* mom up! But then your dad showed up with our dad and bam! He swept your mom off her feet."

I don't know what to say.

"Isn't that just wild? This fact and that they're laughing about it over twenty years later at another *Magda's*?"

Okay, that part *is* wild.

But the rest is just historical accuracy. Mom was clearly supposed to meet Dad. And then go on to have Muhammad and me.

I nod and say, "Yeah, wild," but it's in such a lackluster way that Dania's face falls.

"Oh, wait," she says. "Oh. You're actually not okay with them together."

I remain silent, highly aware of the myriad directions this situation could go.

"Oh," she says again, turning around to walk toward the Orchard. I follow but not fast enough to walk alongside her. "Oh."

Man, her many *ohs* are making me feel like I'm a terrible person.

Maybe I *am* a terrible person.

Because I don't like the idea of Mom being part of a new family. It's strange and unknown, and I'm not ready. I like my world small, limited to just who I allow in.

As I enter the hotel, I shush the thought that comes into my head: *Small and limited, like Dad sees the world?*

I'm not like him, I think as I wait discreetly by the Tree of Red Fluffs for Dania to go into the elevator by herself.

Before I go ahead and wait for another one.

I just don't like awkward elevator silences.

Back at the henna party, when Mom asked why I wanted to bunk with her tonight, I whispered something about there being too many guys around Dad's place.

She'd nodded and then proceeded to tell me how Nuah had looked so happy when she'd seen him outside earlier, when she'd come in to prep me for the henna party with Auntie Maysa. "He's such a sweet kid! You guys are perfect for each other."

Now I'm in the hotel room bathroom wondering how to tell her about Nuah.

She has to know the truth.

Because otherwise, tomorrow, she's going to go out of her way to be chummy with him and then come back to me and nudge me and look in his direction and smile and just be Mom.

Tomorrow.

Ugh.

No ideas come to my mind while I shower, scraping all the henna off my hands and sending the dried flecks down the drain.

No idea of how to tackle this with Mom without her feeling sorry for me.

Maybe I should tell her on our ride home to Eastspring on Sunday.

And keep her from interacting with Nuah in any possible way, by any means necessary, at the wedding.

I wrap my wet hair in a towel, put on Mom's bathrobe that's hanging on a hook by the towel shelf, and open the door of the bathroom . . . to what looks like another party.

Lamya, with her knees up and a phone in her hands, is sitting on the bed we designated as Tats's, while Tats is in an armchair taking off her nail polish, her used cotton balls gathered in a pile on the adjacent side table. Dania's on the bed that I'm going to be sharing with Mom, while Mom sits across from her on the wheely chair from the desk.

Dania's got a facial mask on and is spreading one on Mom's face too.

They're all in their pajamas. And there's music coming from Tats's phone. "Ocean Eyes."

It's her old, chill-out-before-bed playlist.

She abruptly stops the song when she sees me.

Lamya and Dania look over at me when the music ends, and

that's when it hits me: Tats thinks I'm going to cry if I hear Billie Eilish. That I'm going to cry about Nuah—because we always called it the ultimate breakup song.

I back into the bathroom again and close the door.

Because I think Tats is right.

I take a pic of my hennaed hands, the intricate design on them an eruption of blooms, like a floral Persian rug, and share it on my Instagram story.

Then I erase our messages. Nuah's and mine.

All of them.

When that's done, before the emptiness enters me, the emptiness of nothing, no words, no jokes, no pics, no memes, no GIFs, nothing exchanged with Nuah, before "Ocean Eyes" enters my head on a loop, and before it feels like the song's filling the bathroom, reminding me there's nothing between me and Nuah, I click on the link that Layth sent me and watch a baby sloth being fed milk with a syringelike bottle.

I want a sloth. I want to bottle-feed it and have it loop its arms around my neck, and I want it to look up at my eyes once in a while for reassurance. I'd be the best at giving my sloth reassurance, because I'm pretty dependable.

Whoever I pledge my love or even my like to, I'll be around for.

I pause the sloth video and look up into the mirror as it hits me that Dad wanted me to not fall for Nuah, and I stood up to him, but then—

But then Nuah didn't want me to fall for him either.

It's like a double burn.

It's so quiet that I can hear the voices in the room outside. There are more of them out there now.

I unravel the towel and shake my hair out and then bundle it all back into the towel. I'm killing time, like if I wait here long enough, I'm going to come out to an empty room.

Someone knocks. "Janna, just wanted to tell you that Khadija and Zayneb stopped by too. They just got back to the hotel."

Mom. Giving me this info, which is really code for *Come out and be a polite host, girl.*

Sigh. I should have known if I came back to stay with Mom *with Tats*, there'd be a party in the room.

Tats was the one who'd shouted "Come hang in our room!" to Dania and Lamya as we were all getting out of the car. I thought for sure they wouldn't take her up on the offer.

I open the door again, and yeah, it's a party.

Zayneb's orange suitcase is open, and her Canadian treats are being passed around. I smell something really vinegary and suspect it's coming from the big red bag of chips with an outline of a ketchup bottle on the front that's in Mom's hands right now.

I wave at everyone and sit on the long stool at the end of Tats's bed and watch a bit of Lindsay Lohan in *Freaky Friday*, which of course Tats managed to find on the hotel TV.

I need to change into pajamas.

And maybe go out for some fresh air.

After a third visit to the bathroom to change, I'm now at the hotel room door in a super-faded Winnie-the-Pooh pajama shirt atop a pair of black silk pants with pink grinning skulls all over them, my worst set of pajamas (really thought I was going to be alone with Mom and Tats), with my fave black scarf thrown around my head, waving my wallet with a big smile. "Going to get *American* treats from the vending machine. Anyone want anything?"

Khadija rises slowly from the armchair Tats gave up for her, rubbing her stomach enclosed in a long white nightgown with a frilly neck. She adjusts her hijab so it sits more snugly. "I need a walk. I'll come."

I hope my falling face is not too visible.

Noooooo.

Chapter Twenty-Five

✳   ✳   ✳

We walk down the carpeted hallway toward the elevators in silence.

"The vending machine is on the second floor," I say preemptively, to ensure the conversation stays on the topics I want it to. "I couldn't *stand* the smell of those ketchup chips. What's that all about, anyway?"

"Did you try them?" Khadija asks.

"No. I don't think I can get close enough to them to even try one chip." I make a gagging motion.

"They're good. And, really, nothing like ketchup. More of a sweet-and-salty thing. With crazy red coloring that comes off on your fingers."

"No thanks." I push the elevator button. "I'll take my sour cream and onion chips any day."

Silence.

"So what are you in the mood for? I'm thinking chips and maybe M&Ms." I tilt my head, thinking carefully. "Maybe even peanut butter M&Ms if they have those."

Khadija stops rubbing her stomach. "You know what, I'm not thinking that hard about it."

I laugh. "Just snacks."

"Just go with the flow."

"Right. The vending machine flow."

"Or, actually, let's be adventurous," she says with a slight increase in enthusiasm as the elevator doors open. "Let's go to the store down in the lobby. *Lots* of choices there."

"Is it open?" I like this idea. An entire store to roam—separate from each other.

"It said twenty-four hours." She smiles big. "Now I might really go all out and get some MILK."

"Nice." I give her a thumbs-up and watch the floors light all the way down to L. Before silence makes itself known again, I say, "Your baby will like that. And maybe some chocolate chip cookies, too." I add another laugh, but it comes out fake.

"No sugar for Maysarah. She had those gummy bears you gave Nuah. Well, *I* had the gummy bears you gave him, and I couldn't sleep last night." She shakes her head. "This girl can't have any sugar."

As soon as the doors open, I walk fast out of the elevator to leave the mention of Nuah far behind.

She catches up super quick for someone nine months pregnant. "You know that girl I told you about? That Nuah likes? She's vegan AND sugar-free. When I first heard that, I was like, how can anyone live that deprived? But then I saw her. Sumayyah."

My face is melting. I can feel it.

I try to walk faster. But now she puts a hand out to stop me. And holds a phone up with her other hand.

It's a picture of a stunningly beautiful girl. Her dark brown skin is unmade up but glowing. She has a small but confident smile, as confident as the bright yellow head wrap atop her forehead. Her glasses match the wrap and her quiet but proud gaze, her I'm-here-don't-look-away hijab—altogether, it's unbelievably chic.

And she's smart. She has to be, going to Caltech.

And into saving the earth, and vegan. And sugar-free.

Of course Nuah would choose her over me.

Of course *she* was the one that was hard to get—*not me*.

I tear up.

"When I saw her natural-glow skin, I told Nuah I'm signing up for sugar-free-vegan lessons too." Khadija laughs and puts down her phone and then stops laughing when she sees my face. "Oh, I'm sorry. Did I say something wrong?"

"No." I look away and move toward the store.

"What did I say?" She follows me, and her voice sounds so shocked and sad. "Janna, stop. What happened?"

What if she gets so upset that I'm running away from her that she goes into labor? What if her water thing breaks right here on these lobby tiles that are some sort of weird mossy brown to mimic a forest floor? Then what if I have to be the one to deliver Maysarah? In this, the ugliest hotel in the world?

I stop. Right by the tree of fluffy red balls.

Scanning my brain for possible, plausible reasons for my grief, I seize the first one that'll pull her heartstrings. "My mom may be falling for Dania and Lamya's dad, who she knew from college. And I don't know if I like it," I say, letting the tears fall now.

"Oh my gosh. Oh, I'm so sorry." Khadija rubs my back. I turn to the tree. I can't hide my face in its rough bark. But I need to because my nose is running majorly, so I lean hard into it.

When I look back, Khadija's checking her granny nightgown pockets—huge pockets that she turns inside out. "Come on, where are tissues when you need them?"

A fluff ball falls from the tree right onto my head. Khadija stares at me then at the tree above. "What in the world?"

She takes it off my head and hands it to me. It's a mass of cotton balls glued together or something. "This works, I guess? Better than your pajamas?"

"Um, ugh, I don't think—" I protest. Far behind Khadija, the elevators open, and Layth steps out, his jean jacket and backpack on.

I use the fluff ball to wipe my nose.

He notices me and walks over. I turn the fluff ball over and wipe my eyes with the unsnotty side.

Oh my God, I don't even know how old this fluffy thing is. Or how dusty.

"Hey, salaam," he says, coming closer. And then he slows his steps and stops completely when he's a few feet away, as he notices my tears. "Sorry, don't want to interrupt anything. Just about to leave."

I lower the fluff, sucking in a huge breath to drown a sob. I clear my throat and speak as calmly as I can, while sniffling. "No, it's okay. You know Khadija, right? She came with us to the pizza place?" I can't bring myself to say she's Nuah's sister.

"Assalamu alaikum. I'm Nuah's sister. And yeah, we hung out today—of course we know each other." Khadija smiles at Layth.

"Yeah, for sure." Layth looks uncomfortable.

Oh yeah. I have a good idea why he's got a strange expression on his face. He heard me talk about the entire Nuah thing falling apart, and now I'm crying under a fluff ball tree to Nuah's sister.

Why is my life like this?

Tears gather again. "I need another fluff ball," I sputter—to who, I don't know. To the tree, maybe?

Layth takes his backpack off and unzips a side. He holds out a . . . yellow handkerchief.

A handkerchief?

Um, does he live in this century?

"Completely clean. Never used. It's my old Cub Scout necker-chief," he assures me. "I couldn't leave it behind."

I wipe my eyes with it but not my nose. It feels like a strange thing to do so I reuse the fluff ball for my nose instead. I don't want to imagine how I look—with a yellow cloth on my eyes and a clownish red puff at my nose, wearing Winnie-the-Pooh-meets-skulls pajamas. "Thanks. I'll wash it and give it back." I sniffle again.

"It's okay. Keep it. I'm leaving tonight anyway."

"*Leaving* leaving?"

"Yeah, driving to Miami." He shrugs.

The elevator doors open again and reveal Uncle Bilal in a navy bathrobe with green plaid pajamas underneath. He looks surprised to see us all under the tree.

"Layth," he calls out after stepping into the lobby but not mov-ing from outside the elevator doors. "Can I talk to you, please?"

Layth doesn't turn around. "We're done talking." His voice is steely.

"Not if you're leaving. We're not done." Uncle Bilal still stands where he is, but his voice carries.

I check the front desk to see if anyone heard. No one's there. Well, it *is* almost two in the morning now.

Khadija nudges me. "Snacks? Let's go?"

"Yeah." I smooth out the handkerchief. Do I give it back to Layth? It's tear filled but not snot filled, so . . .

Embroidered in one corner of the yellow triangle cloth is LAYTH. In the other corner is MUHSIN.

"We're going to go to the store and get snacks," Khadija says to Layth brightly. "I think Janna's okay. Thanks for the handkerchief."

"Yeah, thanks." I fold it up and hold it out. "Just a bit wet."

"Keep it," Layth says, holding my gaze with his dark eyes, surprising kindness in them. "What if you find yourself without a tissue again? And only have weird fake apples from a weird fake tree to wipe your tears with?"

I laugh. "Okay, then, I'll wash it and mail it to you. To the sanctuary."

Uncle Bilal comes closer, a polite smile taking over his face when he sees me notice him moving. "Assalamu alaikum, Janna."

Layth hitches his backpack up higher on his shoulder and salutes me and Khadija. "Okay, I'm gone."

"Layth, please." Uncle Bilal's pleading voice is calm and steady but loud and firm, too.

Layth ignores it and begins walking.

Khadija looks at me and nudges my arm gently. "Let's get going," she whispers.

But the lobby is so quiet that the whisper draws Uncle Bilal's gaze to us again. "I'm sorry. We're just sorting out a difference in opinions."

Layth turns around. "Why don't you just tell them the truth? You want me to be a bot working for someone else, draining my life away, instead of what I want to do."

Uncle Bilal shakes his head. "No, I want you to use your skills, your talents, to realize your potential."

"By making money for a corporation," Layth says flippantly.

"I never said that. I said take your time to learn what kind of career makes sense. I gave you a few suggestions."

"None of them involved what I want to do," Layth says. "And you promised you wouldn't bring this up. I didn't want to stay here before, and now I'm leaving."

Uncle Bilal's shoulders slump. "Okay, I'm sorry. I shouldn't have brought it up. I thought because it was a green, environmentally responsible company you might be interested. I was wrong. Please, Layth. Just stay for your cousins. They're the ones who asked you."

I'm surprised to hear him apologize. I don't think I've *ever* heard Dad apologize. Or say he was wrong about something.

"I knew I shouldn't have come to begin with," Layth says, low, before turning and walking to the automated doors.

Uncle Bilal looks after Layth, his eyes clearly glistening with tears now. He whispers "sorry" to me and Khadija and walks to the elevators, his feet moving at a much slower pace than before.

"Yikes." Khadija nudges me again and yanks her head in the direction of the store. "Let's go get that milk and peanut butter M&Ms."

I nod, but I've turned to look at Layth's back disappearing into the dark of the parking lot in front of the hotel. "I think Dania and Lamya are going to be really sad to see that he's gone."

"I don't think we should interfere in this," Khadija says.

"Let me just go give this back to him." I hold up the folded scout handkerchief and scrunch the fluff ball to get it ready to throw in the trash can next to the doors. "I don't think I'll have the money to mail it to Ecuador."

"Ecuador?" Khadija follows me.

"That's where he's going." I stop and turn at the doors. "It's okay, you don't have to come, Khadija. I'll only be a minute."

"That isn't going to happen. You're looking at a mosque study circle leader for four years straight. You think I'm going to let you go out there at two a.m. to talk to a boy alone?" Khadija frowns and stares at me. "No way. I'm coming along."

"Oh my God, Khadija! It's nothing like that! No way! Him?" I shake my head and roll my eyes. If she only knew my taste in guys, if she only knew *the one* I really wanted to talk to, to imagine being with, she'd never think this was a big deal.

Layth?

Right.

"He looks like Zayn Malik. I'm coming. Make it fast. It's a bit chilly." She crosses her arms and rubs her hands on them as we step out into the night.

At the far end of the lot, Layth's opening his car door. As he's about to get in, I call out, "Layth, wait!"

He stops and closes the door and leans on the car, his arms folded on top of the roof. I move faster so I can say more before Khadija catches up.

"I wanted to give you your handkerchief back and wanted to tell you that you don't have to stay here at the hotel with your uncle. You can stay at my Dad's. I just have to text Muhammad—I'm sure he's still up. There's a lot of room there. And it'll make Dania and Lamya so happy to see you at the wedding tomorrow."

He doesn't say anything, just looks at me. And then he starts smirking.

And shaking his head. Hard. While laughing.

By the time he finishes all this, Khadija's caught up.

"But why would *you* want me to stay?" He laughs again.

"I didn't say I wanted you to stay." I fidget, aware that Khadija's hearing all this now.

"You used Dania and Lamya's names, but I don't see them here. I don't see *them* stopping me from getting in the car."

"It was just an idea, but if you don't want to do it, that's okay." I hold out the handkerchief. "Here. I think maybe this is special to you?"

He stops laughing.

Stares at me.

And then puts his head down on the top of the car, and from the way his shoulders move, it's obvious he's crying.

Chapter Twenty-Six

❄ ❄ ❄

Khadija and I look at each other. Do we leave quietly? Give him space?

Do we pretend he's not crying right now?

He settles the question by raising his head, wiping his eyes with the back of a hand, and opening his car door.

"Maysarah needs Dunkin' Donuts!" Khadija yells suddenly. "And there's one a few blocks away. Open twenty-four hours. I saw it!"

Layth pauses bending to get in the car, straightens, and stares at Khadija.

"My baby . . . Maysarah. Janna asked what she needed for a snack," Khadija says, pointing at her stomach. "We don't have a car."

He looks at me. I shrug because I have no idea what's going on.

Oh wait, I know. "It's late-night cravings. Pregnant people get them."

"Are you asking me for a ride?" His body's unmoving, but he's still looking from Khadija to me and back again.

"Yeah, I think so." I shrug again. "If you don't mind helping a nine-months-pregnant woman?"

He shakes his head and says, "Get in."

When Khadija convinces Layth to come inside the Dunkin' Donuts because she needs "help carrying stuff back to the car," I start to suspect something.

When she then insists that she needs to have something to drink right then and there and asks Layth to get us a table, I know for sure something's up.

"What are we doing?" I whisper to her in line. The town of Mystic Lake is pretty hopping on a late-night Friday. There are two people ahead of us waiting to order.

It's too bad we're the only ones who look like we rolled out of bed, me in my pajama mishmash and Khadija in her ye olde Victorian nightgown.

"I felt strange letting him drive off like that. I wouldn't want that for my brother, you know?" Khadija scans the menu and sighs. "But I so don't want doughnuts."

"They have muffins and croissants."

"Okay, I'll do a milk and croissant. Ask him what he wants," Khadija says. "Layth. And come back only when you've got something to tell me. Tell him I can't eat unless everyone around me is."

I leave the line and go to the corner table. Layth's chair is positioned so he's leaning against the corner behind him. "Khadija wants to know what you want."

"Nothing."

"She has this thing where she can't eat unless we're all eating." I shake my head. "I don't get it. But I'm not pregnant, either."

He doesn't say anything. Just blinks blankly at me.

I don't like that look of his. It always makes me feel like I need to keep talking, to prove myself or something. "I'm getting a decaf latte. But you might want something caffeinated? Because you're driving all night?"

"I don't drink coffee." He looks away and considers the wall. "Okay, get me a hot chocolate. Small."

I feel weirdly buoyant. To report back to Khadija, who's at the counter now, that I got him to want something.

After giving the cashier our orders, I glance back at Layth.

His head's bent again.

We sit with our drinks. I texted Mom already that we'd be back later due to being at Dunkin', and once word got out to the party that's apparently still in our room, requests came in, so now there's a box of doughnuts on the table in front of us waiting to be taken back to the hotel.

"You okay?" Khadija asks Layth.

Before he subjects her to his signature blank look, I say, "It's okay, you don't have to tell us anything. We just want to know if you're going to be okay to drive."

"I'm fine."

"Good," Khadija says. "So, Ecuador?"

He nods and takes a sip of hot chocolate.

Since he doesn't go on, I feel pressed to explain. "He's going to work in an animal-rescue sanctuary at the edge of the Amazon. He's going to train volunteers."

Khadija nods. "That's amazing."

"Kinkajous, sloths—oh my gosh, you should see the baby sloth there right now. So cute." I wonder if I should show the video to Khadija. To make up for Layth's silence.

Layth sits back and brushes his hair off his eyes. Eyes that are looking at me with slight amusement. "Didn't know you were into animals."

When he turns those eyes warm, he looks so different.

Like I could actually spend time talking with him.

"I love them. My mom's allergic to too many of them, though, so I just never had any of my own." I settle back into my seat too. "I'd like a sloth, actually."

"Yikes. That's one of the reasons that we have rescue missions. The exotic pet trade is the largest illicit market in the world, after drugs and weapons." Layth takes another sip. "That baby sloth you saw was a victim of attempted trafficking."

"I didn't really mean—" I stop and lift my latte to my lips instead of protesting. Because I actually did imagine having a sloth to come home to.

"So how long are you going to Ecuador for?" Khadija asks, breaking a piece of her croissant and holding it in her hand. She doesn't look very enthused about eating it.

"For good."

"Your family's okay with that?"

I'm glad Khadija's asking this, because I've been wondering this same thing, but after seeing that showdown with Uncle Bilal, I wouldn't dare be so brave.

"My mom moved to England. She's cool with it." Layth shoots her that look.

It's a don't-ask-anything-else look.

My eyes are closed. Therefore my soul's closed too.

"And your dad?"

Oh my God, Khadija asked another question.

"He's awaiting trial for drunken driving. For killing my little brother two years ago. So I don't give a shit what he thinks."

I don't move a muscle.

Beside me, Khadija doesn't either.

"I'm so sorry, Layth." Khadija sets the croissant piece down into the bag it came from. "That's terrible."

"I know," he says. "But it'll be okay when I get to Ecuador. I mean, I'll be okay."

I nod. "I'm sorry too," I offer in a small voice. My heart feels like it's been slammed against a wall.

"You know what the funny thing is? My dad was a cook in a halal restaurant. That's what he did," Layth says. "And when the news came out about the crash, some people were more upset that they'd been going to a drunken guy's restaurant than they were about my brother."

Khadija shakes her head. "That's terrible."

"One of the many reasons I need to get away from here." He leans back again and tilts his head so that the top of it is touching the wall behind him. "But Muhsin's buried in Detroit. So I gotta come back and see him."

The embroidered name on the scout neckerchief comes to me. *Muhsin.*

I check Layth's face, still tilted up, and see that his expression's stoic. "How old was he?"

"Eight."

Khadija sighs sadly. "Allah yarhamu. Same age as Dawud."

Now I know why Layth cried about the handkerchief. He thought I was saying it's special because it was Muhsin's.

But I'd just been thinking everything he's going to live on is in a single backpack, so whatever's in there must be either a necessity or special.

"Making dua can help ease your pain," Khadija offers gently. "It's helped so many people in their darkest hours. And God does not give us a burden we cannot bear."

Khadija's offering the teaching most Muslims learn from when we're very young. Which Layth probably already knows.

"I don't know what I believe in anymore, to be honest." Layth straightens his head and looks at us. "He was a little kid. And it shattered my mom. I don't think she knew how to live on. Anyway, I don't want to talk about it anymore. I'm usually not like this. I think it's just being around family again."

I nod, having no words to say for such unimaginable pain. In the time of my biggest pain, Dr. Lloyd helped me through it. "Have you thought of, um, counseling?"

"Been through it. That's why I'm going to Ecuador. It came as a result of counseling. It's my life-purpose action plan." He sits up, like what he said just now is giving him fuel. "It's late. Shouldn't you guys get back?"

"Yeah." I nod, relieved he looks more uplifted. "I'm helping organize the kids tomorrow for their parts, and we didn't get to practice today."

Khadija turns to me. "Oh, I forgot to tell you, Sarah asked if you could help Dawud with his flower ceiling in the morning as well. He needs help putting it together."

I'm about to groan, but then I nip *that* in the bud quickly—groaning about helping a kid the same age as Layth's brother who passed away. "Okay."

I drink the last of my latte, and, when I lower the cup, I notice Layth has stood up and has already started moving to the door, his head bent over his phone. His movements are more confident and determined, the opposite of how he'd come into the doughnut shop.

Khadija gets up, and I stop her from getting the doughnut box and picking up the garbage and just being a mom, so she follows Layth out.

As I gather all the stuff on the table, my phone beeps with a message from him.

Too late to text Muhammad? About crashing at the barn?

No, I'll do it right now.

I dump all the garbage and dial my brother.

It's a beyond-texting emergency.

And then, for good measure, I text Haytham. Layth's going to stay at the barn. He needs space but also a friend. Just don't ask me why.

Ok on all three. Watching a movie so he can join us if he wants.

I'm glad Haytham's awake, so I didn't have to try Nuah, also at the barn.

Layth drops us off, and before he drives away, but after Khadija's begun walking to the hotel doors, I knock on the passenger's window. When he lowers it, I say the words I couldn't find before, when he told us about his brother. "You know how you loved your brother? I don't think you need to bear not loving him now. You can still love him, you know?"

He doesn't say anything, but he doesn't give me that closed-soul look either, so I go on.

"So far I've never lost anyone except an old, really old friend. He was ninety-three. I told you a bit about him before. He's the one who got me to read critically. Anyway, I still think about him and write about him too. And read the books he gave me before he died. It's a way to still love him." I pause and look behind me, and yup, sure enough, Khadija's waiting for me inside the hotel double doors. Man, she's one powerful mosque study circle leader. I turn back to Layth. "I don't know if I make sense."

"Yeah. You're just saying I don't need to forget him."

"And maybe I'm saying you don't need to push the memories away whenever they hit you? That you can be active about remembering him?" I set the box of doughnuts in my hands on the hood of the car, take the yellow handkerchief from on top of it and fold it neatly once more. "Sorry if I don't know what I'm talking about. I've never felt pain like yours. But you should have this. Thank you for letting me using it in my moment of need." I laugh slightly, but my eyes are filling up. And when I hold out the handkerchief, Layth sees them.

He reaches for the cloth and nods, and I back away with the box of doughnuts, but I don't turn to go inside until I see which way he exits the parking lot.

I want to make sure he doesn't turn right to head to the highway.

I want to make sure he turns left to the road leading to Dad's house.

I guess I want to make sure I get to see him one more day.

Chapter Twenty-Seven

❋　❋　❋

Back in our room, I notice that even though the rest of the girls are still here, Tats has already fallen asleep—on top of the bedspread, her hands still painted with dried henna paste. Lamya told her the longer you leave it on, the darker the color.

I wonder what it's going to look like in the morning, the swirly designs on her pale palms.

After everyone else leaves, about ten minutes after the dough-nuts get shared and a subsequent yawn-fest set off by the first con-tagious yawn from Khadija, I brush my teeth, pray Isha, and climb into bed with Mom.

I let her stroke the hair off my forehead for a bit before I turn around, deciding not to tell her any Nuah news today. She seems glowy and happy, and I don't want to make her worried about me.

I'm thinking of a list of new happy things (Tats is here, sloths, dancing with Zayneb) to settle my mind down, to get it to not veer into unhappy territory like Layth's little brother or Nuah, when Mom starts rubbing my back. "Sweetums, Tats set her alarm for six so you can go swimming after Fajr. But now that it's so late, are you sure you want to go to the pool?"

"I don't know if I can," I mumble into the pillow. "I'm tired."

"Okay, well, make sure you wake up in time to join us for breakfast in the restaurant before we head to Dad's at eight. I already packed all our wedding clothes to take with us. Tats's clothes as well. Linda insisted we get ready there."

"Who's us?"

"Us?"

"Us for breakfast?"

"Dania and Lamya, Uncle Bilal and Layth."

"Layth left," I say, wondering if I should bring up the fight between Uncle Bilal and Layth. In case she erroneously thinks they're such a happy family.

"Oh, I'm sorry to hear that."

From a split in the window drapes that allows parking lot lights to cast into our room, I see Tats's form on the bed. Gentle snores accompany the lift and fall of her chest. Maybe watching the rhythm of her sleep will also help me fall asleep.

Mom stops stroking me and lets out a big sigh. "Uncle Bilal was so happy Layth was staying for the wedding, he even went and bought him a jacket today. He was trying his best to help Layth."

"Do you like Uncle Bilal?" I whisper into the pillow.

"What was that?"

"Uncle Bilal?" I ask a bit louder.

"What about him?"

"Do you like him?"

She doesn't answer.

I look at the digital alarm clock and record the time in my head: Saturday, July 17, 3:18 a.m.

The night before my brother's wedding. Well, officially the day of his wedding.

And my mom's gone quiet when I asked her if she likes someone.

"I was honest with you," I remind her, still talking mostly into the pillow. "I told you who I liked."

"But my answer affects your life in a bigger way, Janna." Her voice is so quiet, even though she's not speaking into the pillow but to the back of my head.

"I think I know the answer, then." I can't stop my body from deflating—which is strange, because I'm lying in bed.

It deflates, even though it's actually filling up with all the unknowns ahead.

It feels like the security and safety I began to let myself feel after Mom and Dad's divorce, the sense of home being Mom and me, is beginning to escape through a tiny puncture.

Mom puts a hand on my back once more and starts to massage it again, but I do the one thing I don't want to do, that my mind *and* heart don't want me to do, but that my body on its own, completely by free will, by instinct, does: I shake her touch off.

Hard.

She removes her hand, and there's a frozen stillness behind me that I can feel.

I watch Tats's breathing and mimic it and pretend to have fallen asleep, but my eyes are wide open, my brain imagining Dania and Lamya and Uncle Bilal in our lives always and forever, intruding on the way things are with Mom and me and Muhammad, and even Sarah now.

That's my family.

It's 3:32 a.m. when I hear a noise.

It's a pulled breath. And then a swallow. And then Mom gets off the bed and goes to the bathroom quietly.

When the door closes, I turn around for a moment to rest on my other side.

The lights from the window show her pillow squashed, a strange blotchy shadow on it.

I sit up and touch the dark spot.

It's wet.

I flip back around quickly and close my eyes and close myself so I don't think about what it feels like to cry so much so quietly.

After Mom's fallen asleep—and I'm certain by the way her breath becomes even—I flip to her and stare at her face.

I love her.

And I want her all to myself. Is that too much to ask?

I put my hand out and lay it softly on her shoulder.

She doesn't know how much I love her, I guess.

She opens her eyes right then somehow—like we're cosmically connected or something—and I draw my hand away. But before I turn around, I say, "I love you." Really quietly.

I think she heard, because she places a hand on my back, and I can feel that it's filled with love.

I wake up for Fajr before Tats's alarm goes off, pray, and then text her. DON'T WAKE ME UP TO SWIM.

Mom's reading Qur'an from her phone in the armchair, the light shining on her head, which is covered in her long prayer dress that's one big circular cloth starting from her head—with a hole for her face—and reaching the floor.

I get into bed and pull the covers up over my hair but allow the folds to fall and make a small, open space through which I can watch Mom.

When she wears her prayer dress, she looks like those stacked wooden Russian dolls that you take apart, each doll becoming smaller. Every single morning, her doll self reads Qur'an and does her duas after Fajr.

It's so dependable. I don't want that to change.

I don't want *her* to change.

And, at the same time, I also don't want her to cry. To be lonely. To not have someone who loves her like *that*.

But how can she love people I don't know? That I don't know if I even like?

How can she fall so fast for a stranger? Strangers, plural?

And I don't even know how to talk to her about it.

As I'm about to close up the hole in my blanket, what Mom said about prejudiced people comes to me: *When you see the world as divided . . . it's not about expanding hearts—it's about shrinking our capacity to love.*

I'm not being prejudiced. It's not about skin color or culture for me, this feeling I have about Mom and Uncle Bilal.

It's about preserving what I already have.

Which is what Mom said, a voice whispers after I close myself into the blanket. *That people who are exclusionary want to preserve what they have. That they think others will take it all away from them.*

I take off the blanket and whisper, "Mom?"

She pauses in her reading and looks up at me, with questioning eyes.

"Are you coming back to bed?"

She nods and finishes her reading while I wait.

Then she climbs into bed behind me and wraps an arm around me and laughs. "Aha. So you missed my morning breath, huh?"

Turned away from her, I make a face and then smile.

Maybe I can talk about it with her in the morning.

About her and Uncle Bilal.

Part Three

SATURDAY, JULY 17
WEDDING DAY

To do:

☐ Avoid love at all costs

Chapter Twenty-Eight

✳ ✳ ✳

When I wake up again, it's to Tats sitting up on her bed in a black-and-turquoise burkini, the swim-cap-scarf part off, her long hair rippling around her face, watching TV.

"Finally. Can you get ready fast?" she asks.

"Didn't you get my text?" I throw off the blanket and look at the time. Just after seven a.m. "I can't go swimming."

"Jan, come on. I've been waiting."

"Is it because you want to wear your new burkini?" I roll my eyes. I've been best friends with Tats for years, but sometimes I feel on the cusp of wondering if I fully *get* her. Like I'm thinking right now that wearing a burkini is an "adventure" for her. "Where'd you get it from anyway?"

"Online. It's the same one Lindsay Lohan wore but in blue instead of red like hers." She flips channels. "I wanted to go swimming, but I didn't want to stand out in my swimsuit because you'd be wearing a burkini. That's why I got it."

I walk to the bathroom. "I can't come. My period's gonna come any minute, and so I refuse to go into a pool."

Tats groans. "Oh come on. You don't even have it yet."

I close the door. When I come out, she's still in her burkini, so I decide to bargain. "Ditch the swimming idea and I won't ask about the Jeremy situation. This weekend. I'll eventually ask, but I'll spare you this weekend."

Tats turns off the TV and leans back into the headboard behind her. "What do you mean?"

"I won't ask about how you kept the entire thing from me. Like it was no big deal that you'd started going out with him— without telling me a single thing—when I thought we tell each other *everything*."

"How could it be a big deal?" She tilts her head against the headboard, frowns, and, after straightening her head again, opens her mouth. "I was keeping it a surprise because I thought you'd be happy. He's friends with *you*. And I'd just blocked him EVERY-WHERE. Because he was *actual* buds with that creep who hurt you. But then you were right: He's completely different. I found out how different when I got lonely with you gone for so long. And when he commented on that pic of yours of your dad's lake, I unblocked him for some reason. And saw all the stuff he was into. Next thing I know, I'm talking to him online. And then he picked me up so I could watch him play baseball and we ate tacos after and I kept telling him how much I missed you and so he kept picking me up and . . . Yeah, and."

That was a long spiel. Sort of like there's a teeny bit of guilt underlying it all.

Whatever. I like Jeremy. He's kind. He's good. He's going to treat Tats really nicely.

Who cares that forever ago I fell for him for three seasons of a school year.

"Okay, it's okay. I'm not mad. It was just weird you didn't tell me." I sit on the edge of my bed and then let myself drop down so I'm lying on my back with my feet on the floor. "Can you play 'Ocean Eyes'? Please."

"No. Not a good song for you now."

"Please."

"Janna."

"It's not like that."

She comes over and lies down beside me. "Are you really happy about me and Jeremy?"

"Yeah. How long have you guys been together?"

"From like three days after you left."

"Whoa, that was fast."

"We make sense. 'Cause he's chill and quiet. And I'm not."

"But isn't he leaving for college now? After this year off?"

"No, he decided to work with his dad again for another year. So we'll still see each other." She smiles big.

Tats's going in state for junior college—literally just an hour from Eastspring—so she'll continue living at home.

I'm so happy she's headed toward having a good summer.

The blue skies will be in *her* heart.

"I'm excited for you, okay?" I sit up and twist myself to prop my face on a hand, my elbow poking into the bed. "Really. I want you to have the best, blue-skies summer."

Tats smiles and nods and holds up her hand for a five. I meet my hennaed hand to her hennaed one—the design startlingly dark on her pale palm—and smile big.

Then I sink back into the bed, back to staring at the ceiling.

"Your mom left for breakfast. She told me to tell you we need to meet at the restaurant to eat with everyone," Tats reminds me. "If you don't want to swim, let's at least go down to eat. I'm hungry."

"I saw the girl Nuah likes. She's beautiful and so much better than me in all ways." I say this plainly, with no sadness. At least on the outside.

"Whatever. Janna, you are so not going down that path," Tats says. "Let's go get breakfast."

"'Ocean Eyes.' Please. It's going to help me get ready for today. If I can feel sad here, get it all out, then I'm not going get sad when he's around today."

She sighs and plays the song and changes out of her burkini right there into a strapless short white cotton summer dress that she pairs with a big, bulky, super-faded jean jacket. "It's Jeremy's," she whispers with a sly smile. "I stole it from his car."

I nod, completely lost in the song. No tears fall, but I let myself feel the rejection. I close my eyes and wallow in it.

Then I imagine my recovery—which starts today.

At the wedding. A happy occasion that I'll rise to the challenge of.

When I see Nuah today, I'm going to give him a smile with blank eyes. A blisteringly polite but cool gaze like the ones Layth delivers so well.

Like the someone you're looking at is there but not in a fully charged way. It's like they're fading into the surroundings, and you're acknowledging their aura—present but not robust. Flimsy.

After I let the song loop five times, Tats takes her phone back, and I go to the bathroom to change.

For last-minute wedding prep, I'm wearing big black sweatpants and a big black sweatshirt and a big black scarf. I'm aiming to fade into the surroundings too.

‚ùÄ ‚ùÄ ‚ùÄ

When we get to Dad's, I head upstairs to my room to get the clipboard Sarah gave me. I'm going to be all work, all steely.

Wear a pretty dress, wear a glazed gaze, lock up my heart, and get this wedding done is going to be my mantra.

Just as I get to the second-floor landing, Dad comes out of his room holding several suit jackets on hangers.

Great, perfect timing.

Just get the clipboard from the room. Just check off those to-do boxes one by one.

"So, you can't stay home with me anymore? I'm too old-school for you?"

Old school? Is that what they call racism nowadays?

I'm so glad I've got headphones on. I orient myself toward my room and make my way to it like I don't see Dad.

"You're not going to answer me?" Oh my God, he's still standing there like he expects me to respond. "All because of some boy? Now I'm absolutely nothing to you?"

I open my door and go inside and close it and lean against it.

He's so angry I snuck out to stay with Mom.

I hate this wedding.

Can you please keep Dad away from me

I look out the window while I wait for Muhammad to answer.

There are hired people setting up chairs and running wires and, far off, raking the grass near the lake where the rectangular tables for dinner will be set.

Muhammad must be super busy. He's supposed to be coordinating stuff and arranging rides for friends from airports and doing the million other things grooms have to do.

Tats is downstairs waiting for me. I'll ask her to come up. To walk me down.

Dad will never say anything if she's with me.

Hey come up for a sec

I look out the window again.

Mom's out there now on the grass. With Tats. They're talking to Linda, who's by the chairs being set up in rows, with an aisle in the middle, in front of the gazebo.

Now it's being widened. The space between the two sets of chairs.

Just as I'm thinking that my job is going to be to watch all the action and not participate, right under my window, Dad walks out onto the patio.

YES.

He still has the suits in his hands. He's heading to the barn.

I grab my clipboard and run out of my room, down the stairs, and out the front door to the other side of the house, away from the driveway and the barn and the gazebo, to the space where, when we first drove in, I saw the florist organizing herself.

With Hope Ravson amid her bundles of blue and yellow flowers, I'm pretty sure I'll be safe from Dad.

Chapter Twenty-Nine

✤ ✤ ✤

After a "hi," Hope leaves me alone to contemplate my checklist.

Besides my four main tasks for tonight—welcoming guests, organizing the passing-out of favors, delivering the roast with (cringe) Nuah, training the laddoos and Dawud for their tasks—I have to make sure my uncle, Amu, is all set up for delivering the nikah sermon.

I shoot him a quick e-mail on my phone asking if he needs anything.

On autopilot, I click his website where people ask questions about Islamic topics. Every Thursday, I edit a few for him, and I like to check over how those questions look on the site. It appears this week's questions haven't been uploaded yet, but I do a quick scroll-through to see what's hot right now.

Answers that are read a lot get a flame icon that grows bigger with each hundred views.

The hottest one right now is *Wiping on Socks for Wudu Before Prayer*. Its flame is almost an inch high.

I keep scrolling through topics and watch the fires get smaller and smaller.

If God Doesn't Give You a Burden You Can't Bear, Then Why Do I Feel Like I Can't Bear It has a small flame.

I click it, remembering what Khadija said to Layth and how he responded that he doesn't know what he believes anymore.

Dear Imam, we're always told at the mosque that God doesn't give you a burden you can't bear. But I can't bear what's happening to me. I don't want to list all the hardships in my life right now as it will fill more than the space I'm given. My question: Why do so many bad things happen to some people more than others? Is it that I've been affected by the evil eye? And why does God say I can bear it?

Answer: Thank you for your most sincere question. I believe it shows a deep longing to understand your faith better, to understand the message of the Divine, to better your situation within the realm the One has created.

On the other hand, it may indicate that you're on the ebb part of conviction—as our faith ebbs and flows throughout our lives. It may indicate that you're grappling with how to make sense of where the difficulties of your life lie in the wisdom you've been taught about hardships in our lives. It may even communicate a moving toward a dissolution of your faith, which I pray isn't the case.

Throughout our lives, pain visits us in turns. There isn't a human alive who hasn't been touched by pain. We all carry scars and wounds, but only some rise to the surface to be seen and commented on.

Simply put, the story of pain is common to us all. And no, it's not the evil eye that causes some of us more hardships than others—for a foundation of our faith is that we are not to believe that anything has the power over God to harm us.

But you're absolutely right—the pain varies. And the intensity of pain varies.

While this is all true, also true is that the intensity levels we feel from our pain vary too.

This is where the teaching comes in that we are not given a burden we cannot bear. It's a reminder that we all have differing capabilities to rise, to be resilient, to refuse to let hardships define us.

There's a term in Japanese called gaman, *which loosely translates to "bearing what appears to be unbearable with the dignity of beautiful patience." Humanity in its diversity has had to make sense of painful realities, and there are beautiful teachings all around us on how to not only cope, but to thrive.*

Believing that whatever we've faced and survived we can turn into growth for ourselves and the world is a way forward. We may not believe this in our time of despair and darkness, but we remind ourselves of it in order to climb out, to climb that hidden step placed for us by the All Merciful, to reach a second phase of our life.

Our faith is one built on hope. All good is possible.

Remember: And it is within His power to bring about a second life *(53:47).*

It's so beautiful that I decide to send it to Layth. He needs to read it.

And now, to collect the flower boys.

Haytham. He would know their whereabouts.

I text to find out.

All 3 are here

Where

In the guesthouse

Is my dad there

Yeah

What's he doing

He's handing suits out for us to try on because not everyone came ready

Oh boy. He's helping Layth out.

Because, for sure, *he* never came ready—with his three CHEAP THRILLS T-shirts.

Of course Dad would be so distressed that someone would be wearing clothes like that to a wedding.

Can you please send the kids over to the other side of the house. I need to help them get prepared for their wedding tasks.

I wait, watching Hope organize flowers by their sizes into plastic jugs. She's got boxes full of tall mason jars that I'm assuming are the vases for our tables.

I click a few pics of the flower prep for Instagram, making sure to focus on the pops of blue here and there.

They're not coming. Dawud's working on his flowers here and Logan and Luke think they're helping him.

Okay, moving on to another clipboard task: set up the guest-book-signing table. Sarah showed me the guestbook and tablecloth and other things she'd gotten for the guests' welcome table—and they are all in the basement.

Which means I'd have to go back into the house.

My dad's still there right? In the barn?

No he just left. To go get ties.

I'm coming to talk to the kids.

I take my clipboard and run around the front of the house to the other side. I have to take this route so as to not cross paths with Dad.

I'm glad I'm in my track pants and Nikes.

Knocking on the door to the barn, I open it slightly and

announce, "I'm coming in. Hope everyone's hijabbed."

I open it fully to Haytham sprawled on the couch snickering at my comment.

Wow, the barn is a cool place.

I have no idea why I never ventured in here before—maybe it's because I truly thought it was a garage. Maybe because Linda told me Dad's speedboat was housed in it.

And it sort of *is* a garage. Because one end of the wide-open space, the end facing the barn doors that open to the lake, has the speedboat on a trailer.

But the rest is comfy and cozy.

The space in front of me has a long wraparound white leather couch from Dad's old house with a Persian rug in front of it and a TV set on a low table edging the carpet.

Beyond this setup are two sets of wooden stairs facing away from each other, leading to loft spaces. I can't see into the loft bedrooms as they're closed off by screens.

Behind the couch is an open area that's bordered by big wooden boxes, which, judging from the trail of toys around them, belong to the laddoos.

It's in this space that Dawud is working on his ceiling, a pair of scissors and a spool of green fuzzy wire beside him. Logan is holding flowers out for Dawud one by one, and Luke is running a truck repeatedly into a stack of blocks that he reconstructs after each destruction.

I go over to watch the flower assembly, and Haytham comes to stand beside me. "I found him old plastic netting that your dad didn't need anymore, so he's attaching them to that. I told him I'd help him put it up once he's finished." Haytham lowers his voice to add the next bit. "But I don't think he's got enough flowers."

I nod sadly.

Because the floral ceiling Dawud's making is super sad.

It's woefully empty.

And he's only got a few jugs of flowers left, mostly short, small bits with their petals missing, as well as lots of foliage, mainly ferns that are kind of brownish on the edges.

Even if he were to add these, he's got maybe a quarter of what could cover the center of the gazebo's ceiling.

Dawud stands up to survey his work, his hands unconsciously going to his hips.

Then he drops those hands and looks at Haytham. "It doesn't look real."

I'm about to lie and say it *does* look real when I spot paint cans on a steel shelf on the far wall behind the laddoos. They're regular house paints, but they give me an idea. "It'll look better than real if we add more flowers."

"But I don't have any more flowers except these small ones." Dawud's got a sullen, angry look on his face. At any other time, that bratty look would make me leave the entire thing alone. Walk away from his problem.

But the fact that Dawud is eight years old, like Layth's little brother, Muhsin, gnaws at me and makes me want to overlook his sulkiness and share my idea with him.

"You don't have enough flowers, so that's why we're going to get *more* flowers!" I say excitedly, squashing feelings of impatience rising inside as Dawud's frown deepens and he looks at me almost defiantly, like I don't know what I'm talking about.

He shakes his head. "No, we're not going to because there aren't any more. You don't know anything about flowers! And you said you weren't going to help me. You're mean. You said *I'm so not doing it*. I remember."

"Hey!" Haytham says sternly. "Apologize, dude. That's rude."

"But she said she wasn't going to help me!" Dawud narrows his eyes at me.

"She's not mean. She drove you into town, she took you places, and now she's offering to help."

The steady glare Haytham shoots at Dawud makes him drop the stink-eyes he's giving me. Now he resorts to jutting his chin out. "Where are we going to get flowers? Huh?"

"Don't answer that." Haytham puts a hand up to me before crossing his arms. He's wearing a T-shirt with cut-off sleeves, so his arm muscles make themselves known immediately upon crossing. "Little bro, you're not going to do anything more on this ceiling, and I'm not even going to help you put it up, unless that apology comes out of your mouth."

I want to say it's okay, but then Haytham's so serious, I feel like if I intrude, he'll tell *me* to apologize to him. Maybe it's part of his expertise as an uncle to so many kids.

Dawud slumps down and does this thing where his arms swing slightly, like jiggle, actually, in front of his body and then back behind him. It's like he's shaking the cooties out of himself or something. "Uh. 'Kay. I'm sorry for saying stuff about you."

"It's all right."

"But there aren't any more flowers," he clarifies, pushing his glasses up on his nose.

"Why don't you let me and Logan and Luke get you the flowers?" I say. I turn to Haytham. "Are you busy? If not, maybe you can you help us too?"

"Sure. My duties from Sarah start in a couple of hours, so for now, I'm all yours." He ends this with a sheepish smile. Maybe because he realizes how weird that sounds.

I hope Dawud doesn't catch that and hoot. And I hope I'm not turning red.

Because the truth: Haytham's super cute when he says that.

"Where is he? I brought a ton of ties for him to try on."

I turn around to Dad entering the barn, holding a tie hanger with several ties on it.

I turn back to Dawud quickly.

"He's upstairs," Haytham says. "Nuah! Ties are here!"

What? Nuah?

Dad's dressing Nuah?

I go toward the laddoos and bend down to tell them in a low voice about our adventure providing flowers for Dawud's ceiling, making it sound super exciting. I emphasize how they need to drop everything and come with me now.

I'm trying to get out of there quickly before I have to do a double dose of glazed gazes—at Dad *and* Nuah.

Too late. I turn around with one laddoo in each hand ready to march out with me, Luke with a truck in his hand, and there's Nuah in the middle of the steps coming down from the loft bedroom on the right. He walks to the middle of the Persian rug in a suit jacket that's slightly too big for him but that some man, who came in with Dad apparently, rushes to pin at the wrist.

After taking in Nuah's sudden entrance, hopefully not with my mouth open in surprise, I act like both of them—he and Dad—aren't there.

"He was just going to wear a nice shirt and dress pants and your dad insisted he add a jacket," Haytham whispers to me.

I nod and make my way past Dad, past Nuah, and out the door.

Haytham follows me out.

"I seriously thought it was Layth he was helping with clothes for the wedding," I say to Haytham.

"He did bring stuff for him, too—you should have seen your dad's face when he found out Layth hadn't brought any fancy clothes with him. But Layth left before your dad got here with the suits. Maybe he saw them coming." Haytham laughs.

"Oh."

Oh.

He left.

Without saying anything.

Not that he had to.

But couldn't he have?

Said one word at least?

Like just texted *Leaving*.

Then I would have texted *Let me know when you get to Ecuador?*

And he would have said *Sure but why*.

And I would have said—

I don't know what I would have said.

Chapter Thirty

❋   ❋   ❋

As we walk to the house, I explain my idea for the flowers to Haytham. It's an idea I got from the tacky grove of plants by the Glade restaurant at the hotel. I guess when Tats and I grabbed breakfast this morning, those crafted flowers burrowed into my brain.

My idea: make a ton of flowers, yellow flowers, big ones, medium ones, whatever sizes, out of construction paper and paint. Then use these to fill in the spaces on Dawud's floral ceiling.

"That's an amazing idea!" Haytham's full-on enthusiastic. "Everyone's going to be so wowed."

"Even your family?" I ask.

Because if it turns out tacky, I don't think Sarah's family will be wowed at all. They might even get upset.

"What do you mean, even my family?"

"I mean your aunts and stuff."

"Why wouldn't they be?" Haytham sounds truly puzzled.

Should I burst his little bubble? I think about Dad and his indignation earlier when I arrived this morning. The tone in his voice that indicated that he thought he was so right—he called his prejudiced views "old-school."

His tone had been exactly like Sarah's Auntie Rima's at the henna party.

Is it time for this cultural-supremacy party to be broken up? "Um, because, at the henna party, one of your aunts came barreling to me and tried to destroy me for wearing Pakistani clothes. Which, she said, wasn't honoring your culture properly."

"What? You're joking, right?" Haytham stops walking. So I stop walking too. And the laddoos stop as well and begin to play on the grass right where we stop, a few feet before the porch, Luke trying to hit Logan's legs with the truck while Logan dodges.

"That's what happened." I shrug my shoulders, now weirdly afraid to elaborate even though I'd already blurted it. "So it kind of gave me the impression that some people in your family are super picky."

"Wow, that's rude. Sorry." He scratches the back of his head like he's seriously befuddled by what I'm telling him.

How could he be? Doesn't he know his own family?

Wait, crap. For almost eighteen years, I had no idea that Dad was as prejudiced as he is.

It seems people show their prejudiced hand when family lines get crossed.

I hate it. It sucks. And I'm never going to stop fighting it.

I don't care who I take down doing it.

Even yourself? Because family lines are getting crossed by Uncle Bilal and his family, and you're completely battle ready.

Ugh, I'm not sure why I keep connecting Dad's prejudice and my flare-up with Mom about Uncle Bilal.

This is not about me.

It's about the harm of holding racist views.

Racism is not like being introverted and not wanting your mom to get remarried.

I mean, I just read about Malcolm X's life fighting its devastating effects. About how anti-Blackness leads to whole systems of inequity and brutality and loss of life. The evidence has been in our faces all along. Some of us choose to pretend it's not there, some of us choose to look away.

And some of us know a little about it but don't act on what we know.

Maybe it's because we don't want to be uncomfortable and experience the losses that come with confrontation. Like for me, it means losing Dad's support—including monetary support—and love and everything else that would follow breaking away from him.

But maybe I don't need to break away. Maybe I need to start talking more about things that bother me. Talking in a steady, brave way.

And not just with Dad.

And not just about *some* things, but everything important to me.

I can start by telling Haytham a bit more about what happened with Auntie Rima and gain the courage to talk to Dad— after the wedding.

"Auntie Rima was the one who reamed me out," I say. "Just 'cause the fabric on my body was cut in a certain way and the designs of the embroidery weren't from the geographical area on earth that she approved of."

"Man, I'm shocked, but then not shocked." He puts his hands on his hips and frowns and shakes his head so hard, his floppy hair flops even more. "I'm sorry big-time on behalf of my family. Can I ask what you did?"

"I didn't do anything. I just stood there stunned. But my friend Sausun shredded her." I smile, remembering Sausun's poise. "You might know her. She runs the Niqabi Ninjas YouTube channel? Well, she IS the original Niqabi Ninja."

Haytham stops moving. "What? THE Niqabi Ninja? SHE WAS HERE LAST NIGHT?"

I laugh and start walking, grabbing the laddoos' hands in turn to get them to climb the porch steps. "Oh my God! Are you a fan too?"

"Seriously? How did I not know?" Haytham follows, but it's with a big spring in his steps. He practically bounds up the steps after me. "Wait. That means she's going to be at the wedding?"

I nod.

"Okay, now I'm really nervous. Muhammad asked me to sing when Sarah walks down the aisle to the gazebo. And with the Niqabi Ninja— What's her name again? She never says it on the show."

"Sausun."

"Sausun. Such a cool name." He pauses for a bit in the foyer like he's relishing it. "Sausun. Yeah, so with Sausun as a wedding guest, I'm going to be scared I'll wreck the song."

I wait before descending to the basement. "Why?"

"Because she's amazing. Her channel is amazing. The way she talks about Muslim stuff. And current issues. Even my non-Muslim friends watch and share it. She's funny. She's brave, and she doesn't back down. So she has my mad respect." He's about to follow me to the basement, but I stop him and ask him to get water for our flower painting.

He salutes me and goes toward the kitchen to do my bidding. But then circles back when I'm two steps down. "Hey, I'm truly sorry for what my aunt said. That's not gonna happen again. I'm going to tell Sarah after the wedding's done. And then we'll take care of it together. And I mean it—because we'll let you know what's been done, okay?"

I nod and smile and take the laddoos to their playroom downstairs. I open the cupboard where Linda keeps all their arts and crafts stuff neatly organized to take out a few fat paintbrushes, some jars of paint, a massive pad of heavy white paper, and a bottle of glue. I put these items into a huge canvas shopping bag I brought down with me from the kitchen.

Then we move back to the kitchen, where Haytham's at the sink, water on, filling some jars he found in a cabinet.

We take all this to the side of the house. Hope is still working on her flowers and only briefly looks up when we spread out our stuff.

Haytham goes into complete uncle mode and settles the laddoos down by modeling how to sit against the house cross-legged to listen while I demonstrate what I want them to do. Which is just plop paint any which way on each sheet of the paper I give them. And just keep doing this while Haytham and I use hair dryers to dry the paint and then cut and assemble flowers according to a YouTube tutorial I found while in the basement.

The laddoos, sitting back like Haytham, clap their hands when I tell them they can just go crazy painting.

I was careful to only select jars and tubes of yellow paints. No bold Pacers-blue paint.

Hopefully, it will look tasteful. Hopefully.

"Luke keeps splashing me and not the paper!" Logan squeals for the tenth time, standing up and stepping away from where Luke's flailing around, giggling.

Why are siblings so different from each other?

Luke: erupting in maniacal laughter each time he flings paint on the paper and it splatters or makes some type of a mess. His face, hands, clothes are smeared with paint—mostly on purpose. He occasionally wanders off, at which point I have to run after him and show him a new way to go wild with yellow paints. Exhausting.

Logan: with his sheet of paper positioned far from Luke's mess, he holds his paintbrush stiffly while dabbing or streaking lines carefully, complaining often of a smudge done wrong or of an ant deciding to investigate his work or of Luke's looking at his work "like he's going to wreck it." At which point I have to keep assuring him that life's going to be okay if he just keeps making marks on the page. Exhausting.

After the laddoos do all they can, I get their iPad from the house and set up an autoplay playlist of some kid's YouTube channel that they're really into, which is episode after episode starring a kid who gets new toys and unboxes them and plays enthusiastically with them for other kids to watch and vicariously enjoy. I've seen the laddoos watch the YouTube kid playing for hours, so I know they'll be fine.

Muhammad calls me as I'm cutting out my millionth petal, sitting against the house, my legs extended in front of me, feet splayed. Haytham and I found out that he's better at assembling the flowers, so he's lying stomach-down on the grass, gluing.

"What's Dad doing?" Muhammad asks, his voice low.

"Huh?"

"You told me to keep Dad away from you."

"Oh. He's angry that I didn't stay here last night and is letting me know it." I put my scissors down and pause cutting to sort the painted paper petals in my lap into the piles divided by size—tiny, small, medium, large, and huge. "But it's okay. I've got it under control."

The whole cheery assembly-line production we've got going here in the sun is making me feel mellow. So I'm inclined to not get Muhammad worried right now.

"You sure? I can talk to him if you want." His voice maintains its low tone even though it's loud in the background. "And I've been thinking about what you said; how it's not just Dad being imperfect. Yeah, it's tons worse. So forget my advice to just work around it."

I think about how Haytham said he's going to do something about what Auntie Rima had done at the henna party. "Yeah, I don't want to work around it. We need to deal with it. After the wedding."

"I'm in. And I know just the place to get help with this. I'll send you the link and you can sign us up."

"Why're you talking so quietly?"

"Bunch of people here. I'm picking guests up, rented a big van, well, two big vans, and we stopped to eat lunch."

"Oh, wow. Just for Imran and Adnan? How much luggage did they bring?"

"No, I'm not picking up those goons. They're driving in from the airport on their own. These are other close friends who needed rides."

"Oh my God, *you* calling them goons!" I laugh. "How many people did you pick up?"

"Like forty."

"*Forty* close friends?" I slow my scissors that I'd picked up again to cut a newly dried sheet.

It's kind of wild that Muhammad has *that* many friends he's tight with. I mean, tight enough to invite to what was supposed to be an intimate wedding.

"They're part of the mosque community I used to hang out with in Chicago. But they couldn't afford to ride down to the wedding on their own. When they heard about me and Sarah getting hitched, they were so pumped." He lowers his voice. "I didn't want to forget them, you know? And Dad has all the important people in his business circles and mosque board circles on the wedding list, and I told him to keep at least fifty spots for friends of mine he didn't know about."

"Right. So they're not *close* friends," I say, getting it. He's just doing that thing of inviting anyone and everyone he knows.

"Janna. You know the Prophet said that the worst food is what's served at a wedding where people are invited by class, right? Where only the well-off gather?" Muhammad whispers now. "I didn't want my wedding to be filled with just those who know how to use the right spoon. So yeah, these are my close friends."

I'm kind of speechless.

I'm actually tearing up.

Muhammad's spending the day of his wedding driving guests who wouldn't be able to travel here on their own, who're truly happy for him, guests he calls—who deserve to be called—his close friends.

I look at the flowers Haytham's finished so far. At the drying sheets of paper that are covered in splotches of yellow paint. At the happiness being assembled.

I'm so proud to do this little thing for my brother.

I take a break and go get some blue paint too. He wanted a blue-and-yellow wedding, he'll get a blue-and-yellow wedding.

Chapter Thirty-One

❄   ❄   ❄

When Linda comes looking for the laddoos to feed them lunch, Tats shows up with her.

After marveling at the flowers, Tats drops down beside me where I'm sitting with my back against the house and widens her eyes before tilting her head in Haytham's direction. He's still in his prone position on the ground making flowers, engrossed in his work, singing low, headphones in. Before putting them on, he told me that he's listening to a few songs he's going to be singing tonight.

"Dear child, WHO? Is that?" she whispers.

"He can't hear," I whisper back. "Sarah's cousin."

She turns to me, her hair now in a high, braided ponytail. It's her get-to-work hairdo. It's also a handy weapon—with one mighty flick, she's used it to effectively swipe at people who bother her. And those who bother me, too, like the kids who'd made fun of my hijab in middle school.

"Is he nice?" Tats says, turning to Haytham again, not whispering now, her eyebrows raised high.

"He's making flowers for me. Of course he is," I say confidently, cutting petals from the final sheets *I* painted—these blue. "And he also sings and is into baking."

"So?" She bends her head in front of my face, because I'm looking down at the scissors in my hand.

"So, what?"

"Are you interested?"

"In what?"

"In a guy spending time making flowers for you?"

"You know what, Tats?" I stop cutting. Her face is so low trying to catch my gaze that I'm afraid there's going to be an accident with my scissors and her head. "Do you know about the Bechdel test?"

"The what?" She lifts her head up. "Why are we talking about tests? I know you love them, but we're out of school now."

"The Bechdel test. You can use it to check if two women characters in a film, novel, or whatever talk about something other than men." I go back to cutting. "It's about fiction, but I really don't think you and I would pass it in real life."

"I don't get what you're saying." She sighs like she's bored of this conversation.

Because we don't usually talk about things like this.

I think that's why me and Tats make sense. I can focus on all the important theoretical ideas in essays and in my schoolwork, but then, with Tats, I can just be whatever I want to be, no heavy thinking involved. Me, unfettered. And for a long time, that me unfettered involved boys.

Because yeah, I wanted to be with someone so badly.

Because all around me were people in relationships, making out in hallways, sharing the latest news of who's going out with who, love blooming on-screen, between the pages of books,

Muhammad and Sarah, Dad and Linda, and it felt like if I didn't have it too, I wasn't secure.

Nuah had been that security.

Even if we didn't go out officially.

And it was super unspoken.

I thought *we* knew.

But now I know that it wasn't real—precisely because it was unspoken.

Now I think I'm done.

I'm done thinking that I need a boy to be whole. To be secure.

"I'm saying that I'm not really looking for anyone," I say with confidence.

"Oh." Tats pulls her knees up and then puts them back down when she sees that the skirt of her dress hitches high. "Are you saying you're like Sandra? Aro and ace, like her?"

"No, I'm just taking a break."

"You took a break your entire school career."

"Tats, give it up." I stop cutting and face her. "I don't want to get into anyone, okay?"

"Okay, okay, okay." She waves her hands to calm me down and then stares far out toward the trees ringing Dad's property. "I wish I could get him with my ponytail."

I know who she's thinking of. Nuah. Like how she'd come after Jeremy before. I shake my head. "Oh my God, Tats. Stop. Nuah's his own person. Leave him alone."

"I'm talking about your dad. He's the one who wrecked everything between you guys." She sighs—dramatically yet, strangely, authentically too. "And now it's changed my best friend's soul."

"My soul is not about boys." I start on the last sheet of paper.

"Let's take a break and go in to eat. After I'm done with this sheet."

Or *was* a big part of my soul about boys before?

After lunch—during which we took our sandwiches upstairs to avoid Dad—Tats and I go to find the laddoos so we can practice their roles with them and Dawud before we need to get dressed for the wedding.

We find out they're both taking much-needed naps after getting baths. Linda promises to wake them up with enough time to prep, so we head out to set up the guest sign-in space.

Sarah showed me where she wanted the two tables—at angles in the pathway between the barn and the house, with enough space between them to let families through but not too much, so that it could still serve as a funnel to the reception.

She wanted to make sure everyone passes through to give their in-lieu-of-gifts donations to Syrian relief.

As we're setting the table decor in place, Haytham and Nuah come out of the barn with the floral ceiling netting held taut and low between them, flower side down. Dawud's walking, no, skipping behind them, a bag of zip ties in his hands.

I briefly pause arranging the framed engagement photos of Muhammad and Sarah on one of the white-clothed tables, my curiosity to see how the whole flowers thing finally turned out tugging at me, making me want to turn my head and stare. But I can't.

I'm over Nuah. I mean, I have to be. But it's easier to be over him without seeing him.

Wear a pretty dress, wear a glazed gaze, lock up my heart, and get this wedding done.

I prop up a letter board with Sarah's chosen caption, a verse from the Qur'an: *And among His signs is this: He created mates for you from among your own selves so that you may dwell in tranquility with them. And He has placed love and mercy between you. Surely in this are signs for those who reflect (30:21).*

I feel a tug on my sleeve.

"Don't you want to see it?" It's Dawud with a huge smile on his face.

"Yeah. I'll come in a bit."

"Janna! You gotta see it going up!" Haytham yells as they make their way down the aisle between the chairs to the gazebo.

Tats nods and pulls my hand. Then she leans in to whisper, "I got your back. I'll block your vision of the dude. Let's go see it."

Ugh.

I follow Tats to the gazebo, where one of the hired hands is setting up two ladders. Haytham and Nuah, still holding the net low, are discussing how they're going to affix it, and, after looking up to assess things, they send Dawud to go get a step stool from the kitchen so that he can stand on it and pass them zip ties.

As soon as they lift the floral creation up to check where to center it, and we see the full glorious effect of it, Tats and I exchange glances.

It's just so ridiculously, ecstatically *joyous*. That's the only word for it.

Paper flowers of different sizes, their petal edges curling inward from the weight of the paint but looking naturally so, intermixed with real flowers, amid lots and lots of foliage. A riot of happiness, sprouting unabashedly.

It turned out the opposite of tacky. It turned out sincere.

I imagine Muhammad and Sarah looking at each other while committing to love each other forever and ever, under the joyful flowers, and I feel moved.

My brother is getting married. He's deciding to take this huge, confident step.

Is this why people cry at weddings?

I abruptly turn to the lake, the emotions swirling in me.

It hits me that Muhammad is the closest person to me—in terms of really understanding the particulars of my life. And I know the parts of his life no one else does.

He's the only one who knows what it feels like to live in that space between loving Mom and Dad, separately.

Is that why he always checks on me? And looks out for me? Because he knows what it feels like too—even though he doesn't show it?

But do I do that back for him?

Tears start falling, and I can't believe the amount of times I've cried this weekend. But I've just realized that people cry at weddings, yes, because of happiness, but also because they represent a life change, and part of that life change is that my brother's not going to be as close to me anymore. He's leaving our family for a new life.

Tats puts an arm around me and leans her head on my shoulders. "I'm sorry I made you come to see it." She straightens her head and points at Dad in the distance directing the photographer and crew. "Also, can I get him *accidentally* with my ponytail? While I'm walking by?"

I can't stop the chortle that escapes on hearing that. Tats is just the back-to-earth balm I always need. "Tats, I'm glad I'm here. I actually want to help them put it up."

She looks puzzled. "You know your face is all splotchy, right? Bro's going to know you're crying over him."

"I'm not crying over him. I helped make those flowers. I just want to make sure it's done properly." I turn around and see they've laid the floral ceiling faceup in the middle of the gazebo floor while Haytham and Nuah are on the ladders measuring. "Let's see if my dad's got more ladders somewhere. It'll be easier to put it up if there's more of us up there."

"I thought you were hiding from your dad."

"I just need to do this for Muhammad."

Chapter Thirty-Two

✼ ✼ ✼

Once the floral ceiling is put up—with me, Tats, Haytham, and Nuah each working a corner—Dawud's whole being changes. He's exuding such great happiness that not only does he do a good job listening to all my directions about how to pass out the wedding favors to the guests, he also helps me train the laddoos. After many demonstrations from Dawud, Logan understands that he can't open the boxes "carefully" for people, and Luke understands that he's not to eat the treats himself. They understand that, as soon as I hand them their baskets, they're to pass them out row by row with a smile when Amu finishes his sermon and says "Mabrook!" to the bride and groom. Once we practice with invisible, pretend favors, I let them practice with the real thing, giving some out to the people still milling around doing last-minute things.

The florist, Hope, setting out the vases on the tables near the lake, takes her favor and smiles at Dawud. "You actually did it. You made your own floral ceiling."

"Yup." He rises on his tiptoes like the smile that's taking over his face is making him float, and then drops his heels back down.

"I've never met a kid who's so fascinated by flowers. Can I ask how you got into them?" Hope asks.

"Because in school, my group had to make a field guide to all the flowers near our school. Other groups made field guides to other things, like birds or rocks, but my group made a flower one. And I was in charge of counting all the different ones," Dawud says proudly. "So I know a lot. I like finding the differences between them."

Wow. I hadn't even bothered asking him why he was so flower crazy. It's classification. Like how he knows all the Pokémon species and their traits.

"Well, you're a smart kid. And paper flowers were a genius idea!" Hope opens her box of favors and picks out a candied almond and pops it into her mouth. "Might need to hire you to work at the store."

"I don't live here," Dawud says solemnly.

"Shucks!" She looks at me. "Okay to borrow him to help me right now? If he wants to, that is?"

"Sure! He knows his part for the wedding." I turn to Dawud. "Just make sure to meet me at the guest sign-in table when my uncle starts talking in the gazebo, okay? And remember Haytham said for you to come to the house to shower and change at four."

He nods and takes a step toward Hope, who indicates the jars of flowers in the box at her feet. "There're numbers on the vases. Just match them to the numbers on the tables."

"Okay." He picks a vase up as I turn to go, with Luke attached to me at the hip because he suddenly decided he's tired. "She did the paper flowers. Janna did them," Dawud says.

"What was that?" Hope's already moved on to other tables, with vases in both her hands.

"Janna did the flowers," Dawud repeats, louder. "Because she was mean to me before so then she decided to be nice."

The only thing I can do is laugh.

Because maybe it's kinda true.

Before we get ready, Tats and I take a rest in my room, painting each other's nails (black for me, gold for Tats), and then catch up on messages and socials.

I open a pic that Soon-Lee sent me and shriek. It's a photo of her and Thomas holding up their clothes for the wedding, and it's the cutest thing ever: They've colored their hair to match each other's outfits. Soon-Lee now has hair the same sage green as Thomas's tie, while his hair is lavender like her dress.

Tats looks at the snaps of them I hold up for her and then shows me the pic she took of Jeremy dressed up when they went shopping for his clothes.

He looks good, and I say so to Tats, which makes her lower her phone and say, "Uh-oh, I kinda just had a conscience thing happen right now."

"What do you mean?" I'm watching Soon-Lee's Instagram story of getting her hair done and how hard the hairdresser worked to match the color of Thomas's tie perfectly.

"I mean, I felt guilty just now when you said he looks good." She leans back on the bed beside me.

"Why? You know I have no interest in him in that way."

"Maybe because now you don't have a guy? And before, when you had Nuah, it felt okay?" She sighs. "You sure that guy Haytham is just helping you because he's a nice young man?"

"Bechdel test, Tats. Bechdel test."

"Stop nerding me."

I sit up, looking at a message. "Sandra says she doesn't feel well and might not come. She said she can't drive."

"She never told me."

"What about Jeremy? Can he give her a ride when he comes? And Ms. Kolbinsky?'

"I'm on it." Tats starts texting but then stops. "Oh wait, he can't. He's coming from Lafayette. He went there last night to see his brother."

I think about who else is driving in from Eastspring. Amu. But he never replied to my e-mail from before.

As I'm pondering what to do, Muhammad texts.

Just got here. Linda's getting all the guests I brought settled, thanks for the sign-in table. I'm going to get ready.

Ok, I reply. Btw, thanks Muhammad.

For what?

Duh? For everything?

Are you getting emotional on me? I can't handle that. I like my sis cool and snappy.

I send him a long row of multicolored hearts, and he replies with a vomit emoji.

"Hey, let's go upstairs. To get our clothes," I tell Tats. Mom put our big suitcase in the alcove guest room due to it being a more spacious place for all three of us to change. Maybe Mom's in there resting or something too.

When we get upstairs, Haytham's scrolling on his phone, leaning on the doorjamb of the empty guest room. A guest room with no Mom. "Dawud's almost done. I'm going to help him get ready, then okay if I shower, or you guys need the bathroom?"

"Sure, we're just here to get our stuff," I say. "What are you at now?"

"At?" He moves out of the way so we can get into the room.

"Votes? Still in the lead? Muslim Voice?"

"Yeah, but the girl, Noor, is catching up. She's just a couple hundred behind me." He plays her rendition of Adele's "Hello," a Muslim version that's talking to Allah. "She's really good."

As Tats goes into the room to get the suitcase, I stand outside the room with Haytham. He doesn't have his headphones, so he's tilting his phone to his ear to listen to Noor's song, a look of concentration on his face.

I decide to grant him a wish. For helping me with those flowers.

"Yo, aren't you supposed to be busy?" Sausun's on-screen, but it's with a loose scarf thrown on her head, not her face covered in niqab.

"Niqab up. I want to introduce you to someone. And he's a guy."

Sausun sighs and leans right off-screen and comes back with a towel. She leans off-screen again and spends some time fiddling, and when she comes back, she's wearing the towel on her head in a Mary-mother-of-Jesus style, with the ends hanging down over her shoulders and the scarf that was previously on her head across her face now. "This better be good," she says.

I go to lean on the wall beside Haytham. Tats wheels the suitcase over to us so she can see what I'm showing Haytham.

"Haytham, this is Sausun. Sausun, this is Haytham. Sarah's cousin from Arkansas."

Haytham half lowers the phone that was at his ears before and nods at Sausun. His eyes are large, and there's a tenseness to his face I've never seen before. "Assalamu alaikum."

"Walaikum musalam." Sausun nods back at him.

I shift the phone back to me. "So you know the Muslim Voice competition? Haytham's doing it. And he's currently in the lead. Tomorrow's the last day for votes to come in. So . . ." I trail off and smile up at Haytham, who still has a stiffness to him that's so uncharacteristic. Oh my God, is he starstruck? I look back at Sausun, who looks nothing like a "star" with the towel-niqab deal she has going on right now. "So I was wondering if you could, you know, do a short boost for him? On Instagram and Snapchat? And TikTok and YouTube? Everywhere?"

"Well, I'd have to listen to him sing first. Come to my own conclusions, you know?" She leans left this time and pulls her laptop onto her lap. "I haven't been keeping up with the competition."

"Check it out, please? We'd really appreciate it." I turn the phone to Haytham so Sausun can see him again.

"Thanks, I really appreciate it." He nods again. The tips of his ears are red.

"I didn't promise anything," Sausun responds dryly.

"I know. I just appreciate you considering it," Haytham says solemnly.

She shrugs. "Assalamu alaikum. Janna, are you there?"

I turn the phone to me. "Yup."

"Are we done now? I'm going to look at this Muslim Voice thing, and then I gotta get ready. For your brother's wedding, remember?"

"Yeah, we're done." I think of something. "Hey, any chance you could give someone a ride here from Eastspring? A friend of mine and her grandmother? She was supposed to drive but isn't feeling well."

"Text me the info. Muslim?"

"No."

"Okay, then prep them. About my niqab. Don't want Grandma freaking out that a niqabi's driving her."

I nod, though I know Ms. Kolbinsky will be totally okay with it.

Right before I hang up, I turn the phone quickly to Haytham again as a joke. Just to make him squirm at the sight of Sausun once more. He looks at me, stricken.

"I can't believe you just did that. You actually asked *her*." He puts his fingers through his hair.

I laugh and follow Tats, who's pulling the suitcase down the stairs to my room. "Hey, I just want you to win."

Before I shower and change, I check Sausun's accounts and see not a peep about anything related to the Muslim Voice. She's probably still researching.

I'll check in again later.

When I open the suitcase, there's only Tats's and my clothes.

Where are Mom's? I try calling her but don't get an answer.

I call Linda.

"Your mom went back to the hotel to change. She thought it would be less crowded. She hadn't known that the boys were also using the bathrooms here," Linda explains. "But she's coming back earlier to get her makeup done. So meet in my bedroom around five, okay? Tats, too."

I hang up and stare at my dress in the clear plastic dress bag.

In my head, I imagined Mom and me and Tats getting ready together, helping each other zip up our dresses and stuff.

I *wanted* Mom to zip me up. Like she had when we'd tried the dress on at home. When she'd lifted my hair and twisted it in a bun and stood next to me, looking in the mirror, declaring me "stunningly beautiful," and even if I hadn't believed her, I'd still felt a glow from how much she meant the words.

Is she zipping Dania's and Lamya's dresses up?

I pick *my* dress up by the hanger from the suitcase and lay it on the bed. Tats is still in the shower, so I sit beside my dress and, without thinking, start tapping on my phone.

What are you guys up to?

There's typing happening on Dania's end.

Getting ready

Just you guys?

No

Typing happening.

We're in Khadija's room, helping her.

Zayneb's there? And my mom? There. Slide it in like that so there's no notice of my insecurity.

Typing.

Typing.

Typing. *Still?*

Zayneb's with her fiancé and brother. They got ready early so they already left. I think she promised Sarah she'd do something for her so look for her there. And Adam, her fiancé. We'll be over soon too.

She didn't say anything about Mom.

My mom?

I thought she was with you?

I smile. Unconsciously.

"Tats?" I say when she emerges from my bathroom in my bathrobe, a towel around her head. "Is it okay if we drive to the hotel? To go get ready with Mom? Haytham said we can use his car."

"Now? Is there enough time?"

"If we leave this minute, there is."

"Okay," she says, sliding into my yellow flip-flops. "Let's go!"

"Like that? You're in my bathrobe."

She opens the door. "Janna, do you know me or not?"

I pull the suitcase, and we go out the door, down the stairs, and out into the day.

Chapter Thirty-Three

❄ ❄ ❄

When Mom opens the hotel room door in *her* bathrobe, Tats wheels in the suitcase and beelines for the bathroom. We worked out that she'd change first.

I need to talk to Mom.

Maybe because I let her, Mom tells me everything.

How Uncle Bilal and she reconnected when she sent the wedding invitation to him and his family in the spring. How she got to know him better in the last three weeks while I've been at Dad's.

And how, just last week, he asked her to marry him.

"But only when I was ready, he said. And I'm not ready until you are," Mom says.

We're lying down on the bed, staring at the ceiling like when we talked about Nuah in my room.

"What about when Muhammad is ready too?" I ask, wondering if she's told Uncle Bilal that I'm the "difficult" one.

"I spoke to Muhammad last week. He thought we should wait until after the wedding to introduce everyone to each other." Mom sighs. "The dinner on Thursday was supposed to be for me to meet

Dania and Lamya. I wasn't trying to hide it from you. I just knew there was a lot going on with the wedding, and I wanted you to be ready to hear about it."

"Why did you tell Muhammad last week and not me?"

"Because you're my baby," Mom says. "And you feel things in a different way than Muhammad does. And just so you know, he's not completely convinced about Uncle Bilal either."

It's my turn to sigh now. I feel Mom's pain.

She's gotta check in with so many people, even though she knows how her heart feels.

I decide to be the mature one now.

I reach out and touch her shoulder to turn her around to face me. "The important thing is, do you like him? Is he a good person with similar values? Do you both like running mini marathons for charities? And wearing T-shirts to outdo each other's commitments to bettering the world?"

She laughs and then looks at me with a probing mom look. "I'm sure I like him. Really like him, alhamdulillah. But do you really mean that?"

"I don't want to stop you from being loved, Mom," I say. "I know you'll still love me." I pause before adding, "Right?"

"Don't even ask me that. Nothing will ever come between me and my kids. Are you sure?"

"Yes, because I don't want you to be alone."

"I'm not."

"I want you to have someone to go on your charity walks and stuff with. He seems to be into that as well."

Mom laughs. "He isn't. He actually works for a nonprofit that connects corporations with merchandise for charity initiatives and sometimes he gets leftovers."

"Oh, well, he's into eating breakfast and authentic Italian, like you, so . . ."

"*That* he is." We both lean forward for a hug at the same time.

I draw away first because I can't help adding something. Because I need to be honest. "But remember, I don't know him, so it's going to take me a while to, you know, go with the flow of it all."

"Of course, sweetums. You have to come to your own conclusions. And let your own heart open as it wills." She sits up as Tats emerges from the bathroom, all dressed. "Let's get ourselves changed?"

My dress is dark navy blue with thin dark ribbons around the waist, at the neck, and high above the wrists—all these ribbons end in perfectly looped bows, and that's the simple elegance of this dress. That and its gossamer fabric that just falls lightly all the way to the top of my feet, like it's made from darkly dyed fairy wings.

It's just a perfectly goth dress, the only dress that screamed *Janna Yusuf!* from all the dresses we looked at in the five stores Mom and I visited.

Each time I tried the dress on at home, I felt like walking taller, straighter, prouder.

Mom lifts my hair and zips the dress up in the back, and I instantly feel better. *More alive.*

I help her with hers, a periwinkle-blue silk that has a flounce at the bottom. She's so pretty with a darker blue hijab to top it off.

Tats also looks pretty in her off-the-shoulders sunny mustard-yellow dress, which hangs in ruffles around her chest and then flows down to right above her knees, with a thin gold belt cinching her waist. On her feet are gold gladiator sandals and at her left wrist, a gold cuff, her only jewelry.

She—very beachy, boho-looking, with her now-blond hair spread wavy all around her shoulders, two thin braids at the sides that meet in the back and hang in a slender single braid all the way down to her waist—looks the opposite of me.

She looks perfectly Tats: approachable, sunny, with no pretenses.

Me: reserved, still learning to open my heart to a bigger circle of people. Still learning about my capacity to give and love.

As Mom drives us back, I see that Haytham's posted his latest haiku.

He must have just finished his shower.

> *To spend time with you*
> *Means to fill the sky with blooms*
> *Then to disappear*

The sky with blooms?

Is he talking about the floral ceiling? That we made together?

Oh no, Tats's questions about him are getting to me.

But, I ask my stupid heart, *do you actually like him in that way?*

No, I don't, my stupid heart answers. *He's cute, but we're on different wavelengths.*

Then why make a narrative, a love story, a world in your head? If your heart isn't officially ready to participate in one in real life?

After we get our makeup done quickly, Tats and I take a walk-through of the wedding grounds before more guests come.

Everything looks perfect.

The guests Muhammad drove are already seated in chairs,

dressed in diverse cultural clothing, vibrant, bejeweled, and some understated, too. I get this surge of goose-bumpy happiness just seeing them there, waiting to witness Muhammad's commitment to love Sarah. A smile immediately takes over my face, and I find myself leading Tats to mingle with everyone, moving between the rows, me saying salaam and introducing myself to each person, Tats following behind, waving happily, a big welcoming smile on her face.

"Janna!" Zayneb's standing in the gazebo with a sheet of paper in her hands. She's wearing the lengha she showed me a picture of before. It's grayish mauve with gold beading, the full high-waisted skirt and the short top, and the chiffon shawl on her shoulders all in the same color—even her hijab matches it exactly. It's just really elegant all around. I have to say, even though I'm not into the colors she's into, Zayneb has really good taste in clothes. Like, I can see myself being okay wearing what she has on right now.

Or maybe it's just the confident way she's wearing it.

There's a guy leaning back against the gazebo railing, his arms crossed. He's got a pretty full beard and looks very close to Zayneb's age. It must be Adam, Zayneb's fiancé.

Tats and I finish saying hello to Muhammad's guests and then walk between the sets of white chairs toward the gazebo.

"This is my brother, Mansoor. Mansoor, Janna and . . . sorry, forgot your name!" Zayneb says to Tats.

"I'm Tats. Short for Tatyana!" Tats says with a flourish to Mansoor, the guy with the full beard, who nods back.

"I'm just practicing my little roast of Sarah," Zayneb says, which reminds me of—groan—my roast with Nuah. "It includes a slide show, so I brought a portable projector, and Mansoor's helping me figure out how to use it."

We hang around for a bit, fiddling with the projector, when Zayneb suddenly looks beyond me. Her expression changes, like actually transforms. Softened, lit up, buoyant.

Now *that's* the look when sunny skies invade your entire self.

I glance behind me, and there's a guy walking toward us with a cane, though he's young. He's kind of tall and thin, and looks like maybe he's partly East Asian and white, and really handsome in a quiet, old-time-movie-star way. He's in a trim suit, also grayish mauve, and when I notice the color, that's when it hits me: *This* must be Adam.

"How did it go?" Zayneb asks, her voice rising as she goes down the gazebo steps to meet him.

He stops walking, and they talk a bit away from us, and just from the way they're looking at each other, and the way their clothes match so perfectly, I know for certain that this really *is* Adam.

Tats and I exchange glances, our eyebrows rising at the same time. She leans over to me and says, "Why can't you get yourself one of *those*?"

I poke her, and we slip off the other side of the gazebo to check in at the house before we have to work the guest sign-in table.

As soon as I come into the house, the first person I see is Dad. He and Linda are both trying to brush the laddoos' hair, each tackling one of them, while Mom watches from near the kitchen island, smiling.

Dad turns around to me and says, with no ill feeling, "Janna! You look stunningly beautiful!"

I'm surprised, but I give him a weak smile. "You look good too. And you, too, Linda."

"We were thinking that we'd all wait and see Muhammad come down first. You know, like the bride walking down? Sarah's doing that with her family, so let's receive our groom?" Dad puts the brush in his hand down on the counter and picks up Luke. "I want to get pictures."

I nod, but I still don't know how to handle Dad, so I turn to the glass sliding doors. The guests are chatting happily with one another in the distance, and I kind of wish I was mingling with them again. There's no tension over there.

Mom clears her throat. "Haroon."

I turn from the door, surprised at Dad's name coming from Mom's lips. It's been a long time since I've heard it.

"Do you want to go up and walk Muhammad down? With Janna?" Mom looks at Dad and then at the stairs.

And a photograph blooms in my head.

It's a photograph Mom has hanging in our apartment, right outside her bedroom. Of Dad and Mom sitting on top of the stairs at their first house, the one they had before I was born, with a toddler Muhammad sitting between them. His hands were resting on both their knees in trust, and sometimes when Mom would look at that picture, she'd tear up, but she'd always tell me it was from happiness.

"Shouldn't it just be you and Dad, Mom?" I say, thinking of that photo. "And Linda, too—the parents? And I can take the pictures of you all coming down?"

"No, you three would be beautiful," Linda says, nodding her head encouragingly. "Muhammad will like that."

"Are you sure, sweetheart?" Dad's voice is hesitant.

"Yes." Linda reaches over to take Luke from him and looks at me, her voice certain. "Janna, go. I'll join in on the photos when you all get down here."

"I can take the pictures!" Tats says. "And Logan can help me, right, Logan?"

He nods and lets Tats lift him onto a chair so he can see the camera set up on a tripod, and I follow Dad and Mom upstairs.

Chapter Thirty-Four

❊ ❊ ❊

We wait outside Muhammad's door in silence, me close to Mom.

Dad suddenly turns around completely to me. "Janna, I'm sorry."

I'm so caught off guard that I freeze.

Mom looks at me, confusion on her face.

"We don't have time to talk now. But please, let's make time." He turns back to Muhammad's door. "I don't want this day to be a bad memory for you and me."

I nod. And whisper to Mom, "I'll tell you later."

After the wedding, I promise myself.

And it won't be just telling.

The door opens, and Muhammad, in a royal blue tuxedo that actually looks really nice on him, jumps back, frightened. "Oh my God! What are you guys doing? You almost gave me a heart attack! On my wedding day!"

Mom, Dad, and I laugh at his hyperbole and also his face.

"We came up to walk the groom down," I say. "You have to position yourself between Mom and Dad, and I'll walk behind you all."

But when we take the first step, a tsunami of bittersweetness pours into my heart, and I can't move. Maybe it's the fact that when Muhammad takes those steps down the stairs, he's actually moving on to his new life.

"Janna!" Muhammad, now at the top of the stairs, looks back at me. "What are you doing?"

"You realize you're moving away, right?" I lift my hands to my face.

I can't cry. My makeup.

"Yeah, you mean like how I moved away for college?" His voice is playful.

"No, for good. 'Cause you're getting married." My hands are still in front of my face. This is the best makeup I've ever had. It's not coming off or getting messed up.

My hands are in front of my face so I don't have to see Muhammad's face.

Because if I do, my makeup will most definitely get messed up.

"Janna, come here." He calls me but actually moves back to me and wraps me in a hug. "I'm not going for good. You think I would have said yes to Sarah asking me to marry her if I'd had to leave my family for good? No way!"

Uh-oh, tears are starting. I try to quickly think about something else.

Layth handing me the yellow handkerchief comes to mind, the handkerchief with the name Muhsin.

And suddenly it hits me.

I'm not alone and won't be.

I'm surrounded by love. Mom, Muhammad, Dad, Linda, Sarah, the laddoos.

So is Layth—he just can't see it. Uncle Bilal, Dania, Lamya, his mom—they all love him.

Wait . . . did Muhammad say *Sarah* asked him to marry her?

I start giggling into Muhammad's jacket, my shoulders shaking lightly. He hugs me tighter and says, "Come on, don't cry. When you find out that I'm never going to be out of your life, you'll regret these tears. You'll be like, I wish I'd said good-bye and good riddance to him!"

"I'm not crying. I'm laughing." I break away from his hug and show him my face, tearless. "Yeah, right, as if *Sarah* asked you to marry her."

"She actually did. She cleared it all with her parents and then invited me to dinner with them and pretended to pop it out of a fortune cookie. A slip of paper that said *Will you marry me?*" He says all this seriously.

"You're joking. You're the one who was after Sarah from day one!"

"But *she* was the one who said I was a keeper." He grins and puts his hands on his hips. Dad loops his arm through his left one, and Mom loops her arm through his right one and then holds out her arm for me to loop mine through.

"Okay, let's do this. Walk me down, guys."

As we walk down the stairs, I'm kind of in awe of Sarah. My sister-in-law-to-be.

To have that kind of guts is goals.

After the pictures, Tats and I head to the guest sign-in table.

We get there as several people walk toward it from the driveway, and we see more leaving the parking field and getting ready to cross the road.

I turn to a fresh page in the guest book and prepare myself to receive guests.

I realize I'm actually standing taller now, more proudly, and I let the smile I feel take over my face.

The first few families all have girls around my age—Aalya, Varisha, Lybah, and Hanaa—but I don't know any of them. I realize from their dads and moms exclaiming in delight at how much I've grown that they're people our family used to hang around with in Chicago, when I lived there as a kid. It feels strange that there's this whole bunch of girls I could have played with long ago that I don't remember now. At their parents' encouragement, they lean in to hug me, and I appreciate the way they do it so lightly, so respectfully. I give them all a smile as they go to find seats.

After that, it's a blur of people coming, smiling, signing, going to sit down.

The blur is interrupted by the arrival of family from Dad's side, including Imran and Adnan, who pause to take pictures with me and their wives. From Mom's side, only Amu and his wife, Khaleh, who packs so much sweetness into her tiny quiet self, were able to come to the nikah. The rest of Mom's family live too far—Mom's other brother and my little cousins are in Dubai with Teta—so they're coming to the reception next year, insha'Allah.

Then Soon-Lee and Thomas arrive, and I run ahead to greet them.

"I missed you so so much!" Soon-Lee is almost jumping up and down while hugging me in her lavender dress—which is officially the cutest thing I've seen so far.

We squeal some more as Thomas stands apart with his hands in the pockets of his—are those jeans? With a really nice suit jacket?

"What? Dress jeans are a thing. Look it up." Thomas shrugs, his hands still in his pockets.

"Just stay away from my dad," I warn. "Oh my gosh, I have to get a pic of you two. This is going in my personal wedding album."

I take pics of them posing cutely with each other, and as I'm finishing, I notice someone else who makes me scream again.

Sandra. And Ms. Kolbinsky. Dressed to the nines.

Who knew weddings could be so much fun?

Sandra has on a black pantsuit, which looks perfect on her, while Ms. Kolbinsky is in a raspberry-colored lace dress with a black hat that reminds me of those hats British royalty wear in pics. Fascinators, I think they're called.

I give them hugs, and Sandra, who's usually quiet and more of a listener, gives me a quick update on her summer so far, while Ms. Kolbinsky keeps pinching my cheeks, telling me she misses sharing food with me. After I promise her that I'll be back in Eastspring tomorrow, I lead them all to the table to sign in.

That's when I remember Sausun. Why wasn't she with Sandra? "Hey, where's Sausun? The girl who drove you?"

Sandra points toward the barn. "There. Talking to some guy."

I stand on my tiptoes to see, and, yup, Sausun is talking to Haytham, with her sister by her side. Her sister doesn't wear niqab, and I can see from all the way down here that she looks impatient. She keeps turning her head and looking around and moving away then coming back.

After I watch Sausun and Haytham for a bit, in between directing my just-arrived friends to their seats, I decide to go over there to check if all's okay, leaving the table in Tats's capable hands. There's something weird about how Haytham is unmoving, while Sausun's sister keeps moving, and Sausun's talking nonstop.

I introduced them, so I feel a bit of responsibility for whatever's going on up there.

"It just doesn't feel authentic to who I am. No one would even believe me," Sausun's saying as I get closer. "Country music? So totally not my thing."

Haytham's everyday, confident stature is gone. It's like his muscles all deflated, and he's standing there shriveled. "But it's *Muslim* country," he protests weakly.

"If we're talking Muslim music, I'm more of a Khalil Ismail fan. Perfect Tupac vibes, you know?" Sausun sees me. "Janna knows. Tell this guy it doesn't make sense for me to tell people to vote for his singing. My followers would see right through me. They'd think it was a plug."

I never considered that. It's true that Sausun has pretty uncompromising taste, but I really thought she'd just help.

"But can't you make it an unpersonal thing? Can't you just say if you had to choose for the Muslim Voice competition, you'd say Haytham?" I appeal.

"But that's the thing. I *wouldn't* choose Haytham. I'd choose Abdul Kareem."

"Who?"

"Abdul Kareem. The man who sings those traditional nasheeds."

"The *old* man?"

"Yup, the old man. From Sudan." Sausun turns to Haytham. "He's amazing. Study him."

Haytham swallows.

"The thing I like about him is his entries are all without musical instruments, just pure vocal melody," Sausun says, nodding at me. "Thanks for getting me to check the Muslim Voice out. I'm actually going to do a video tonight asking everyone to vote for Abdul Kareem."

Oh man, I just made everything worse by asking Sausun to get involved. I'm afraid to look at Haytham.

"Okay," he squeaks.

I risk a glance and see he's still standing there in the exact same I've-been-run-over-by-a-truck pose, and I realize he'll be like that all day unless somebody scrapes him off the road.

"Let's go? To the wedding?" I suggest brightly.

Sausun nods and begins walking, her black abaya rising a bit with her steps to reveal a pair of sparkly turquoise Doc Martens.

She's an iron-willed queen.

I follow behind with Haytham, who's walking slowly.

"I'm so sorry. Really. I thought she'd just do it," I tell him quietly.

"No." His voice is low and sad, but then he clears his throat and continues slightly more upbeat—as though he's mustering energy. "She's right. She has to stick to her principles."

His voice is still tainted with the squeak from before.

I nod, and as we make our way to the wedding site, I glance at his face to gauge the level of hurt. The level of burn.

But, weirdly, he's actually looking at Sausun walking ahead, with starstruck eyes again.

Truly, I don't think I'll ever, ever understand guys.

Thanks for sending that Q & A

A text from Layth, as I'm sitting at the sign-in table in a respite after a horde of guests.

That Imam has got some cool stuff

He read more of Amu's answers? And likes them? I feel a surge of pride. That Imam's my uncle. My mother's brother.

Cool uncle

Yours is here but I'm avoiding him

Hey he's not a bad guy. He's just on another wavelength.

Still avoiding him. I have my own reasons that Layth doesn't need to know.

I'll get to know Uncle Bilal after the wedding.

You know he actually paid for everything. My brother's funeral, our bills, helped my mom get to England. Even my counseling. And he's not loaded.

Then why don't you like him if he's so kind? I hope my skepticism doesn't show.

He did this thing a year ago that got me mad. When he found out I wasn't going back to school, he set me up with a job I hadn't asked for. So he was off my list for a long time.

Because he doesn't believe I'm ok being me. He thinks I'm going to Ecuador to get away from everything but I'm actually going towards everything I believe in.

I read that over and over again, feeling like I want to know more but can't ask everything I want to know—about him, about his mind, what he believes in—because then he'd wonder why I'm so interested, and then explaining that would be weird.

But I can show interest in some parts of him without sounding weird.

Or is that also weird?

I hesitate briefly and then just do it. Can you send me videos from Ecuador? Of the animals?

Sure. I'll let you know whenever I upload my stuff onto the Friday stream. Especially if I'm helping a sloth.

I smile.

Chapter Thirty-Five

✱ ✱ ✱

"The nikah is a simple concept in Islam. It's a contract that is essentially an offer and acceptance. Either partner can initiate the offer, and the acceptance has to be willingly given—it is forbidden that one partner be forced or be reluctant to enter the marriage contract. Thus, I always check with both parties before a ceremony to ascertain that neither has been compelled or unduly influenced to say yes to the marriage."

Amu looks from Muhammad to Sarah and then smiles at the guests, his white beard nodding as he continues. "In this case, being the maternal uncle of the groom, I know for certain that the bride and the groom are quite enthusiastic about entering the contract. So enthusiastic, in fact, that it had to be pulled up a whole year so that they could start their life together earlier. So enthusiastic, I can see Muhammad's foot tapping as he waits for me to finish this sermon so he can be Sarah's husband, finally! Don't worry—I won't be long, ya walad."

The audience laughs.

I'm sitting in the back, still at the sign-in table with Tats—and now Jeremy's joined us—and we have a beautiful view of the entire ceremony. In the gazebo, under the floral ceiling that made both Muhammad and Sarah gasp when they first saw it, Amu is standing in his long white thowb, with a crisp navy thowb jacket that reaches the ground. Behind him, sitting on either end of a modern white chaise sofa with Sarah's father between them, are Muhammad and Sarah, both looking up eagerly at Amu with smiles on their faces.

When Sarah entered the grounds with all her family flanking her, to Haytham singing Jason Mraz's "I Won't Give Up" with Muhammad standing beside him beaming, I left the sign-in table to give her a hug, and we both teared up. She'd been trying to save the whole dramatic wedding-dress-entrance for the wedding itself, and had originally planned to wear something a little simpler for the nikah than the elegant dress she'd already picked out for next year. But she told me that when her parents realized that Dad was making this party huge, they said she needed to show up "worthy of their family's stature."

So there she is in a fairy-tale white wedding gown that only she could pull off. The heavy dress is slathered in intense white beadwork from the wrists up the arms, all over the bodice, to the full skirt that puffs out Cinderella-huge all the way down to the hem from the trim waist, at which a taffeta bow sits facing the front, like she's a present. A veil, just as pouffy as her skirt, its edges as intricately beaded as her dress, sprouts from her white-silk-hijabbed head. It's pushed back now onstage so she can smile at the audience, especially at her family sitting in a curved row on the right, adjacent to the gazebo, all gazing adoringly up at her.

I actually admire her for doing this thing to make her family happy tonight. It's not something I would have done—and I know Mom and Dad wouldn't have expected me to—but Sarah, with her "saintly" ways, remembered the bigger picture *for her*. Which included a family wanting her to "choose them" at this point in time.

Sarah's words in the cleaning closet come to me: *Janna, it's never simple. No relationship is. It's a back-and-forth dance where sometimes you give more, sometimes you take.*

". . . the part of love that we wish to receive and give, that we crave but often don't know how to articulate or communicate, is mercy. Mercy can be defined in different ways. It's the ability to see the other as one worthy of your care, as worthy as you. It's the realizing and the receiving of each other's vulnerabilities. It's the committing to safeguard those vulnerabilities, so much so that you become a protector, a comfort, a shield for each other to grow safely, without the hard shells we humans wear—must wear, it appears—to be resilient in this harsh world. Mercy is love that lets us be, that grants us the serenity and refuge of true love. And that is what I wish these two young ones today." Amu ends his nikah sermon and begins the nikah itself.

"I'm going to go sit up front with my mom to see this and be there to congratulate them first when the ceremony's done," I tell Tats. "Are you coming?

"No, there are guests still arriving. Jeremy and I will take care of the table."

I make my way to the curve of chairs at the left of the gazebo where our side of the family's sitting, facing the audience like Sarah's family. On the other side, I catch Dawud's eyes as he stands up to wiggle a bit, favors basket in his hands, before being yanked down by someone.

His eyes are not the only ones I see. In the audience, Uncle Bilal is in a seat at the far right in between Dania and Lamya, but his gaze keeps turning to the left. Up front to our family row.

Mom.

Dad's sitting a few chairs away, so puffed up, proud, and happy. Linda sits beside him, leaning into him, her elbow fitting into the crook of his arm.

Is that what Amu meant about the "serenity and refuge of true love"?

I look at Uncle Bilal once more. He's trying to look at the stage, but there go his eyes again, just taking a tiny look before darting back.

Will he show love and mercy to Mom?

Because I know she will to whoever she's with.

After the ceremony we all hug one another. Even Sarah's family is hugging us, even Auntie Rima's hugging me, even Sarah's mom is, and it's so so tight that her face dissolves into a smile when she pulls away, and this is weird, but the more I let everyone hug me, the more I just relax into hugs.

So much that I go and find Dania and Lamya and hug them, too.

As dinner's winding down, the ice-cream truck chimes, and Haytham takes the mic and makes an announcement that children of all ages are invited to buy treats but only if they hold their money tight in their hands and make "the longest, straightest, silentest line in the world." When he says this, I glance with raised eyebrows at Sausun, sitting beside me at my specially chosen table of nine. "He's a Super Uncle already."

"And?" Sausun shoots back.

"And Super Uncle needs votes," I remind her.

"Janna, quit it. I'm already following Abdul Kareem on all my socials. His rendition of 'Tala'al-Badru' is impeccable. Unbeat-able."

"That's because you haven't heard Haytham's rendition. I have, and it's amazing." I shrug and get up. "I have to go help him, since I arranged for the ice-cream truck to be here. Anyone want ice cream?"

Just as I ask this, Dad takes the mic from Haytham and makes an announcement of his own. "Perfect. Will the balloon artist please head to the ice-cream truck? To entertain the children?" Dad watches the artist, who's been waiting for his gig, go off. Then he turns back to the guests. "The kids can get their ice cream, and the adults can get dessert. As you may all know, I run Lite Indian Desserts. Rich, traditional desserts with a twist: They're not rich in calories! Twists are what I specialize in. So of course, in com-memoration of my son's wedding . . . Sorry." He pauses and looks over at the section where Sarah's family is seated. "I mean, my son's *nikah ceremony*—a reminder, the real wedding reception is next year, folks—I've decided to unveil my newest twist. Will the LID Inc. gentlemen and gentlewomen standing by please come and serve the dessert selections to each table?"

Servers immediately move in with trays that they set three to a table, with three sweets on each.

"These are just a small sampling of my new line, more of which are available at the dessert table at the back." Dad stands taller with pride and continues. "Honored guests, may I present you with my fusion line of Indian and Arab sweets, playfully titled Desarabi, launching on Monday! Taste and note the names of your favorites, which are easy to see on the specially made, clearly labeled trays."

I lean over and look at the white cardboard tray of three sweets that's been placed between me, Sausun, Tats, and Jeremy.

Baklaburfi (baklava and burfi), *basboodda* (basbousa and lad-doo), and *kunakheer* (kunafeh and kheer) stare back at me. I raise my eyes to the table up front where Muhammad and Sarah are seated, to see their reactions.

Sarah looks somewhere between amused and impressed while Muhammad appears shocked.

I decide not to check out Sarah's family's reactions and just go help Haytham.

Chapter Thirty-Six

❀ ❀ ❀

Alex, the ice-cream-truck guy, is smiling, with his sister Katarina beside him. The balloon artist has already started making animals for the kids waiting in line.

"Aha!" I tell Haytham. "See? I was right. Happy ice-cream dude!"

"Look at the line," he counters. "Of course he's happy. The guy's making a killing. Hope he has enough ice cream."

"I still won."

"Okay, you won." He smiles at me, and Tats looks over with raised eyebrows from where she's helping the laddoos peel their ice-cream treats.

Great. The story about Haytham she made up is going to grow in her head.

"And tomorrow, *you'll* win. The competition. Insha'Allah," I tell him.

"About that. Your cousins, Adnan and Imran, they taught me this song, apparently one of your brother's favorite songs. I'm going to sing it without any music. It's just the first lines and the chorus. They're going to help me keep tune in the background a cappella, with hums and snaps."

"But I thought the entries were done."

"No, I don't mean for the Muslim Voice. I mean for right after this, when I'm singing in the gazebo. Do you think she'll like it?"

"Who?"

"Sausun."

"Oh, now I get it—you're trying to sing a cappella to get her on your side." I smile.

Uh-oh, Tats is looking over again. She's probably thinking, *They're smiling at each other—it's true love.*

I look at Haytham. He's looking back at me expectantly.

"I like it. Great idea," I assure him.

"No, do you think she'll be interested?" He shifts uncomfortably. "In me?"

I break out in the hugest smile ever. I don't care if Tats is staring like a hawk.

The skies are blue, my brother just got married to the love of his life, there's a jolly ice-cream truck and driver right beside me, balloon animals are being made, and Haytham likes Sausun.

After Muhammad and Sarah, that's the best crush of this whole too-much-love-happening wedding yet.

Chaahe tum kuchh na kaho maine sun liya.

Holding his phone in front of him for the lyrics, Haytham sings the opening lines of "Pehla Nasha," a Hindi song Muhammad and I heard from Dad all the time growing up.

Haytham is so good the laddoos try to sing along from the audience, mistaking it for the real thing.

I move over to where Sausun's standing, a glass of pop in her hand. "What do you think?"

She raises her glass to me. "Better. Also, what are you? His agent?"

"No, just a gal tasked to find out if you're open to looking into an eligible young man who can sing whatever song you want, train and subdue any child within a five-mile radius, bake cupcakes, and also glue flowers together." I add quickly, "Oh, and compose poetry in the shower."

"You're kidding me, right?"

"No, I witnessed all those things."

"No, you're kidding me that he asked you to check if I'd be interested."

"No, he actually did."

She looks over at the gazebo. Haytham's turning off his mic, and after he does, he glances right at Sausun's face.

Well, at Sausun's eyes, because that's the only part of her face that's visible.

She doesn't say anything and just finishes drinking her pop.

I don't speak either—because 'tis a fragile moment when Sausun doesn't have anything to say back.

After Haytham sets up the sheets for Maghrib in the field behind the gazebo (one of his clipboard tasks), and after he gives the adhan, and after Amu leads salat for the guests who join, Sausun finally speaks as she's putting on her Doc Martens and I'm putting on my open-toe, black summer-mesh boots, the shoes we removed for prayer.

"Tell Haytham to go back to his roots. Because that's one beautiful adhan I just heard. Dare I say, almost as beautiful as one of Abdul Kareem's nasheeds."

"What would he find if he went back to his roots?" I ask playfully, zipping up the back of my second boot.

She straightens up. "He'd find a purity of purpose, by which he can see clearly the parts of the world that don't last and the parts that do."

"Oh my God, Sausun." I shake my head. "The guy's just asking if you'd be interested in getting to know him. He's not trying to find a guru."

"Have him declare his intentions to my father first. Who's in South Africa at the moment. So he'd have to wait a month before we even exchange a word." She looks at me. "Tell him I don't play games. If he's serious about finding out whether we work, he'll find me serious. If he's not, he won't find me at all."

I nod, ecstatic. And then I pull a total Tats. I lean in to hug her.

"Stop. It's just a guy. Lose the drama," Sausun commands, before walking back to where her sister's waiting for her.

I'm about to run to Haytham when my phone pings.

Will you introduce me to your uncle? Just want to say salaam.

Layth.

I look up at the gazebo. Then to my sides.

Oh, wait, he means when he returns for a visit.

Sure. When do you come back again? To America?

You mean after I leave?

Yeah, after Tuesday.

Idk, maybe next summer?

Ok so next summer, I can introduce you.

You can't introduce me now?

I look ahead and to my sides again, confused.

Then I turn around, and I see him by where the men are putting on their shoes.

He's there in jeans and a gray suit jacket with a black CHEAP THRILLS T-shirt underneath.

Chapter Thirty-Seven

❋ ❋ ❋

We sit at the table where I left Dad's desserts.

He says he's not hungry, but he's interested in trying the *baklaburfi* because those are his two personal favorites from both cultures. He gets me to agree to split the piece with him.

He divides it neatly with a fork.

We agree to close our eyes and bite at the same time, so that we don't see each other's reactions, so that we just choose our own feelings on the *baklaburfi*.

But I open my eyes right away.

Because I want to see how he's doing. If the sadness I saw when he drove away from the hotel is still raw on his face.

"Your brother asked me to help him drive the vans back from Chicago, so I went with him. Then when I got back here with the guests, I was going to leave. And I did leave. But then, when I stopped for a restroom break, I saw that you'd sent me your uncle's site. And then I kept scrolling through all his stuff. For an hour, in a gas station diner. And then I thought about your brother being so nice, and your uncle, and, yeah, you." He doesn't look up when he speaks, just keeps seesawing a fork on the bump of an upside-down spoon. "And I had this thought: *Let me go to this one wedding before I leave this place.* So I drove back. Lucky for me, my uncle had a jacket he'd bought for me still in his car."

"I'm glad you came back." I don't care that I said it so plainly.

"You are?" Now he looks up.

"Yeah."

"Why?"

"Because now I can ask you why sloths are so bad as pets."

"Still after sloths?" He laughs. "Hey, you want to know why I asked to follow you on Instagram right after we met?"

"Because I'm mysterious and compelling?"

"No, because you had a comeback that involved Che Guevara and education. And I was like, *Who's this nerd with an edge?*"

"Do you want to know why I didn't accept your follow request?" I say.

"Because you thought I was an asshole?"

"No, because I thought I'd never see you again." I unzip my purse and take out my phone. Then I request to follow him.

He smiles again, but this time he does it after he clears his hair from his eyes, and I see that they're not sad, his eyes.

They're open. Like something—*a shell, like Amu said?*—might be breaking.

Amu hugs Layth when I introduce him as Uncle Bilal's nephew, and add how much he likes Amu's website.

As they're talking, I look past them and see Nuah sitting with Khadija, Dania, and Lamya, on the steps to the gazebo. I've done a good job of avoiding him, and he's done a good job of it too.

Hopefully, one day it won't be like this between us.

I really pray it's so.

I'm still trying not to think of the roast—which is scheduled to happen in ten minutes. Maybe Nuah will just recruit Haytham to do it with him.

Someone puts an arm around me, and as soon as I feel the gentleness of it, I know who it is.

I turn to Mom.

"He came back?" she whispers, indicating Layth with a tip of her head in his direction.

I nod, waiting for more, but she doesn't say anything. Her eyes wander to the gazebo, to Nuah, so I take a deep breath.

"Mom, I can't talk much about it now, but I wanted to tell you . . . just forget about me and"—I lean in to whisper—"Nuah. It's a no-go."

She draws away and looks at me in concern. "Oh no, are you okay? What happened?"

"Can you not ask about it now? I promise to tell you on our ride back home."

In answer, she puts a hand on my back, and I let her rub it, grateful for it—all of it. The silent way she accepted my request, that she didn't look over at Nuah again, and that now she's just gently letting me know she cares.

Uh-oh, I see Haytham waving me to the gazebo.

It's for the roast.

With Nuah.

Haytham looks at his clipboard. "So you guys are on right after my little cousins do their thing for Sarah. Right before Zayneb. You have about five minutes to prep if you want."

Nuah and I stand behind the gazebo, in the space before the row of trees that surrounds Dad's property. There are other people waiting for their turn onstage, and I'm surprised by how many of us there are.

Nuah's tilted away a bit and gazing toward the water. "Assalamu alaikum."

I have to answer that. It's a greeting of peace. "Walaikum musalam?"

"No, I mean that, Janna. I want us to both stand on peaceful grounds when we're around each other. I don't want you to feel anything except okay when you're talking to me." He clears his throat and swallows. "And I hope we'll talk to each other. Ummah-wise, you know? Because I care about you. And I always will."

I'm just going to be transparent. I have nothing to lose. "Then why were you so distant from me? From the moment you came up here?"

"Because I was caught up in this thing with Sumayyah, and then, the more I realized that you were interested in me, the more scared I got. So yeah, I retreated from it all."

"I wish you'd just texted me before." I won't dissolve, I tell myself. "To tell me about her. Like a friend would."

"I should have." He looks right at me, before looking down at his feet. "I'm really sorry. It doesn't make sense how I acted. I think I just completely pushed it out of my mind, the possibility of me and you, and so it was easy to not involve you in what was happening. Maybe it was a coping mechanism—to keep you out of it."

I think about that. I just took it for granted Nuah would always be there. Which was my fault.

"It's okay," I say. "You weren't the only one who did that. Keeping people away. Maybe I'm the one who should really say sorry first."

For taking you for granted.

"Sorry." It comes out of us at the exact same time, with the same somber inflection, which makes us both laugh.

Even though, inside, I'm hurting.

"Are we on peaceful ground? As friends? Salaam?" Nuah asks, a smile left over from laughing still on his face.

I'm glad that I'm able to say in a steady voice, because it's so true, "Yes. Always, insha'Allah."

It's only at the end of saying it that emotions rise, and I need to swallow the lump filling my throat. And though it's hard, I know I have to apologize for something else. "And I'm sorry for not seeing the way my dad was. The way he *is*. I guess that makes me a part of his problem—to be able to close my eyes to it all."

He nods. "There's more going on than what you see. Or think. Microaggressions are hella hard to put a finger on if no one's paying attention."

And I'd thought it only happened *out there*—from non-Muslims to Muslims—and so I failed to see it right under my nose. I tear up again. "I'm so, so sorry."

"Don't feel sorry *for* me, though. Hey, I got my job at my dream company that I'm returning to on Monday."

And you've got Sumayyah to look forward to, too. "And a roommate who'll supply you with Haribo halal gummy bears for the rest of your life," I add, feigning jealousy on my teary face.

He breaks out in a smile at that, a genuine Nuah smile, and a wish for him blooms in my heart: that he find happiness on his road ahead—even if it's with Sumayyah.

So I'm able to give him a real smile back.

"When you consider the potency of Muhammad's unsocked feet, it's troubling," Nuah announces on the gazebo stage.

Oh man, I realize before I add my part, we sound like the 'Arrys, who Sarah had so not wanted to have at the wedding. *How did this make sense to me and Nuah before?* "But when you consider he takes a biannual approach to showering, it makes sense!"

When I look up from reading that out from my phone, I see Muhammad doubling over in laughter. Okay, this was a good call. To dish out humor at his level.

And, in a way, Muhammad got what he wanted all along: a blue-and-yellow wedding featuring bad humor.

Nuah and I go on and on, and there are a lot of groans and cringes from the audience, and squealing laughter from the laddoos.

And then we're done. But I don't get off the stage. I add one more that I do on my own.

"When you consider the relentless kindness of Muhammad, it's awwww. But when you consider he's the best brother in all the land, someone whose footsteps I wanna follow, one of the purest souls I know, you just wish him the most beautiful life possible in this life and the next." Then I get off and go hug my brother.

Afterward, there's a dabke that starts small with just a few of Sarah's relatives—including Haytham near the lead of the line dance—but which begins to pick up guests as the drumming becomes livelier. Pretty soon, Thomas, Jeremy, and Nuah are holding hands with Sarah's dad and uncles and cousins, trying to keep up with their steps, and I'm marveling at how this weekend all the various parts of my universe have collided into one.

Auntie Rima is smiling huge, clapping her hands to the beat of the dabke, and seated beside her, Auntie Razan winks at me like, *See? There's so much joy here.*

Layth and I sit in the back row of chairs, watching the dance and the groups of people taking pictures with Muhammad and Sarah in the gazebo. We already did our family pictures, so now I'm pointing out everyone I know to Layth, who nods in between looking at his phone.

"You said you want to see videos I upload when I get to Ecuador. What about some I already did?" He passes me his phone.

It's a younger Layth, with super-short hair and a more innocent look about him. He's smiling at the camera with a gray baby monkey attached to his arm. The monkey's reaching for his black leather cord necklace, trying to chew on the round pendant hanging from it.

I wonder what the pendant is and whether he's wearing it now, but I'm too shy to look.

I say cute, and he tells me about the monkey, how her mom was shot and she was saved from being sold as an exotic pet and brought to the sanctuary and how she was so clingy.

"This was Muhsin's favorite animal at the place, so I uploaded a ton of videos for him." He takes his phone back. "The way it is in my head is that he watched this one before he died. 'Cause I'd just uploaded it the week before."

"He must have." I don't know what else to say. I'm just happy to hear him tell me something about his brother.

"Here, this isn't one of my videos, but I thought you'd like to see this guy."

"Aw, a sloth!" I watch the sloth slowly stick his head out of an animal carry case set on the forest floor and, as if starring in a slow-motion movie, grasp the mossy reedlike tree in front of his cage and climb. His head rotates in mellow motions as he climbs higher.

It's like he wants to take in—and consider—everything around him.

"It's a release-day video. After being treated at the sanctuary, he's ready to be on his own again."

I'm so enamored with this sloth and his handsome eyes and gentle appreciation for the world around him. I press pause on the video, my black-nail-polished fingers enlarging the picture to look at the sloth's cute eyes. "Can anyone go there? To this place to volunteer?"

"Yeah, why? Would you want to?" He turns to me, his eyes wide. Surprised. Happy.

And . . . is that excited?

"I don't know. Maybe sometime in the future . . . It just seems peaceful. And important."

"That's why I'm going back. That's what I was talking to your uncle about. I read his whole article on the environment that he just posted a few days ago, and even though I've heard it from other Muslim scholars before, it's never like the way he wrote about it. He basically said it's one of the most important fights for all of us." He stops speaking and looks at Amu, who's talking to Mom and Auntie Ameera and Auntie Maysa in the aisle just a bit ahead of us. "Besides, it's the last thing that's keeping me believing. Nature, and how perfect it is."

"Yeah, my uncle's always been an environmentalist. He says there's no escaping the environmental messages in the Qur'an. It's a Muslim thing."

"Then why are Muslims some of the worst when it comes to the planet? Why are there so many illegal animal trade hotspots in the Middle East? Have you seen the disgusting videos?"

"Okay, sorry, I shouldn't say it's a *Muslim* thing," I clarify. "It's an Islam thing."

If I defined my faith by the evil that some Muslims do, I wouldn't follow it. Like the monster who assaulted me.

Who thought he was a great Muslim, even after attacking me.

But I know the opposite is true too. I can define my faith by the amazing things some Muslims do. Like Amu and Muhammad and Sarah and Khadija, who, because she wouldn't let Layth go driving off upset, got him to come back . . . and now I'm so happy he did.

Something about sitting here with him is therapeutic. Like when I sat by the water yesterday in my sari.

Like Layth had been sitting by the water—when I *really* met him for the first time.

Maybe it's because we're both introverts. And recharging like this, together, in the midst of a big wedding is what we both need. And it's weird, but he's the first person I find easy to talk with about "big" things. Like issues and topics I care about but would only share with the paper I wrote essays on before.

That I wouldn't really say out loud to the world or my friends, even.

No one—not Tats, not Nuah, not even Sausun.

I glance at Layth, and he glances at me right at that moment.

"Janna, come on." Tats is in the aisle, walking over to us, her hand in Jeremy's behind her. "Muhammad wants us all in a picture. The Eastspring crowd."

After I get up, I look at Layth. "Don't go. Okay?"

"I won't. Not yet." He nods at me, and again he does it with his hair pushed off his eyes.

Chapter Thirty-Eight

❋ ❋ ❋

We take so many pictures—Sausun, her sister, Sandra, Ms. Kolbinsky, Soon-Lee, Thomas, Tats, Jeremy, Nuah, Khadija, and a bunch of people I don't know that well who are friends of Muhammad's and Sarah's from the mosque. Mom's friends, awaiting their turn, joke they're going to turn off the floodlights set up to shine on the gazebo if we don't stop hamming for the cameras.

We're shifting and moving to shuffle off when Sarah yells, "Wait! Zayneb, you too, and get Dania and Lamya as well!"

Suddenly more people crowd the gazebo, including Layth, who Lamya brought with her.

Zayneb stands in front of the gazebo, before the steps, waiting for all of us to get ready.

"Why aren't you coming up?" Sarah asks her.

"You guys done shifting?" Zayneb's arms are crossed.

We all nod, some of us looking at others. In the short time I've known Zayneb, I've never heard her voice so stern.

"Okay, we're coming." She turns to her fiancé, who's sitting in the front row of the guest seating, the cane he was using before leaning against the back of his chair. She helps him up by turning another chair around, so he can grab the back of it, and then gives him his cane. They make their way up the steps, Zayneb matching her speed to Adam's.

"He's got MS," Lamya whispers to me.

"And Zayneb's super protective of him right now," Dania adds. "Because he just had an attack a couple weeks ago and he has to use a cane for a while.'"

We watch them get to the landing and take a spot near the front, making room beside Sarah.

People start leaving soon after.

Zayneb comes to say good-bye, and I talk to Adam for a bit. He says he likes the floral ceiling I helped make, and Zayneb tells me I should be proud as he's an actual artist who does installations. After Zayneb reminds me to keep in touch, they go off together because Zayneb's brother has come back to pick them up. Apparently, they're all heading off on a road trip to California tomorrow to visit Adam's friends.

Khadija also comes to say her good-byes. "So remember I told you about *someone's* nutrition routine? Well, friend just posted an entire how-to on it. I'll pass you her Instagram profile."

She does it right then and there, sending me a link to Sumayyah's profile via DM.

I nod, starting to call up my mantra—*Wear a pretty dress, wear a glazed gaze, lock up*—but I don't need to finish it in my head.

I just nod at Khadija and embrace her tightly, promising to visit her when Maysarah's born, thankful for her sweetness.

After hugging the Eastspring crew good-bye, except for Tats, who's going to stay with Mom and me at the hotel and then drive back with us tomorrow, I'm about to find a spot to sit down when Dad shows up at my elbow.

"What did you think of the *baklaburfi*? I saw you and Bilal's nephew eating it," Dad says, bending down to pick up a napkin on the ground.

"It was good." I'm unsure of how to respond to Dad. I don't want a scene, and I don't want to act like everything's okay, either.

"I wanted to tell you that I got to know Nuah a bit more." Dad crumples the napkin. "He's a good kid."

"Dad, he doesn't like me. And I don't want to talk about it."

"What do you mean, he doesn't like you?" Dad turns to me, surprised. "He's studying engineering at Caltech."

"Yeah?"

"Bilal's nephew didn't finish high school."

I breathe in to calm down. "Dad, remember you said earlier that we're going to talk about things at a better time? Maybe this isn't a good time?"

Dad looks at me, and I can tell there's turmoil happening inside him. "Look, what you said about me and Linda, how I thought that made sense, but not you and Nuah—*how I thought that at first*, I may add—got me thinking."

I tilt my head and wait. He's looking at the gazebo behind me, but his eyes are not still. They're moving around like they're searching for something. Maybe more careful words to say.

Which, in terms of growth from being prejudiced to not being prejudiced may be good? I don't know.

But I wait.

"It got me thinking, because . . ." He suddenly looks down, sheepish.

I've never seen Dad look like that. Like *humble*. Ever. "Because

I didn't like it when I was treated like that myself. And that's why I stay away from Linda's family. I've never even met them, because of what happened with Mom's family before. I just imagined it would happen again."

He finally looks at me. "I realize I don't want to drive you away, because I love you." He nods like he found the right words. "And I don't want to break up our family. Even more. So I want to say sorry."

That nod almost makes me relent, because there's humility in it—but the image of finding *The Autobiography of Malcolm X* on *his* bookshelf comes to me.

I'd told Dad that I didn't want to talk about it all now. I made it seem like it wasn't the right time or place.

But when is it the right time or place, except exactly when it's in front of us?

And it hits me: I'd just said that to *avoid* talking about it. Ever.

My heart's real action plan had been to just chalk up Dad as prejudiced and lessen my interactions with him and go on with my life. Maybe, at the most, talk about it all with Muhammad and let him do the work.

But then that leaves Dad as he is in my mind.

A father who thinks he's gotta be not-so-racist in order to "not break up our family."

And it leaves me without the skills to deal with this properly—when I see it again. Prejudice, racism, anti-Blackness.

And I will see it again.

I can't be a person who only thinks about stuff. Who theorizes. Who makes a great world in my mind.

All of this living in my head just gives me a feeling that

things are good, that what I believe is enough. That I don't need to expend any energy to make the good happen.

That I don't need to learn more, too.

I look at Dad's face and decide I'm moving out of my head into the real world. Toward becoming someone who actually addresses things—like Sausun and Sarah always do and like how Haytham said he was going to deal with Auntie Rima. Like how Layth decided to move to Ecuador to fight for what he believes in.

Maybe that's what I need to secure before I go to college—not a boy, not a relationship, not romantic love, but learning how to act and take risks and first steps and be decisive and become bolder and move out of the safety of my head and into the disruptive and messy realm of making life better. For me and others, too.

And I start right here.

"It's good that you're saying sorry, Dad. But you didn't wound *me*." In trying to keep calm as I speak to him, I realize how much easier it is to blow up and yell at someone or deal with them passive-aggressively—coconut-ice-cream style. I'm squashing a lot of impatience at the moment and it's a real inner struggle to keep it all contained. "It's not about me and Nuah. And it's not about you and what happened with Mom's family. Or Linda's. It's about harboring something in your heart and mind that wrecks people's lives and is unjust and leads to brutality and lives lost. You know that. I've seen you shake your head whenever you see news about police brutality against Black people. It can't just be something we feel we believe or have on our shelves in books. It's something we have to act upon."

"But wouldn't you say I'm acting on it now? That I recognized I was wrong about Nuah?" Dad lifts his hands, palms up, like he's holding something in them, something he's asking me to assess.

I feel relieved for a bit to have his upturned hands, still sheltering a crumpled napkin, to look at. It's a relief to take a break from gazing directly at him while holding a bunch of careening emotions at bay. Discomfort, fear, anger, worry, sadness—great dollops of sadness about what happened with me and Nuah, and me and Dad.

What happened, unbeknownst to me, with Nuah and Dad.

And especially about what more could happen, now and in the future, to other people in our lives.

That's why I have to keep going. Strong and steady, while piercing Dad's armor—gently, though, because he'll always be my father. "Did you recognize you were wrong because you found out Nuah's studying engineering? And so he makes sense in your world now? Especially when your daughter is so upset?" I look right at him, holding his eyes this time and not fixating on the space below them like I'd been doing when I first started talking. "What if Nuah wasn't going to college or wasn't so polite? What if he hadn't accepted the suit you gave him and instead had run away from you dressing him up like Layth did, Dad? Would you still think he's a 'good kid'?"

"I'd think of him like I think of Bilal's nephew."

"No, Dad. I know you wouldn't. Because you didn't bring any of the same things up about Sarah, or Linda, or even when you found out about Jeremy, any of the things you brought up about a potential relationship with Nuah. Any of the extra scrutiny. And that's why it's not just you saying 'sorry' that will solve this. The only sorry that works is if you promise to learn more about why you acted differently about Nuah—learn with me. And Muhammad. And Mom. We all need to learn about it."

He stares at me.

I've never spoken to him in such a calm yet forceful way before. While not looking away or trying to escape the conversation.

He breaks his gaze, glances behind me, and returns his eyes to my face with a sigh. Then a nod.

I decide to take that nod as commitment. "Muhammad knows where we can get support on this. I'll sign us up."

He nods again and it's a surer nod, so I let myself spring forward lightly and give him a quick brush of a hug.

He's caught off guard and his arms are not ready to hug me back, but when they do, when they reach forward to bring me back to him, it's tightly, with a whispered, "Thank you."

There's going to be a lot more work to do—for both Dad and me. Antiracism work and openness work and just the work of taking filters away from our eyes, filters that block the true worth of the people who come into our lives.

When I reach the driveway, there's one more good-bye.

Layth's parked there, and he's leaning on his car, speaking to Dania and Lamya, who smile and wave me over when they see me.

We do small talk about the wedding, and then it peters out. When it looks like it's going to get awkward, Layth says, "If you're still thinking about volunteering, let me know and I'll send you links to stuff."

Dania looks at me and says, "Oh, I didn't know you were into it as well!"

"It looks cool. And the animals are just so cute," I say, hoping they don't think I have a thing for their cousin. "I've always liked animals."

"That's neat," Lamya says, exchanging a glance with Dania. "Dad's waving from the side of the road. He's brought the car, so we'd better go."

"Did you say salaam to Dad?" Dania asks Layth.

"Yeah, when he was going to get the car. And we talked before when he gave me the jacket."

"Okay, then, don't be a stranger. You'd better message us each Friday . . ."

Dania's about to go on talking when I stop her with, "Hey, I'll let you guys say salaam in peace."

It feels odd to be intruding when they're saying good-bye as cousins.

I turn to Layth. "Assalamu alaikum, drive safe. I'll look for those links."

He nods and I nod, and then I turn and walk to the front of the house, to the porch.

It's full of guests waiting for people to bring cars up, so I'm able to disappear into the crowd and go stand by the front door, with my back against the brick of the house, wondering why I feel so down suddenly.

After a bit, I see Dania and Lamya going to their car. I'll see them tomorrow at the hotel—we made plans to eat breakfast together before checking out.

I better go into the house and pack up the stuff in my bedroom.

But I don't go in.

I know what I'm doing: I'm waiting to see Layth drive off.

But it's not happening.

I move to the corner of the porch, where it wraps around the side that faces the driveway, and stick my head out a bit to check if his car's still there.

It is.

And he is.

He's still leaning against the car, looking at something in his hands. Something he's turning over and over, his head tilted like he's considering something.

I step onto the side porch and pretend I just came upon him. "Oh, you're still here!"

He looks up, and I swear his entire face lights up. I'm not imagining it. "Hey, I was just thinking of coming to find you."

"Really, for what?" Maybe I'm lighting up too.

"'Cause I wanted to give you this. I'm selling my car in Miami, and I stuck this on the dashboard to remind me of Merazonia, the animal rescue. So I peeled it off." He takes a few steps and reaches over the porch railing to pass me a plastic frame with a picture of a woolly monkey in it. The back of the frame has an adhesive band on it. "It's not a sloth, but maybe it'll still make you interested in volunteering?"

"Aw. Is it the same monkey in your video?" I look at it to see any distinguishing features, but I can't tell.

"Yup."

"Thanks. I think it *will* remind me of volunteering," I say, my mind jumping leaps and bounds ahead. Maybe I can go next summer. Or even during the Christmas holidays.

"So it was a good idea. To give it to you."

I nod. And we look at each other for a few seconds, and then he turns around to go to the car. He gets in, starts the engine, rolls down the window, and says salaam.

I just nod again, and then he's gone.

But I don't feel sad like I did before—because now I have a woolly monkey picture that I'm going to stick onto the dashboard of the car Muhammad's passing down to me before he leaves for California.

It'll remind me of the animal rescue.

And other things.

Part Four

❈ ❈ ❈

SUNDAY, JULY 18
SENDING THE
BRIDE & GROOM OFF

To do:

☐ Love

Chapter Thirty-Nine

❋   ❋   ❋

We're in the water. Tats, Dania, Lamya, and me.

I'm pretty sure the Orchard's pool has never seen so many burkinis at once. Dania's and Lamya's aren't *technically* burkinis, because they're in tracksuits, but Tats and I are in full Muslim swimwear.

Tats is finally having her Lindsay Lohan moment and even has her big hair stuffed into the attached cap on her head. Though we arrived late to the hotel last night, she convinced everyone to agree to a swim before breakfast.

"Promise we'll go swimming again in our burkinis this summer?" Tats asks me as she floats on her back.

"For sure." I float, gazing at the gray ceiling. "Though I'm going to need to order a new one. One that doesn't fall off," I add, giggling as I remember my introduction to Haytham.

"Oh my God, you should order this same one I'm wearing!" Tats lifts her head and yells out to Dania and Lamya, "Guys, Janna's going to order the same burkini as mine! Like you guys are!"

"I am?"

"Yeah, and we can do synchronized burkini swimming!

Maybe to that mehndi song? Do a TikTok in the water?" Tats nods, like we're set. And then she smiles. "Ah. I feel so free in this thing."

I let out a laugh.

I'm so glad I have Tats in my life.

Breakfast at the Glade is a quiet symphony of clinks of cutlery until our entourage arrives. It's Tats and Dania who are the loudest—discussing the possibility of Mystic Lake being a mini Area 51 because of a vast space devoid of trees they both glimpsed—while Uncle Bilal and Mom walk behind them, amused, and Lamya and I follow exchanging memes on our phones that we can't figure out but are too afraid to ask anyone.

After we get our food from the buffet, Mom sits right beside me. Uncle Bilal is still at the toaster waiting for his toast to pop, so I lean over and say, "I charge chaperoning fees, remember."

She laughs and says, "Don't worry—ours will be a long-distance arrangement. Though I hope it's okay, I invited them to come meet us in September in Chicago? When I drive you to settle in at college? Uncle Bilal's going to bring the girls from New York for school too, and I thought we could have dinner together and do something."

I nod. And then lean over and put my head on her shoulder, like always. "Layth says he's really nice. Uncle Bilal," I say low, just so she can hear, and then look up at her. "And I liked hearing him say that."

"Thank you," she whispers. She pauses before adding, "Then maybe you'll be okay if we decide on a nikah date?"

Uncle Bilal is coming over with his breakfast plate and bowl, his eyes crinkling as he smiles down at his oatmeal.

"Yes," I tell Mom, straightening up. "Really, why wait for your breakfast dreams to start?"

She laughs and gives me a side-hug.

Dania brings her plate loaded with potatoes to sit on the other side of me, and when Mom passes a piece of her omelet for Uncle Bilal to taste, Dania looks at me, a slightly concerned expression on her face, like *You okay with this? Our parents into each other?*

I shrug and smile at her. She'll know soon enough.

My heart feels pretty ready to make my world bigger.

Muhammad and Sarah come by to say good-bye before they leave for their "little" honeymoon to Niagara Falls (Muhammad's idea) before the *real* one they're taking next year (Malaysia and Thailand), with Dad and his family following in their SUV. We're all out at the front of the hotel, and it almost becomes a bawl-fest when Logan realizes that everyone's leaving.

He runs toward the hotel doors, all the while heaving dramatically.

I channel Haytham, go after him, get down on my knees, and tell him that when I come back, I'm going to make cupcakes with him, so if he cries now, he's acting like I'm not coming back, and that's not true, is it?

He shakes his head. "Can we make the same cupcakes that Haytham made?"

"Yup, I'm going to get his recipe."

"And the same frosting?"

"The same everything."

He shudders once more, swallows, and nods, satisfied, and then holds my hand so that we can walk back to the others.

Sarah lets out a big whoop from where she's clustering with

Dania, Lamya, and Mom, her phone out in her hands. "Haytham won the Muslim Voice!"

Oh my God, he won!

I check my own phone and see that he beat Noor by 103 votes.

I can't stop myself from checking Sausun's Instagram and Snapchat.

She'd posted something late last night.

"Soooo, many of you are going to wonder why I'm wading into THE MUSLIM VOICE competition of all things. But that's because you haven't heard Abdul Kareem. And I HAVE." There's a cut to Abdul Kareem singing "Tala'al-Badru Alayna" from her laptop, and then Sausun's back. "I'm here to tell you all to vote, cast your ballot, press that button for him"—fast cut to Abdul Kareem singing again—"or him." A cut of Haytham singing "Hold On" from her desktop computer, after which there's a screeching sound. "Yeah. That was indeed country music. Of which I do not approve. But the dude Haytham does. Thus, the choice is yours—you'll never know mine. Even though you know I don't like country. But voices sometimes make you rethink your choices, which is terrible but also, I don't know, weirdly satisfying? To know humans are not stagnant? Even humans with superior tastes? Okay bye, go vote!"

So that's how he won.

I smile.

Sausun and Haytham.

Muhammad and Sarah.

Tats and Jeremy.

Mom and Uncle Bilal.

Me and—

Well, all I'm going to say is this: *Let there be all kinds of love.*
And taking first steps.
And changing my world.
Insha'Allah.

From: jannayusuf@uchicago.edu
To: haroon@lidinc.com, Muhammadandsarah34@gmail.com,
husna_librarian@yahoo.com
Re: our tickets for MuslimARC

We're all in for the October Chicago session—mark your calendars. And Muhammad, let's do Baba's Pizza and Pasta afterward for old time's sake?

Forwarded message: from info@muslimarc.org
Re: Registration Confirmation for Anti-Racism Seminar 101
Thank you for registering for our upcoming seminar: Anti-Racism 101. We look forward to you joining us for this informative session exploring the historical roots of racism and its continuous social impact, with an emphasis on Muslim spaces. . . .

From: jannayusuf@uchicago.edu
To: layth_ahmed3@gmail.com
CC: sausun@niqabininjas.com, haytham@haythamthevoice.com,
Muhammadandsarah34@gmail.com
Re: raingear packing list for ecuador in december

Thanks for the list! Cc'ing Sausun and Haytham and Muhammad—Sausun wants to know if there'll be enough sunshine to power a small solar generator for the cameras we're bringing to shoot the fundraiser. Haytham wants to know if we'll even be able to shoot. We're worried about the rain.

And Muhammad wants to know if there are good pizza

places in Mera. (Sarah doesn't need to know anything. She has her "Ecuador clipboard" already filled.)

Let me know answers for the others. When you next go into town for wifi.

Adios and see you soon.

Insha'Allah,

Janna

PS Also, Sausun and Haytham both wanted me to ask if you're sure you can't come to their nikah on Thanksgiving weekend. It's a simple, everyone-drop-in nikah at the Eastspring mosque. They hope you can come. (I hope so too.)

Thank You for Being Part of This Big Day . . .

Planning a celebration of love involves the efforts of many hearts. Here are those who were important to ensuring Muhammad and Sarah's nikah weekend unfolded as intended.

To thank the people who guided this book, I'd like to call them by the table number they'll be seated at during next year's "official" wedding reception (the one decorated tastefully in a matte-gold and gray color scheme).

Table one: Jez, Hamza, Bilqis, Jochua, Ahmad, Zuhra, Hajara, Johanne—thank you for helping me understand love deeply enough to write about it.

Table two: Jamilah Thompkins-Bigelow, Margari Aziza Hill, Nevien Shaabneh, Kenyatta Bakeer, members of the MuslimARC team—thank you for helping me *begin* to learn about anti-racism and being an ally. Any and all of the good offered on these topics in *Misfit in Love* comes from those seated at this table while all the deficiencies come solely from me. Please note: as a non-Black author, I could not explore the impact of anti-Blackness on Black characters; I chose to explore how non-Black characters are complicit in perpetuating anti-Blackness and how easy it is to practice

complacency even when confronted by prejudice in our midst. But this is only one sliver of insight into the subject. I urge all readers to seek out narratives written by Black authors, particularly Black Muslim authors, to more substantially understand the impact of racism in our communities.

Table three: Uzma, Ausma, Safiyyah, Aisha, London, Huda, Fartumo, Natalie—thank you for being in my writerly-worries-sharing friends crew. (Jamilah and Nevien, you totally need to table hop to this table too!)

Table four (seats more than eight, this one): Zareen Jaffery, Kendra Levin, Sara Crowe, Dainese Santos, Justin Chanda, Amanda Ramirez, Lisa Moraleda, Brian Luster, Marinda Valenti, Lucy Ruth Cummins, John Cusick—thank you for helping me continue Janna Yusuf's story.

Tables five, six, and seven: Faisal, Shakil, Anwaar, Amanda, Sana, Sakeina, Sahar, Bushra, Muhammad, Khalil, Khalid, Zenyah, Chiku, Saira, Dawood, Alain, Shaiza, Rania, Amie, Naseem, Soobia, Mehjabeen, Bilqees, Nhu, Thayyiba, Zakiya, Farzana—thank you for being in my crew of beloveds.

Tables eight and on and on: All of the readers who've shared their love for Janna, Nuah, Adam, Zayneb, and other characters with me via e-mails, messages, and in person—with members of the *Misfit in Love* street team sitting at the head of each table. Thank you so much. I write for *you*.